Dying for a Cruise

A TRAVELLING COOK MYSTERY

Dying for a Cruise

A TRAVELLING COOK MYSTERY

Joyce Cato

ROBERT HALE · LONDON

ISBN 978-0-7090-9852-2

Robert Hale Limited
Clerkenwell House
Clerkenwell Green
London EC1R 0HT

www.halebooks.com

Typeset in 11/14½pt Palatino
Printed in the UK by the MPG Books Group,
Bodmin and King's Lynn

ONE

JENNY STARLING PULLED her rather distressed-looking but nearly always reliable cherry-red van to a halt on the crest of a hill and turned off the engine. She removed the ignition keys and put them in the pocket of her lightweight linen jacket, then walked to the edge of the road and looked down at the winding River Thames below.

It was July, and in the fields the barley was just beginning to think of changing its mantle of green for a more mellow hue. The sun shone high and powerful overhead, and somewhere in the distance a church clock struck one. She hoped that it was the church clock in the village of Buscot, which, so her map assured her, was positioned just down the road.

Beside her, in a hawthorn thicket, a yellow hammer whistled merrily for his bread-and-cheese, whilst corn buntings trilled cockily from the highest bushes in the hedges that ran in patchwork lines across the valley. Dog roses and wild poppies bloomed like mad things.

Jenny took a big breath of fresh air and smiled with satisfaction. It was nice to leave the city of Oxford behind every now and then, although she was quite content with her present job as head chef at St Baptista's College.

What she wasn't so happy about was the two weeks' holiday she was being practically forced to take. Union rules, or so the college bursar had said.

She sighed glumly.

Jenny didn't particularly approve of the – to her mind – somewhat ludicrous habit her fellow holidaymakers had of flocking to some foreign coast every summer in the hope of turning lobster red in the sun. She didn't find the prospect of getting sand in her shoes exactly appealing, she objected to children depositing sticky ice creams on chairs and benches, and, most of all, she disliked having to eat somebody else's cooking. All of which meant that Jenny inevitably stayed firmly put during the annual summer migration of the great British public. And usually became thoroughly bored in the process.

Which was why she was always on the lookout for the odd strictly temporary job, to tide her over the slow, boring weeks of her supposed vacation time.

She straightened her majestic shoulders with another sigh. Wallowing in the pastoral beauty around her was all very pleasant, she supposed idly, but she had an appointment at 2.15 with a certain Mr Lucas Finch, who was in need of a cook for the weekend, so she couldn't dawdle about indefinitely.

A light breeze lifted a few dark glossy curls across her broad forehead as she walked back to the van. At six feet tall, and with a figure that could best be described as Junoesque, she had some difficulty in squeezing her curvaceous frame behind the steering wheel and not for the first time promised herself that she'd look around for a bigger van. One that could hold even more of her catering equipment, and perhaps even come with power steering, air conditioning that worked and, best of all, more leg room for plus-sized drivers!

She steered the old van (which now had painted on one of its panels a very twee scene of unicorns and fairy-tale castles, courtesy of her artistically frustrated mother) slowly down the narrow country lane. She hadn't passed a single vehicle since turning onto it, and it had a little-used and rather forlornly neglected air.

She had gone only about half a mile down the hill when,

coming up the other way, she noticed a man on a rusty and badly squeaking bicycle, who was pedalling away with something less than enthusiasm. He was wearing a personal stereo system and some kind of classical music, leaking past his earplugs, was keeping an eerily accurate tempo with his squeaking front wheel. A moment later she pulled up in front of him and once again switched off the engine and got out. Her van's ancient internal combustion system was apt to be very loud and noisy and wasn't above giving the occasional backfire, which tended to make people jump. Herself most of all. The cyclist's head was well down as he attempted to urge his squeaking steed up the hill, and at first he simply didn't realize that she had stopped right in front of him. A bag of what looked like groceries lay firmly strapped across the handlebars, which were wobbling rather alarmingly.

Jenny coughed. Loudly.

The man's head jerked upwards and the handlebars corkscrewed, promptly pitching him head first off the saddle. He landed, rather artistically Jenny thought, right at her feet. He looked as if he were coming up to retirement age, with a small white moustache and more wrinkles on his face than a candlewick bedspread.

She quickly moved her considerable frame into action and went to see if he was all right.

'Hell's bells and buckets of blood,' the man muttered, but the lack of heat in his tone made it sound more like a greeting than a curse. No doubt, Jenny surmised, pedalling for miles on a reluctant bike in the hot summer sun would sap the passion out of anyone. But at least he wasn't hurt.

As she knelt down beside him, the man rearranged himself so that he was sitting on his bottom (as opposed to his elbow and nose) and stared at the fallen bike in the road. The front wheel was still spinning jauntily, if rather uselessly.

'Damn the useless piece of junk,' the cyclist huffed. 'I'd be better off walking.' He took off his headphones, and Jenny recognized a passage from Dvorak before he switched the CD off.

And then, as if suddenly remembering the cause of his downfall, his head turned and swivelled sharply upwards, the visor of his cap shading his eyes. What he saw was a wonderful figure of a woman. She was dressed in a very long, very sensible summer dress of cornflower blue with a matching jacket that perfectly complemented the shade of her large and quite beautiful eyes.

The man blinked.

The last time he'd seen a woman of this shapely a size was in the far-gone days of his youth when women had hips and breasts, and the hour-glass shape that made a man's mouth water.

'Excuse me,' Jenny said politely, looking down at the man who happened to be sitting on one of her feet. 'Could you tell me if I'm anywhere near Buscot?'

The cyclist blinked again. Then, rather reluctantly, he struggled to sit upright, grunting and groaning with theatrical vigour as he did so. He put his hands in the small of his back and stretched. Then winced. Then nodded.

'Buscot's just round the bend … er … love. You can't miss it.'

Since Jenny hadn't actually considered the possibility that she *might* somehow manage to drive through an entire village without noticing it, she gave him a brief smile of agreement.

'Thank you. Now, could you tell me how to get to—' She quickly stood up and delved into the van's small glove compartment and withdrew a letter '—Wainscott House?'

The old man, forgetting his various bruises for a moment, gave her a rather odd look.

'You'll be wanting Lucas Finch then?' he asked. His eyes, which the cook guessed were rather short sighted, narrowed ominously.

Jenny, as a rule, didn't go about discussing her private business. But since she had – albeit unintentionally – been the cause

8

of his rather abrupt introduction to the tarmac, she supposed that she owed him at least a little something by way of recompense. Besides, she might learn something about her erstwhile employer. She nodded, briefly. 'That's right.'

The old man suddenly shrugged. 'Wainscott House is the last house in the village, right next to the river. Big, square, solid lump of a place it is. You can't miss that, either.'

Jenny smiled, and almost knocked the poor man flat for a second time. She had, the cyclist mused with a wistful sigh, the loveliest smile he'd ever seen on a woman. Including those of his favourite screen goddesses of yesteryear such as Rita Hayworth and Veronica Lake.

Then he shook off such silly maundering and reached for his bike, hefted it onto its wheels and stared glumly down at it. 'Another two miles to go,' he muttered and sighed so heavily that Jenny thought he'd pop the buttons off his shirt. He set about readjusting the shopping bag onto the handlebars, and Jenny bent to retrieve a small jar of instant coffee from the roadside verge that had escaped from between the knotted handles of the carrier bag.

He thanked her for it, shoved it back inside, then turned rather abruptly and gave her a very long look. 'Lucas Finch ain't all that popular around these parts, love. Just thought you should know that.'

Jenny, who'd just started to lift one foot in the direction of her van, put it very firmly back onto the ground. 'Oh?' she asked, her voice arch and just inviting confidences or downright gossip.

Jenny had had quite a few experiences with people who weren't 'too popular'. And sometimes, those occasions had ended in murder.

'Ahh. A bit of a villain, we reckon.'

Jenny's left eyebrow began to elevate towards her hairline. 'Oh? How so?'

The old man sniffed. 'Well, he's a cockney for a start,' he said judiciously. 'Everyone knows what them big city fellers can get up to. You can't trust even the so-called professional classes neither nowadays. I blame the bankers for the mess everyone's in now, I can tell you.'

Jenny bit back a smile and the urge to say 'Don't we all?' but nodded gravely. 'Anything else?'

The man took off his cap to reveal a sparse crop of grey hairs, and scratched his scalp. 'Oh, there's rumours all right. He reckons he grew up in a poor slum, but now he's rolling in lolly. Well, how did he get it all, hey, if he's not crooked?' He thrust his jaw out pugnaciously. 'That's what we'd all like to know.' He sniffed again. ''Sides, he's got a parrot. One of them big, colourful things, with a long tail and a vicious beak,' he added ominously, as if that somehow clinched matters. 'You just watch yourself, love, that's all,' he finished, giving her a concerned look. 'You just watch yourself.'

Jenny smiled again, and the cyclist reared back. He'd managed to stay a bachelor for all of his life precisely because he'd avoided women with lovely smiles. 'Well, I'd best be off,' he muttered hastily and gave his bike an experimental push. It squeaked like a mouse catching sight of a pound of cheddar.

Jenny winced and quickly set off in the direction of the village.

The old man, after a few moments' thought, turned to watch the woman in the oddly painted old van disappear into the distance. She'd climbed into her seat with that very fetching kind of grace that some very large women seemed to possess. She'd walked well too. Almost flowed across the road.

The man frowned. He rather liked the gal. She looked like a good, honest sort. He only hoped she knew what she was doing, getting herself mixed up with the likes of Lucas Finch.

He shrugged, and pushed his complaining bike all the way to the top of the hill, before re-mounting it and wobbling his way precariously to the next village but one, where he had his home.

*

Wainscott House was indeed situated less than a stone's throw from the wide River Thames. Jenny parked her van off the road under the shade of a tall horse chestnut tree, locked it up carefully and walked to the white picket gate.

It was not that she suspected that anyone would want to steal the old clunker, especially since her mother and her paintbrush had vented their spleen upon it. But she did have a lot of cookery equipment stored in it, and it would break her heart to lose it if some drunken louts took the van for a joyride and wrecked it.

The house was a solid, square structure, no doubt an old farmhouse in former days. It had a delightful front garden; a 'proper' garden, as her grandmother would have said. At the side walls grew hollyhocks and delphiniums, foxgloves and Canterbury bells. A stone path led straight down the middle to the front door, and was edged by pansies, marigolds, love-in-a-mists, feverfew and Sweet Williams. A honeysuckle grew up the front porch, framing the old wooden door with fragrant blooms. Bees and butterflies wove their happy pollen-drunken way through the warm air, filling it with sound and fluttering colour.

Jenny sighed in rather envious bliss at the picture-postcard perfection of the scene, then glanced at her watch. She was early. Too bad. She marched up the path, set down her small case that she kept permanently packed for such short-term assignments like this one, and very firmly thumped on the door.

And Jenny *could* thump very firmly when she needed to.

A moment later the door was opened by a tall, thin, grey-haired man, with watery blue eyes. On his left shoulder sat a large blue and scarlet macaw. Its yellow and black beady eyes settled on her as the bird cocked its head curiously to one side.

'Hello,' it said. Quite clearly.

Jenny smiled at it.

Lucas Finch gaped rudely at the shapely giantess in front of him, and his jaw fell comically open. 'Bugger me,' he said at last.

Jenny, not a whit put out by the rather unconventional greeting, smiled politely and held out her hand. 'I'm Miss Starling,' she said firmly.

As if she could be anybody else.

Lucas started, making the parrot's tail upend in an effort to keep his balance, and then thrust out his own hand to take hers in a hearty grip. 'Lucas Finch,' he said jovially.

'I wrote in answer to your advertisement for a cook for the weekend?' she prompted, when he made no move to either speak or invite her in.

Lucas blinked, then suddenly seemed to recover his equilibrium. 'Oh, right. Yes. That's right. Er … yes. Er … won't you come in?' He stepped back, and led her into what, just forty years ago, people referred to as the front parlour. It was now decked out to be something of an office-cum-study with a splendid view across the river and to the copse of trees on the opposite bank.

'Er … won't you sit down?' he asked. He looked for all the world like a man who, having got what he wanted, now hadn't the faintest idea of what to do with it. 'Er … drink?'

Jenny smiled. 'A cold glass of squash would be nice?' she asked, hopefully.

'Squash?' Lucas, who had gone automatically to the drinks cabinet, put down the decanter of whisky he was holding, and half turned. 'Er … right. Squash.'

He was indeed, as her cyclist friend had informed her, most definitely a cockney. His words came down his nose with a cockney twang that would tarnish silver. 'Squash,' he said again, and stared forlornly at the drinks cabinet.

'Or cold milk, if you prefer,' Jenny added, guessing correctly that Mr Lucas Finch had probably never purchased squash in his life.

'Milk!' He brightened at once and disappeared briefly, returning a minute or so later with a glass full of the white liquid. It was so cold the glass had developed tiny beads of condensation, and Jenny took it gratefully. She and hot weather didn't always see eye to eye. Eagerly she took a few good hefty swallows.

Lucas watched her generous chin wobble just slightly as she drank, and backed into a chair, unable to take his eyes from such an impressive sight. As a self-made man, and definite 'character' himself, he instinctively knew another 'character' when he came across one. And, because he was at heart a gregarious, people-friendly sort of chap, he found himself quite taking to his temporary cook.

Jenny put down the glass on her left knee, and glanced at him patiently.

Lucas smiled. 'Right. You're the cook,' he said, then suddenly brightened. 'Of *course* you are.' As if, he might just as well have added out loud, you could possibly be anyone else.

Jenny caught on at once, and far from being offended, positively beamed at him. 'My father always says you can't trust a thin cook. It makes people feel uneasy,' she said promptly.

Lucas Finch laughed.

The parrot laughed.

Jenny laughed. Then, typically, got straight down to business. 'Now, Mr Finch,' she began briskly. 'I understand you require a cook from Saturday breakfast to the Sunday evening meal?'

Lucas nodded, relaxing back into his chair. 'That's right.' He was suddenly very much the businessman now, and potential host. 'I have guests coming for the weekend. I don't often entertain, but when I do, I like to do it right. I hate anything to be stingy. I have a housekeeper here, of course, but for guests, I like to push the boat out.' And he laughed, as if at some private joke.

'Exactly,' Jenny concurred, her voice rich with approval. 'Now, how many are you expecting?'

13

'Well, there's young David Leigh and his wife, Dorothy. She's just discovered she's up the spout, by the way, so if you see her barfing into the river, don't think it's something you cooked.'

Jenny's polite smile froze. 'Don't worry,' she said, ever so sweetly, if through gritted teeth. 'I won't.' *As if!* The damned cheek of it. Even pregnant women, *especially* pregnant women, found her food sheer ambrosia.

Lucas, if he'd known her better, would have started grovelling in apology immediately. But since he didn't, he merely nodded, and carried on blithely. 'Then there's that old codger, Gabriel Olney and his wife, the luscious Jasmine. Now I wouldn't mind planting her in my garden, I can tell you.' And he drawled the double entendre with such a childish delight that it was almost impossible for Jenny to take offence. Although a woman's libber would have jumped right down his throat at such an openly sexist remark, she mused with a wry twitch of her lips. 'Bugger me, if she ain't a little goer. She's not so young, actually, but all the better for it, if you know what I mean?'

Jenny, stifling a sigh, began to understand what her friend the hapless cyclist had meant. Politically correct Lucas Finch most definitely wasn't. Suddenly, she was not at all surprised that Mr Finch wasn't 'any too popular around these parts'. Even in this day and age, villagers, as she knew only too well, tended to be an insular and conservative lot.

And for different reasons entirely, he was beginning to become very unpopular with his cook as well. Any implied slur on her cooking was guaranteed to get her gander up.

'So it's just the four guests?' she clarified. She'd have to keep Dorothy Leigh's delicate condition in mind, of course. Plenty of vegetables and rice dishes for her.

'Right. Oh and myself, and yourself, of course, and Captain Lester and the engineer. Oh, and Francis. My manservant,' he added. He said the final words very much like a magician might say 'abracadabra' before producing a rabbit from a hat.

14

Jenny found it, much to her chagrin, rather touching.

That Lucas Finch must indeed have had a poverty-stricken upbringing, she didn't doubt. The way he liked to throw his money about when entertaining was a sure sign. And now, the very reverence with which he referred to Francis by the ultra old-fashioned title of manservant made her heart contract in compassion. No doubt to the young Lucas Finch, growing up in London's grime, the thought of him ever having a servant must have been as fantastic a dream as owning a goldmine.

Of course, what the absent Francis felt about being described as a manservant to Lucas probably didn't bear thinking about. Jenny shrugged the thought aside. She was allowing her mind to wander off the point.

'So you have—' she made a quick mental count '—five guests, and … er … the engineer? And Francis and myself.'

Lucas frowned, looking puzzled.

'No,' he said. 'There's just the Olneys and the Leighs.'

'And the captain?' Jenny prompted. He counted as a guest, surely?

Lucas looked at her as if she was mad. 'The captain steers the boat, love,' he explained with a gentle patience that would have been kind, if it hadn't been so patronizing.

Jenny fixed him with an eye that was beadier than the eye the parrot was giving her. 'Boat?' she echoed sharply.

'Course,' Lucas said, looking surprised now. 'The *Stillwater Swan*.' He said the name as lovingly as Romeo would have addressed Juliet.

'The *Stillwater Swan*.' Jenny repeated his words flatly and felt herself flush. She was beginning to feel as if she and the parrot might have a lot in common, after all. 'I don't recall the mention of any boat in our correspondence, Mr Finch,' she said, her voice like steel.

The fact was, Jenny was not so sure that she liked the sound of the word 'boat'.

Her father, who'd been a top chef in both London and then

Paris for most of his career, had told her once about working on the *Queen Elizabeth II*. And all about some of his more harrowing experiences during a typhoon just off Bora-Bora. She still, to this day, had nightmares about trying to cook a seven-course dinner in a kitchen that wouldn't keep still.

Lucas Finch suddenly slapped his forehead in a well-blow-me-down gesture, making the parrot on his shoulder jump nervously.

'You silly sod,' the parrot said, quite clearly.

Jenny glanced at the bird in some surprise, then shrugged. No doubt the bird had picked up quite a few less than salubrious phrases from its master over the years. It was just a sheer coincidence that it had chosen to utter the comment at such an appropriate moment.

'Of course, I didn't say, did I?' Lucas grinned at his own neglect. 'Come on, er … Miss … er….'

'Starling.'

'Starling. I'll show you my pride and joy.'

Jenny wasn't any too sure that she wanted to be shown Lucas Finch's pride and joy. Nevertheless, she got rather reluctantly to her feet, and followed his tall, white-haired figure through the house and out into the vast back garden where, at the bottom, the River Thames meandered by, like some stately relative just calling in for a visit. And there, moored to a large wooden landing, was the most beautiful sight Jenny had ever seen.

The 'boat' was a large, flat-bottomed, two-storeyed paddle steamer – obviously purpose-built and to spec, in order to traverse England's biggest river. Not exactly a Mississippi riverboat special, it was certainly unusual and undeniably elegant. It had, in fact, class written all over it.

It was also, as its name suggested, painted a bright, almost blinding white, with black and orange trim. As they approached it, the cook noticed how the steam whistle that rose above the structure was carved like the neck and head of a swan, with its orange-painted beak wide open, to allow the steam through.

The riverboat had tiny balconies on the upper storeys, with hanging baskets affixed to the walls, frothing over with blue, red, green and yellow. Its brass fixtures gleamed like gold. Its planked decking was dry and clean, and a light gold in colour. The windows on both floors were wide and pristine, and glass sliding doors led out onto the lower deck. It was most definitely a rich man's toy.

'Isn't she summat?' Lucas Finch asked with masterly understatement and beaming pride, and Jenny nodded.

'Oh yes,' she agreed, her blue eyes sparkling. 'She certainly is summat.'

'Want the guided tour?'

Jenny nodded. If she was to spend the weekend cooking on this lovely vessel, she most certainly did want the guided tour. Especially of the kitchen. Or, she supposed she should say, the galley.

The *Stillwater Swan* didn't so much as bob at her mooring as they stepped from the jetty, through the open boarding gate and onto its lower deck. Jenny went straight to the rear and looked at the large paddles below.

Long, elegantly curved paddles rested in the still, clear water of the Thames. She could just imagine them turning, gently and smoothly pushing the boat along. What was it about paddle steamers, she mused meltingly, that so boggled the imagination? She felt like a giddy schoolgirl about to go to her first dance. She'd cooked in castles, in colleges, and indeed in some of the stateliest homes of England in her time. But this was something special. Perhaps it was the magic of steam, or simply the call and romance of a bygone era that made her heart flutter.

'This here's the engine room.' Lucas briefly opened the door, giving her a glimpse of a large but modern boiler, and a row of technical-looking, state-of-the-art dials. 'The coal and water are stored here.' He nodded to the side, where a small door led off to the storerooms. 'We also have another freshwater butt on the starboard side, in case of fires, or if the tanks run low.'

Jenny nodded but in fact knew nothing about the mechanics of how such a boat must work. Nor was she particularly interested. Just so long as, when she turned on the taps in her kitchen – no, *her galley* – the water came on, then she was happy.

'But the guests, of course, have nothing to do with the dirty, smelly end,' Lucas laughed. 'Up there—' He nodded above, to the balconies on the second storey '—are three bedrooms and a bathroom. Double beds, mind. And thick carpets. And real antiques. When I had the *Swan* built, must be twenty years ago now, I had her fitted out with nothing but the best.'

Jenny ignored the boasting, having got her measure of the man by now.

She didn't doubt that Lucas always had to have the best of everything, and for once she was not amused or touched by his extravagance. The *Stillwater Swan*, it was plain, *simply deserved* the best of everything.

She followed him as he led her to the main salon, that also served, she saw at once, as the dining room.

In the centre of the room was a large, gleaming mahogany table that could easily have seated twenty. The cook could just imagine it set with a snowy white cloth (what other colour for the *Stillwater Swan*?) and awash with gleaming crystal, a towering candle-and-flower centrepiece, and silver cutlery set for a seven-course feast.

She began to practically quiver in anticipation.

Lucas Finch watched her reaction with a smile of satisfaction, and nodded. In that instant, he knew that this surprising cook would not let him down. His guests would be treated to nothing but the best. 'I've got flowers arriving later on tonight, plus the delivery of food.'

At the magical word 'food', Jenny turned to him, her blue eyes sparkling. 'Yes?'

Lucas smiled. 'Don't worry, love, you can check it all out for yourself, and if I've forgotten anything, then tell me. I have an arrangement with the butchers and greengrocers around here. What I want, I get.' And his eyes glinted, just for a moment losing their jovial, laid-back twinkle.

Jenny made a mental note to watch out for that particular gleam. Only truly ruthless men could get quite that expression in their eye. She followed with a rather wry smile as he led her to the galley, which was nowhere near as poky as she had feared and imagined.

A large gas cooker stood in one corner, surrounded by adequate top-space. Cupboards were arranged in that very neat way that was peculiar to boats, taking up the minimum amount of space, whilst at the same time making the most of every square inch. A large sink and a small table completed the ensemble. All in all, not too shabby.

She made a quick inspection of the utensils – plenty of pots, pans, and cutlery. She had with her, of course, and packed securely in the van, her own portable set of knives, spoons, spatulas etc. No cook worth her salt travelled without them.

After a long, thorough inspection, she nodded, turned to look at him, and smiled. 'This will do nicely,' she said judiciously.

Lucas Finch grinned.

The parrot on his shoulder coughed.

'I'm afraid you'll have to kip in the adjoining cook's bunkhouse,' he said, and went to a small door set in one bulkhead. It opened into a tiny bedroom, that contained one single bed, and a narrow wardrobe with one drawer at the bottom. There wasn't so much as a porthole, and Lucas pulled on a cord that turned on a rather weak light. Jenny eyed the bed with a jaundiced eye, and then shrugged her massive shoulders. It was only for one night, after all.

'It'll do,' she said shortly, and turned back to her galley. 'So you'll be wanting a full English breakfast for Saturday and Sunday mornings?'

'Right. Might as well start the cruise off on a good nosh-up,' he said cheerfully, and Jenny positively beamed at him.

He was a man after her own heart, despite the rather rough edges.

'Then, something light for lunch – salad, paté, something like that,' he agreed enthusiastically, 'then as lavish a meal as you can manage, say, round about eightish at night?'

Jenny gave him a long, considering look. 'I can manage a very lavish meal, given the right ingredients,' she warned him. It was her dream to be let loose on a no-holds-barred feast. She tended, she knew, to go rather over the top though.

Lucas laughed. 'I bet you can.'

Jenny looked at him archly. 'How many courses had you in mind, Mr Finch?'

Lucas leered at her. 'Surprise me, darlin'.'

'Give us a kiss,' the parrot interpreted helpfully.

Jenny looked at the bird thoughtfully, then glanced at its laughing-eyed owner.

'I might just do that,' she murmured.

And then smiled. Well, he'd asked for it!

TWO

JENNY HAD NO intention of sleeping in the narrow and cramped room on the *Stillwater Swan* that night if she could possibly help it. And certainly not when Wainscott House itself was standing nearby practically empty and presumably just full of comfortable bedrooms with nice big beds! She'd arrived on a Friday afternoon strictly for Mr Lucas Finch's convenience, and she intended to sleep in one of the spare rooms at his country residence that same Friday night for her own.

A labourer was still worthy of her hire, after all. And so she set about securing these sleeping arrangements with all her usual tact and diplomacy – not to mention downright sneakiness. As with most things, timing was all.

Just before the deliveries of food were due to arrive, Jenny was sitting on a garden chair under a large plum tree, with her small case by her feet. She had deliberately kept it by her side, and now she gave it a thoughtful glance. She was waiting, very patiently, for the opportunity to deposit it where she wanted it and, inevitably, her patience was eventually rewarded.

Catching sight of a grey-haired figure at the kitchen sink, she promptly rose to her feet, grabbed her case and made her way to the kitchen through the well-tended vegetable garden. The housekeeper, busy filling a glass vase with water ready for a spray of gladioli, jumped a little as a large shadow fell over her, then turned sharply, her rather frosty face thawing a little at the sight of the cook. She obviously had no objection to her employer asking an outside agency to cook for his weekend guests, and Jenny guessed that the woman was glad to have a weekend off. So much the better – in her subconscious at least, she probably already felt as if she owed the new arrival a favour.

Jenny smiled at her pleasantly. 'Hello. You must be Mr Finch's housekeeper?' She held out her hand, forcing the woman to put down the vase. 'I'm Miss Starling – please, call me Jenny.'

The older woman shook her hand, looking a little flustered now.

'I was hoping you could show me to my room?' Jenny said, and looked at her case helplessly. 'I'm expecting the food to be delivered soon and I must go over it all. I wouldn't put it past the greengrocer to try and palm me off with bruised peaches or marked plums.'

The housekeeper, who introduced herself as Beatrice Jessop, tut-tutted and agreed that nowadays shopkeepers would indeed take the most atrocious liberties, should you let them.

'Exactly,' Jenny agreed, as if she'd been listening to the Wisdom of Solomon. 'So I'd really like to just unpack my night things and stow away my case before rolling up my sleeves, so to speak, to do battle. I imagine I'm to be put up in the room next to yours? We are the only two ladies in the house, I presume? Or does Mr Finch have a partner?'

The housekeeper, who'd obviously had no such orders from her employer to prepare a room for the cook, very quickly agreed that, obviously, Jenny was to have a room next to hers. Where else? Professional women should stick together after all. And no, her employer was so far very much a bachelor.

Soon Jenny was helping the by now thoroughly thawed housekeeper to make up a fresh bed in a pleasant and large room at the rear of the house. It had a charming view overlooking the village, with its old church, well-maintained village green and picturesque cottages.

Mrs Jessop then very tactfully withdrew, and Jenny slipped a voluminous – but quite sexily diaphanous – white nightdress under her pillow and straightened up again. She gave the sturdy double bed a satisfied smile, nodded once in satisfaction, and left the room. On the landing she couldn't resist stopping at the window to look down at the winding, wide river, and the *Stillwater Swan* at her mooring. From the second floor, the boat looked even more impressive. Having an overall, prow-to-stern look at it, she saw at once that it was surprisingly large. It was a good thing, she mused, that the river had been recently dredged and enlarged or she'd doubt the *Swan* would be able to clear it. Although she supposed that good old Father Thames had seen – and accommodated – much more prestigious boats in his time.

She'd spent the afternoon minutely exploring every inch of the beautiful paddle steamer, being unable to resist it. It had, she knew, three large bedrooms on the top floor, including the master suite, which faced the front. A spacious bathroom had every modern convenience, including flushing toilet, shower and full bath. Down below, as well as the main salon/dining room and galley, it had a games room, and another toilet. At the rear was a large expanse of open decking, on which to play quoits or even, if you didn't mind being just a touch cramped, a game of tennis.

Jenny looked at the gleaming white vessel and felt herself smile. She couldn't have stopped herself from falling in love with the craft even if she'd tried to. It so effortlessly brought back memories of the elegance and elan of days long since perished. She could just imagine Greta Garbo lounging on one of the main salon's white leather couches with a gold cigarette holder about a foot long in one hand, and swirling a fluted glass of champagne in another. Clark Gable wouldn't have given a damn whilst playing poker in the games room, and Noel Coward wouldn't have looked a whit out of place holding court by the mock fireplace in the salon. It wasn't very often she got an assignment as glamorous and as different as this one.

She took a long deep breath of pleased anticipation. She could hardly wait for the morning to come. The lure of a short river cruise was beginning to make her feel as excited as a little girl on Christmas Eve.

With her bed-finding mission now satisfactorily accomplished, Jenny made her way tranquilly back to the garden.

Wainscott House, she saw at once, had been built around a large quad. In the middle of the quad there had been placed a large square lawn, with a sundial in the exact centre, which looked both old and original, and she wondered if it had truly come with the house. This lawn was in turn surrounded by colourful and tightly packed herbaceous borders. The house occupied two sides of the square, and on the opposite sides were two small converted cottages, that had once been stables, and a variety of outbuildings.

From one of the large cottage doors, wide enough to have admitted the horses that had once lodged there, a man stepped out and into the sunshine. He wasn't a tall man, and he wasn't a young man, and from the way he moved down the path in a curiously circular, rolling gait, Jenny had no difficulty at all in labelling him as an old sea-dog. Only sailors walked like that in her experience. Which was considerable. Either that or he was someone who had had way too much grog. This, then, she surmised, could only be the captain.

Jenny left her seat in the shade in order to waylay him. 'Hello. You must be Captain Lester?' she asked pleasantly.

The man jerked to a halt, obviously taken aback by the sound of a woman's voice. Jenny wasn't surprised. She hadn't thought that the housekeeper, Mrs Jessop, was the kind of woman to take to crusty old sea-salts, and from what she knew (or rather, guessed) of a sailor's lonely life, they probably preferred to keep themselves to themselves. Not that she supposed that piloting a riverboat was the same thing as taking to the oceans.

Still, one sailor, or so she'd discovered in her early twenties, was very much like another.

'Aye, that's right. Tobias Lester, ma'am, at your service.'

Tobias Lester was, she supposed, in his mid-fifties. His hair had once been golden but had now settled into that silver-blond salt-and-pepper shade that could be so attractive on a man. His eyes were the same blue/green of the sea, and looked attractive in a rather round, pleasantly creased face. His skin had the look and consistency of leather – no doubt as the result of years of working outdoors.

'I'm your cook for the weekend,' Jenny introduced herself, instantly liking the older man's warm smile of greeting.

Tobias Lester's smile widened. 'Pleased to meet you, ma'am. A sailor's always glad of a first-rate cook. I joined the Merchant Navy when I was just eighteen, and reckon I've sailed every sea that's out there. But I can't say that any of the ships I was on had what you might call a first-class cook – not a priority, see? But with pleasure cruises, well, that's different, isn't it? Got to keep people happy. Will this be your first cruise?'

They began to walk in unspoken mutual consent down the path and out towards the river. Jenny took the captain's assumption that she was, in fact, a 'first-rate cook' for granted. But it pleased her nonetheless. What a *nice* man Captain Lester was.

Jenny nodded. 'Yes, it is my first time on the water.' And then, thinking rather uneasily of Bora-Bora and typhoons, she added a shade uncertainly, 'I hope the going won't be too rough.'

Captain Lester laughed heartily. 'Good grief, no! The river's as flat as a mill pond. It'd have to be, I reckon – the *Swan*'s a flat-bottomed boat, you see. She can't take much rocking about.'

Jenny nodded but didn't, really, quite 'see' at all. What she knew about boats could be written on the back of a pea. And a *dried*, very shrivelled pea at that.

'She hasn't got a V-shaped hull,' the captain continued,

showing remarkable patience at a landlubber's obvious ignorance. 'If we hit a wave, she has no real way of riding it out
comfortably. That's why Lucas called her the *Stillwater Swan*,
see? There's a vast difference between the way river craft are
made and ships that have to put out to sea.'

Jenny smiled, much relieved. 'So it's a guaranteed smooth
ride then, is it?'

The captain laughed his hearty laugh again, his eyes crin-
kling attractively at the corners. 'That I can promise you,
ma'am. Even if it rains. Which—' He looked up judiciously into
a bright blue sky '—it won't.'

And sailors knew these sorts of things. Or so she'd been led
to believe. And, in truth, she was quite prepared to take his
word for it.

The captain had an easy-going manner that would enable
him, she imagined, to get on well with anyone who crossed his
path. But he also had that unmistakable air of competence
about him, that made you feel you could trust him, as well as
like him. It came as no surprise then that the socially active
Lucas Finch had chosen this experienced and presumably
retired seaman for his captain. He looked the part, he wouldn't
embarrass him or his guests with too much social ineptitude,
and he so obviously knew what he was doing.

The perfect man for the *Stillwater Swan*, in fact.

The cook glanced back at the house, her face thoughtful. 'You
live in the converted cottages, Captain?' she asked, slightly
curious. She hadn't expected Lucas Finch to be such a considerate employer.

'Yes, that's right. Me and Brian O'Keefe, the engineer.'

'Mr Finch must use the *Swan* a lot then – if he likes to keep
his staff so close?' she probed, wondering why she was so
curious. Perhaps, she thought wryly, it was the siren call of
wanderlust catching up with her rather late in life. But she
found herself, rather unexpectedly, envying Lucas Finch and
Captain Lester the idyllic life they appeared to lead.

'Oh yes. Lucas loves the *Swan* almost as much as I do,' the captain mused, casting such a loving look over the gleaming white boat that Jenny very nearly felt uncomfortable. 'When I first came here, I'd been in the Merchant Navy for so long, it was getting harder and harder to keep finding a ship to take me on – they like their tars young these days. Can't say as I blame 'em,' he added, sighing, then shrugged. 'It's a young man's game, I suppose.'

Captain Lester, Jenny realized, like a lot of solitary people, could become very loquacious when given the opportunity. Not that she minded. She was at a loose end until the food came anyway, and she was genuinely interested to hear about a life led on the water.

'So when I saw this advertisement, like, for the skipper of an old river paddle steamer, I was down here like a shot. Especially when it came with board and lodging on site. Thought it was going to be one of those touristy things, though. You know what I mean? Take a cruise up the Thames for fifty quid a day, with a licensed bar thrown in. That sort o' thing. I was expecting wedding parties and rowdy office outings and what not.'

He shook his head sadly at the thought of it, and Jenny nodded glumly in sympathy.

'So you could've knocked me down with the proverbial feather, like, when I came here and met Lucas – Mr Finch. When he told me he was a private owner, I was quite surprised. And then he took me out to the *Swan* ...' His voice trailed off, and Jenny once more nodded in perfect understanding. Yes, she could well imagine his reaction.

As she herself looked at the boat, it wasn't hard to understand what a dream come true she must have been to someone like Tobias Lester. He must have felt himself approaching the scrap heap, with nothing but rented accommodation in some anonymous town to look forward to, and a slow and lonely descent into old age. To find himself in charge of a beauty like the *Swan*, and with the added security of a full-time job as well, it must have felt like all of his Christmases and birthdays had come at once.

As if sensing the direction of her thoughts, Tobias Lester leaned back against a large wooden pole that marked the beginning of the landing stage, and folded his arms across his muscular chest. 'I'd more or less resigned myself to a life with my sister, see, up Banbury way. She's a widow. Got a nice enough little semi, a bit o' garden. Shops nearby. Nice enough, I suppose. If you like that sort o' thing.'

But a bit of a graveyard for a man like you, Jenny instantly surmised, and shuddered. She could well imagine the gloom and despondency with which Tobias Lester must have considered a semi in Banbury. The fact that his words confirmed her hypothesis on his character came as no surprise to her at all. She'd always been good at reading people, and their situation in life.

'And then I saw her.' The captain nodded his head towards the beautiful white vision, his voice so full of love and slave-like devotion that, for the first time ever, Jenny understood why men would insist on calling a ship 'she'.

'Course, when Lucas said he intended to take her out at least once a week, I took it with a pinch o' salt, like. He'd just had her commissioned, see, and I thought ...' Aware that he was becoming a little less than discreet, he shrugged his shoulders and trailed off.

Jenny, of course, had no such scruples. 'You thought it was just another rich man's toy?' she stated flatly. 'That he'd soon get bored with it, and leave it to slowly rust away, out of sight somewhere?'

Tobias gave her a thoughtful glance, and then nodded. 'Yeah, that's what I thought, right enough. And glad I was to be proved wrong. Lucas has had her for years now, and we still go out in her near enough every week. Course, he likes to show her off, so we often take guests up to London or Oxford and back. Sometimes even further – though the river gets narrower the further north you go, and it wouldn't do to get the *Swan* stuck. Not that I mind the company of guests, you understand?' he added anxiously. 'A boat like the *Swan* deserves to be shown off. She was made for folks to enjoy. But I like it quiet too – when it's just us.'

Tobias settled himself more comfortably against the post. 'I remember, deep one winter, we took her out just after an ice-breaking barge had been through. We'd had a hoar frost the night before, and the sun came up next morning, as pale as a lemon. Well, we took her out, and she was the only boat on the water. All the weeping willows was hanging over the banks, like them silver strings you put on Christmas trees. Must have been a Sunday morning, too, cos as we went, we could hear the church bells a'going. No one was with us on that trip, neither. Just me and Brian, Lucas and Francis. I'll never forget it. People tend to think that a riverboat's just for the summer. T'ain't true.' He shook his shaggy, leonine head, and Jenny, who'd been almost hypnotized by the vision of it in her mind, suddenly opened her eyes a little wider and gave herself a mental shake.

This would not do!

'Well, I suppose I should inspect the cupboard space on board. I don't want to take any food that might spoil.'

'Oh, we've got a refrigeration unit on board, didn't you see it?' Tobias asked, as proud as any father talking of his daughter's prowess.

Jenny, thoroughly delighted now, admitted that she hadn't seen it, and she followed him happily to the galley to be shown a small but handy fridge, tucked away under the sink.

Hundreds of yards away, in a neat and newly renovated cottage in the middle of the village, David Leigh looked up from his desk and glanced through the window towards the river.

He should be at the office, by rights, but Archie Pringle, senior partner of Pringle, Ford & Soames, Solicitors, had been more than happy to give him the afternoon off, when informed that the junior man had been invited to join Lucas Finch on a weekend river cruise.

Not only was the *Stillwater Swan* something of a 'celebrity' around and about, having been featured in several lifestyle magazines and local newspapers, but Pringle, Ford & Soames would be very happy indeed to get their hands on some of Lucas Finch's much-vaunted business dealings. It was well known that Finch had made the majority of his fortune in biscuits, and owned several factories that still produced such delights as 'Jimmy Jammy Fingers' and 'Peach Puffs'. There was a lot of mileage to be got out of a biscuit king, so Archie Pringle was more than happy (if a little envious) to let his junior have a little leeway in the hopes of landing some of Finch's business. And if, as rumour had it, the start-up money for Lucas's empire had been a shade, well, shady, then that was just too bad. In this uncertain economic day and age, it paid even well-established and respectable solicitors not to be too choosy who they did business with.

David Leigh, however, was not feeling particularly grateful for his unexpected leisure time. In fact, as he looked out at the river and thought about tomorrow morning and the start of the cruise, happiness was the furthest thing from his mind.

He pushed the papers he'd been working on away and rose to his feet feeling stiff-necked and badly knotted up. It was his nerves, he knew. The tension was getting so bad that he thought, just sometimes, that he might go stark staring mad any minute now. He felt like he wanted to scream and rant and rave, but didn't dare to, because he was not sure that he would be able to stop, once he'd started.

Instead, he walked slowly towards the window, and his eyes went immediately to the almost fairy-like figure of his tiny wife, who was busy picking some raspberries at the bottom of the garden. She looked incredibly lovely, dressed in a pale, floating summer dress, her ash-blonde hair blowing in the breeze.

Although the doctor had assured them that she was indeed three months' pregnant, she still looked as slender as a reed. At only five feet two, with tiny wrists and ankles, David could hardly imagine her big with child.

He sighed, then winced, as a haunting note filled the air.

At the bottom of the garden, Dorothy Leigh looked up, and frowned. She knew the sound well, of course. Everyone who lived in Buscot did. It was the hauntingly lovely steam whistle of the *Stillwater Swan*.

Brian O'Keefe must be testing the boilers in preparation for the cruise tomorrow.

Dorothy paused in picking the luscious, tart berries, a small frown tugging at her pale brows. She wasn't looking forward to tomorrow. Or Sunday. She wished, in fact, that they weren't going at all.

She knew that Lucas Finch had what her mother coyly called 'a thing' for her, but it was not the thought of fighting off Lucas's rather coarse passes that worried her.

Her green-eyed gaze turned back to the house and she thought she saw a figure step hastily back from the bedroom window. Not possible, of course. David was hard at work on old man Filey's last will and testament. The silly old goat was always chopping and changing it about, much to the amused annoyance of his loving kith and kin. He'd probably left his imagined fortune to his cat this time, or to his sour-faced sister who was, for some reason, currently in favour with the old man.

Dorothy sighed and resumed picking the berries. If asked, she couldn't have said quite *why* she was so uneasy.

She only knew that she was. She just couldn't shake off a feeling of … well … of … doom, almost. Her old granny would condescendingly have put it down to her condition, whereas her more modern doctor would have reassured her that it was only natural that she should sometimes feel so restless, but Dorothy knew it wasn't that.

There was something wrong with David.

But she knew that her husband would only give her one of his long-suffering, lightly amused looks if she tried to ask him about it, so she didn't bother. But a wife knew these things.

And so she went on patiently picking berries, and wishing that Lucas hadn't asked them out on the boat.

Inside the house, David Leigh walked back to his desk and pulled out a piece of paper. He looked at it for a long, long, time, his face curiously pinched and grim. Yet anybody looking over his shoulder wouldn't have seen anything remarkable about the correspondence at all. It was simply a long, hand-written letter from one of Pringle, Ford & Soames' clients, outlining some conveyancing work that he wanted done on a property out Farrington way.

But what David Leigh did next might well have surprised any observer.

For, slowly, carefully, and on a separate piece of paper, David Leigh began to write an exact replica of the letter. Word for word. And in a handwriting that was fast beginning to look indistinguishable from the real, original thing.

With just a bit more practice, David thought with a near-hysterical and grim twist of his lips, he could have a lucrative second career as a forger ahead of him.

In the beautiful old town of Woodstock, Gabriel Olney checked his tie in the mirror. It was perfectly straight and impeccably knotted. It was navy blue, and bore the insignia of a very good public school. He stood ramrod straight in front of the mirror, looking every inch the colonel he had once been. He was not tall, at five feet eight, but the very rigidity with which he habitually stood to attention made him *seem* taller. He was going to be sixty-one on his next birthday, but he was as lean and fit as a whippet.

His dark grey eyes checked that his moustache was properly trimmed, and that his dark blue 'sailing' jacket was without a crease. He gave a brass button an eagle-eyed check, but it shone as only good old-fashioned spit-and-polish could make it shine. He gave a grunt of satisfaction.

Unlike David Leigh, Gabriel Olney was looking forward to the weekend. Very much so.

He smiled, a rather hard, gimlet-eyed smile as he took off the jacket and began, very carefully and very neatly, to pack his small, overnight case. His wife's larger case already lay half packed on the bed, crammed with garments she'd simply tossed in, willy-nilly.

He gave it a scathing look.

When his shaving things were neatly stowed, and his deck shoes (encased in polythene, of course, to ensure that they could make no dirty marks) were neatly tucked away at the side, he shut the lid and zipped it up. Then he straightened and reached into his wallet. From it he exacted a cheque.

It was a very *large* cheque.

As he looked at the rows of noughts, he smiled with gloating satisfaction.

And if the same fictional somebody who might have been watching David Leigh had now been stood peering over *his* shoulder, they'd have been very surprised indeed. For the cheque was not made out *to* Gabriel Olney, but was made out *by* Gabriel Olney to Lucas Finch.

But still Gabriel Olney, late colonel in what he considered to be one of the best regiments in the land, smiled with eminent satisfaction as he considered the vast sum of money he intended to part with.

At that particular moment in time, Jenny Starling was also smiling like the Cheshire cat that had had the cream. And found a canary in it to boot.

She was standing in the large kitchen of Wainscott House, going over every item the butcher, fishmonger and greengrocer had brought in their smart little refrigerated vans.

The butcher had arrived first, bearing lean cuts of venison, dark, marbled steaks, prime lamb, fresh pork and smoked bacon. Not even Jenny had been able to find a single fault with the tender meat.

The fishmonger had arrived just as she'd finished carefully storing the meat in the large fridge at Wainscott House. She would only remove the food to the *Stillwater Swan* first thing in the morning.

The fishmonger had fared rather less well than the butcher, for Jenny had insisted that he take away his mussels and return with a batch that suited her fastidious tastes better. She'd compounded his misery by rejecting two of his trout, which, she insisted, after a beady-eyed look at their gills, could be chucked in the bin, thank-you-very-much. But she was happy with the prawns, crab, salmon and whitebait, although she did reject his oysters.

Jenny disliked cooking oysters, ever since that very distressing incident concerning the Russian ambassador's wife, and the six bottles of vodka.

The greengrocer, last of all to arrive, had to watch and wince as she minutely inspected every vegetable and piece of fruit that he laid out for her, from the leeks to the quinces, the asparagus to the grapes. He left with only a few bruised apples, some (admittedly) unwholesome-looking bananas and a dented kiwi.

All in all, not a bad haul, Jenny thought, looking at her list of goodies. Already her heart was thumping. Breakfast was easy enough, of course, for a full English breakfast was a must. She could make some fresh sausages with the pork and the herbs she'd already gathered from the kitchen garden, and smoked bacon, grilled tomatoes and kidneys. And of course plenty of fried eggs always went down a treat with the men.

For the ladies, though, and especially Dorothy Leigh, Jenny would include the options of delicately flavoured omelettes, porridge and perhaps a little kedgeree on the menu.

Lunches, too, would be a snap, with plenty of salads, a cold chicken and ham pie, perhaps even a huge fruit salad, to help keep the guests cool and refreshed on a hot summer's day.

But the evening meal....

Jenny sat down eagerly, pulling the list of goodies towards her, and letting her imagination run riot.

There would have to be hors d'oeuvres, of course – cheese and anchovy biscuits, Bengal eggs, salmon croutes, sardine and olive canapés. She sighed in bliss. Then, for a second course, perhaps some lobster cocktails followed by a chicken liver savoury or maybe halibut rarebit. And she mustn't forget soup, of course. A rich game soup, or, no, perhaps something lighter … Jardiniere soup, or lettuce and spring onion soup. Yes, very nice on a sultry summer evening.

And for the main course.... Her heart very nearly sang a song. Well, Lucas Finch had promised her she could go wild. Perhaps eels. No, perhaps not. Not with a pregnant woman seated at table. Fricassee of veal, perhaps, or venison à la royale. Hmm....

And desserts that looked as beautiful as they tasted. They'd have to be cold, of course. A pity that, but it *was* high summer. Almond cream with greengage jam would go lovely with a variety of things. Apple gateau, or apricot soufflé … yes, especially for Dorothy Leigh. And for the gentlemen something a bit more substantial. Chestnut and pineapple trifle, or floating island, or lemon sponge....

Someone coughed.

Jenny looked up ferociously. She'd just begun to elevate herself into the lofty heights of foodie nirvana and she wasn't too pleased to be brought down to earth with such an unkind bump.

'Yes?' she snapped. To a perfect stranger. Jenny blinked, and immediately apologized. 'I do beg your pardon. I was miles away.'

The stranger inclined his head. And in that instant, Jenny

was forever to believe that this man did *everything* silently. She had certainly never heard him come in, and since the kitchen was tiled, she *should* have heard him. And when he spoke, his voice was little more than a whisper.

'I'm sorry to disturb you, Miss Starling, but Mr Finch wondered if you would care to prepare this evening's meal, or would you prefer for Mrs Jessop to do so?'

That this was the famous 'manservant' of Lucas Finch, Jenny was in no doubt. He was dressed in a white houseboy's jacket that reminded the cook of all those films set in India, where the pukka sahib was waited on by expressionless Indians with round, soulful eyes.

But Francis Grey didn't have round, soulful eyes. He was about fifty, she supposed, slim, and had such an air of being so neat and tidy he hardly looked human. Not a hair was out of place. On this hot July afternoon, not a bead of perspiration dared quiver on his forehead.

'Oh, I'd be delighted to cook the evening meal,' Jenny said quickly, and with some considerable relief. She knew that Mrs Jessop could make a decent bed and arrange a mean gladioli floral display, but Jenny believed – quite rightly – that *nobody* could cook like she could cook.

'How many are going to dine?'

Francis Grey blinked. 'Just Mr Finch. Mrs Jessop and myself eat in here.' He indicated the kitchen, at the same time, and in some mysterious way that not even the perspicacious Jenny Starling was quite able to fathom, indicating that she also was to dine in the kitchen. Not that Jenny had ever intended to do anything else. Still it rankled to have a 'manservant' make it quite so plain. She inclined her head somewhat stiffly. 'And the captain and … er … Mr O'Keefe?'

Francis smiled. His face, Jenny noticed in disconcerted surprise, was so bland, so *nondescript*, that even though she was looking right at him, she'd have been hard pressed to actually describe what he looked like.

'The crew see to their own meals,' Francis said, somehow relegating the *Stillwater Swan* and her servants to another planet.

Jenny nodded. 'Very well. What time would Mr Finch like to dine?' she asked stiffly.

'Eight-thirty is the usual time,' Francis allowed. Bowed. And left. Or rather, not so much left as somehow floated away.

Jenny watched him go and then, for some strange reason, shivered. Hard.

THREE

JENNY AROSE, SOMEWHAT reluctantly it had to be said, with the dawn chorus. She tiptoed stealthily down to the kitchen, not wishing to disturb either Lucas or Mrs Jessop, and yawningly made herself a cup of tea. This she sipped for a moment before deciding to take it out onto the lawn.

All around her, the cool early-morning air resonated with birdsong. The grass was still moist with dew, and far in the distance she could see a farmer, riding a red piece of farm equipment to the slope of a hill, no doubt in order to turn the hay. She sipped her delicious hot brew and watched the bees disappearing up the fluted bells of the foxglove flowers.

It was going to be another glorious day, as Captain Lester had so ably predicted yesterday. Already the sun was promising to blast its furnace-like heat down on her head as she made her way to her by-now favourite spot under the plum tree. It looked, to her experienced eye, to be an old-fashioned variety Victoria plum, and she wished she could be here in the autumn to sample its fruit. Victorias made perfect plum tarts.

The very rustic-looking wooden bench groaned just slightly in protest as she sat down on it, and a thrush, who was in the process of whacking a snail against a stone, paused to eye her with rather dubious interest. He needn't have worried – she was not that interested in sharing his breakfast. A nasty French habit, that. Snails. She could cook anything but snails were the exception.

Jenny ignored the bird and continued to sip blissfully away at her tea. It was so nice to be on holiday, after all. She was just down to the final mouthful when she heard a cheerful whistle (of the non-avian kind) coming from the direction of the river. The tune was 'Messing About On The River' – a rather apt title under the circumstances, she mused with a smile.

Curious, Jenny strolled to the gate and stood leaning against what had probably once been a chicken hutch, to watch a dark young man step lithely aboard the *Stillwater Swan*. As he did so, he hefted a large bag of coal under one arm as if it was nothing more than a feather pillow. No doubt, the impressed cook surmised, this was Captain Lester's neighbour and fellow worker, the engineer, Brian O'Keefe.

She wondered idly whether his name could be put down to Irish or Scottish ancestry, but when he disappeared into the *Swan*'s boiler room, she shrugged and glanced at her watch. It was still only a quarter to six. She had plenty of time.

She returned to the kitchen and began the task of moving her precious food packages to the *Swan*. Although from time to time she still caught snatches of 'Messing About On The River' issuing from the boiler room, Brian O'Keefe never stuck his head out to ask who was about, although he must have heard her.

Perhaps, she thought rather dourly, he was one of those obstinate individuals who did nothing more than that which was strictly their job, and resented doing even that. She hoped not. She was looking forward to this cruise, and didn't want anything to spoil the ambience.

By seven, her galley was fully stocked. She'd added plenty of herbs and some more fresh vegetables from the kitchen garden to the final tally, and her last act was to place her knives and assorted instruments reverently into a drawer. She gave the oven another look over, although she'd already tested it thoroughly yesterday afternoon. One of the disadvantages of being a travelling cook was that you were always using ovens that you didn't know. And, as every cook knew, sometimes to their cost, all ovens had their own idiosyncrasies and funny little ways that could trip you up. Flat soufflés and burnt duck being amongst the worst that could happen. But she was confident that the specimen on the *Swan* didn't have too many surprises in store for her now.

One of Jenny's worst nightmares was the thought of an oven giving up the ghost altogether. Although she was perfectly capable of producing a good meal using rings and grill alone, she didn't much care to have her ingenuity put to the test. (Using microwaves didn't even cross her mind.) But the gas bottles were full and the cooker was a relatively new and trustworthy brand. She nodded, gave the boiler room a passing look as she left, and returned to the house.

Mrs Jessop looked surprised to see her, and then looked faintly approving as she realized that the cook must have already been hard at work for some time. The younger generation didn't know they'd been born, Mrs Jessop was wont to say. Not that she'd said it to this Miss Starling. She had infinitely better sense than that!

The two women were cosily drinking tea together when the parrot, in a flurry of scarlet and blue excitement, fluttered by and landed squarely on the teapot lid. Apparently the creature had little feeling in its scaly feet, for instead of squawking and hopping off the hot ceramic rather smartly, it merely turned, cocked its head to one side, and fixed Jenny with a curious, pale eye.

'Wotcha,' the parrot said amiably.

Jenny blinked. 'Good morning,' she replied.

Lucas Finch came in at that moment, yawning mightily. It was an experience somewhat similar, Jenny mused, to that of peering down the Mersey tunnel on a smoggy day.

'Mornin', ladies,' Lucas said, and scratched himself vigorously under his left armpit before fixing the teapot with an avaricious stare.

Mrs Jessop quickly and competently shooed the bird off, and poured him a cup.

Jenny wondered what the oh-so-correct Francis would make of this cosy little domestic scene. She somehow doubted that he would approve.

Lucas pulled out a chair and sat amicably next to his temporary cook, took a hearty slurp of tea, and then sighed blissfully. 'The gannets will be arriving in another half an hour or so, love,' he warned her cheerfully. 'David and Dot only live down the road aways, and old Gab and Jasmine like to be on time. He's an ex-soldier, you know,' he informed her a trifle glumly, then rolled his eyes. There was something about the way he spoke that roused the cook's instinct for trouble.

Jenny glanced at him curiously. 'Were you once in the army, Mr Finch?' She fished for information gently and was somehow not surprised to find that she had hit some kind of nail right on the head.

Lucas jumped as if he'd just been goosed, and Mrs Jessop began to studiously study her teacup. She stared at it so hard that Jenny wouldn't have been surprised if she'd been attempting to read the tea leaves, which was definitely a fine art in this day of the ubiquitous teabag. So long as there were no tall, dark, handsome strangers lurking about in the bottom of her cup, Jenny wished her luck. Tall, dark, handsome strangers, in her opinion, were far more trouble than they were worth.

'Yeah, I was in the army a lifetime ago,' Lucas finally and rather reluctantly admitted. 'A solider, too. Saw action in the Falklands.' He sounded definitely defensive about it – a strange reaction for a man most people would automatically call a hero. He slurped another great mouthful of tea. 'Well, I'd better make sure Brian and Toby are on the ball. Er … you all set then, love?'

Jenny nodded, and promptly outlined the very varied and substantial breakfast menu she had planned. 'When would you like it served?' she added, and watched him swallow the last of his tea, before wiping his mouth with the back of his hand. Far from finding his coarse mannerisms off-putting, they roused in her a sort of amused affection.

'About nine will do,' he said, after thinking about it for a moment or so. 'We don't want too early a start. We'll take an hour, have a leisurely breakfast on board, and then set off about ten. I don't like to eat and cruise at the same time – you miss too much, stuck in the main salon.'

Jenny, who didn't like anything to compete with her food (including a paddle steamer), smiled happily. 'I quite agree. That sounds like a very good idea.'

She watched him leave, looking rather better for his morning slurp of tea, and smiled wistfully. For all his uncouth ways, she rather liked Lucas Finch. She would bet a fairly substantial amount of her wages that he was not half as bad as he'd like people to think. Or maybe not, she added mentally, after another moment's thought.

'If you don't mind me giving you a piece of advice,' Mrs Jessop's tentative voice broke in, and Jenny quickly turned back to her.

'I'm always willing to listen to advice,' she said, quite truthfully. Whether or not she took it was an entirely different matter, of course.

'I shouldn't talk about the Falklands war too much in front of Mr Finch, if I were you. He's apt to be a bit sensitive about it.'

'Oh?' she said mildly – and craftily. It had been her experience that the less you seemed to want to gossip, the more gossip came your way.

Mrs Jessop's genteel face took on a look of mild distress. 'People can be so ... unkind, sometimes,' she said, her hands fluttering over her cup. 'There are all sorts of nasty rumours going around that ... well, I really don't know how they start. But in a village ... people can be so *spiteful*, can't they? And I'm sure there's nothing in it, really. Just because Mr Finch was a Londoner, you see. And, well, sort of very aggressively working class, so to speak.' She gulped out the last words in a slightly embarrassed rush. 'And just because he grew up in a neighbourhood with some rather, well, shall we say, *undesirable* men, people will take on so,' she finished firmly, looking faintly relieved to come to the end of her somewhat rambling sentence.

Jenny had no difficulty in interpreting this rather obtuse explanation. It was quite obvious that people in these parts believed Lucas Finch to have been one of those parasites who had somehow profited from war. The kind of man who'd made a fortune from other people's misery, in fact.

Jenny sighed. She rather thought – realistically – that the locals probably had it right. Men of Lucas Finch's ilk could turn a war into a goldmine – and regularly did. So had he been an arms dealer in the not so distant past? Or simply one of those men who could supply whatever was needed, cheaper than anyone else, and thus rake in the readies? It was, she supposed grimly, just as well that she wasn't a gambler by nature. Lucas Finch probably *was* just as bad – or worse – as he made out. And liking him just showed spectacularly bad judgment on her part!

But she smiled kindly at Mrs Jessop (who obviously needed to consider her employer more in the light of being a rough diamond, rather than an out-and-out crook) and agreed that, yes, people, could indeed be very spiteful when they wanted to be.

At half past eight, a rather impressive-looking Jaguar XJS pulled up on the gravelled entrance at the front of the house with just a little jaunty spurt of gravel. Jenny, who was just walking back to the boat, found herself curious, and paused to watch the couple who emerged.

In spite of the sports car being what she considered to be a young man's toy, it was a silver-haired man who climbed out from behind the wheel. From the ramrod-straight way in which he marched to the passenger's side and held open the door, she had no trouble in recognizing an ex-soldier.

This then was Gabriel Olney.

Expecting a similarly silver-haired, genteel officer's wife to make up a matching set, the cook was faintly surprised by the woman who stepped very elegantly from the car. She was, Jenny saw at once, extremely stylish. Everything about her fairly screamed it. Her hair was dark and shaped into a very chic, short, geometric cut, and when she turned and smiled rather perfunctorily at her husband, Jenny caught a glimpse of liquid chocolate eyes as dark as her hair. But she wasn't quite as young, perhaps, as she was trying to make out. Jenny put her somewhere in her mid-forties, but her figure was as smart as that of a twenty-year-old and her clothes must have cost the earth. She wondered, without so much as a single pang of envy, how many times Jasmine Olney did her shopping in Paris.

Then the pair passed on into the house, and the curvaceous cook returned to the *Stillwater Swan* to tend to her tomato and herb omelettes and the nicely sizzling bacon.

Ten minutes later, Jenny glanced with satisfaction at the browning sausages and checked her watch. It was nearly nine.

She didn't like to prompt her employers, but food should be enjoyed when at its premium. She turned down the heat on the stove and, wiping her hands on a pristine clean towel, made her way out to the open decking at the *Swan*'s stern. She could see at once that the planking had been freshly marked for quoits. So Brian O'Keefe *had* been busy after all.

As she moved across to the open landing gate, she saw the engineer himself walk past, a block and tackle draped casually over one shoulder. He paused and gave her a brief but all-encompassing look. It was the kind of look that missed nothing, and left you feeling somehow unnerved – and not in a nicely feminine and appreciative way either.

Brian O'Keefe, Jenny saw at once, was tall, dark and extremely handsome, which was three strikes against him right from the start. He was, she guessed, of Irish ancestry, and had the dark, brooding good looks of that race, and their clear, dark blue eyes. He had the bad manners to look at her as if he found her wanting.

Jenny sniffed. Hard.

Just then, Gabriel and Jasmine Olney appeared at the landing stage, with Lucas Finch and two young people of almost remarkable appearance. Remarkable in that they seemed to go together like two halves of the same coin.

These, Jenny surmised, must be David and Dorothy Leigh.

Dorothy was a small, elfin, fairy figure of a woman, and no sign of her condition yet showed. She tucked a long lock of pale hair so blonde it was almost silver, rather nervously behind her ear, and looked up at her husband. On her face was a look of such adoration that Jenny very nearly winced.

David Leigh was a perfect foil for his wife. He was taller, but not so tall that he made Dorothy look dwarfish. He was lean, but had a look of strength about him that was in perfect contrast to her rather ethereal figure. His hair was a rich shade of brown, very earthy, to offset Dorothy's own silver hue. What he made of her look of adoration, though, the cook couldn't tell.

He hadn't seemed to notice it.

'Ah, just coming to round us up, hey, love?' Lucas's voice seemed to suddenly galvanize the tableau into action.

Jenny smiled and nodded. 'Breakfast is ready,' she agreed. 'I've written out the menu and left it at the table.'

'How marvellous,' Gabriel Olney said, patting his ridiculously lean stomach. 'I'm starving.'

Jenny was distressed to see just how lean the old soldier was. Although she didn't suspect him of being ill, she did suspect him of not eating enough. Stripped off, she could probably count every single rib the man had. She made a firm note to pile Gabriel Olney's plate with extra sausage and black pudding.

Jasmine Olney made no comment on her husband's starvation, real or otherwise. Her eyes had gone straight to Brian O'Keefe, and had stayed there.

It was not surprising. With his shirt undone all the way to his waist in an effort to beat the heat, he was really something to look at. Especially since, with the block and tackle slung casually over his shoulder like a bag of swag, he reminded the cook of a pirate from one of those 1940s films, the kind that Errol Flynn had done so well.

Nor was O'Keefe himself unaware of his new audience, she noticed, with a wry twist of her lips, for he turned on Jasmine Olney the same kind of quick but comprehensive glance that he'd given the cook just a few moments earlier.

His own lips, Jenny noticed, turned up into a twisted smile that was almost, but not quite, downright insolent. Jasmine Olney flushed. She looked annoyed. And pleased. The sexual tension between them was so rife that Jenny wished she had a knife about her person, just to see if she could actually cut it.

Lucas Finch was too busy ogling Dorothy Leigh to notice, but Dorothy had seen the speaking look that had passed between the dirty, sweating engineer and the impeccably groomed Jasmine Olney, and she quickly looked away in embarrassment.

Her eyes skidded to a halt as they met Jenny's probably equally embarrassed expression, and the two women promptly pretended not to notice that there was anything at all amiss.

'I've cooked some porridge as well as some tomato and herb omelettes, for those who might not prefer a full English breakfast,' Jenny said, clearing her throat. In her opinion, food was an excellent choice of conversation whenever a social gaffe had been committed. It was so comfortingly safe.

'Hmm, lovely,' Dorothy quickly said.

Jasmine Olney merely smiled.

Brian O'Keefe nodded and strode off, rudely not saying a single word to anybody.

Gabriel Olney's lips tightened a mere fraction. 'A surly fellow, that,' he muttered, to nobody in particular.

Lucas tore his eyes from Dorothy, and met those of his guest. 'Hmm? Oh, yes, I dare say he is. But he's a damn good engineer.'

'Did you see that positively *torturous* thing he was holding?' Jasmine purred. 'It looked like he was taking off to a dungeon with it. I do hope you don't have a prisoner's brig on this boat, Lucas,' she laughed, and gave her husband a highly amused glance.

She was, Jenny thought with some surprise, deliberately baiting him. In her experience, wives with a roving eye usually tried to hide it from their spouses, not rub their noses in it.

For the first time since arriving at Buscot, Jenny began to feel distinctly uneasy.

'It was only a block and tackle,' Dorothy Leigh said, damp-eningly.

'And how would a pretty little thing like you know that, my dear?' Gabriel said, allowing his words to drop to a caressing whisper. His eyes smoked over Dorothy with such undisguised approval that both David Leigh and – more comically – Lucas Finch, stiffened in anger.

Jasmine looked more amused than angry at this attempt to upstage her. No doubt, Jenny surmised, she thought her husband was merely trying to make her jealous in his turn. Getting his own back, so to speak. Jenny thought it all rather childish, and wished they'd bang it on the head.

She had good food waiting!

And then she noticed how David Leigh was looking at Gabriel Olney and caught her breath. Her unease intensified into something solid and ugly. She was beginning to think that this river cruise might not be as pleasant as she'd hoped. For there was more than mere pique in the look that David was giving the old soldier. Now, any man with a wife as pretty as Dorothy was bound to have to put up with a fair bit, Jenny supposed – men did so like to ogle after all. But whereas David Leigh had been faintly amused by Lucas Finch's obvious infatuation with her, he was looking at Gabriel Olney as if …

Well, as if he'd like to kill him.

'My father worked on building sites for most of his life,'

Dorothy answered Gabriel's question as if he'd been serious. She seemed unaware of the undercurrents passing around them, and her voice was still rather matter-of-fact. 'He owned his own construction company. I often used to meet him at work in the summer holidays,' she recalled, her face softening in remembrance of those happy days. 'He used to let me help to mix the cement and put some bricks in place. He even let me use the crane once. I sat on his knee, of course, and he guided my hands. It was great fun,' she finished, with a seemingly genuine, carefree laugh.

Gabriel smiled. 'You could sit on *my* knee any time, my dear,' he purred, so archly à la Terry Thomas that Jenny almost expected him to caress his moustache villainously as well.

Dorothy gave him a rather furious look.

'Well, let's get at this breakfast,' Lucas Finch said, a touch icily, giving Olney a rather speaking glance as he moved past him. Then, just as everyone, with varying shades of relief, turned to follow, he suddenly stopped and gave a loud piercing whistle.

Jenny was not the only one who jumped.

From the direction of the house came a long, scarlet and blue streak of colour, and a moment later the parrot headed unerringly for Lucas Finch's shoulder. Jenny felt the slight breeze on her face as its wings whirled past her.

'Oh Lucas, do you have to bring that filthy thing along with you?' Jasmine asked petulantly. 'I'm sure I read somewhere that they carry some horrible, unpronounceable disease or something.'

The parrot, firmly settled on its master's shoulder, turned and eyed Jasmine keenly. It cocked its head to one side.

'Don't get your knickers in a twist, love,' it advised.

Everybody laughed. Including Jasmine.

Jenny added a sprig of basil as a finishing touch to the plate of omelettes and then turned around, only to find Francis standing right behind her in the doorway. Once again, she hadn't heard him enter. She managed not to jump.

He was dressed in white trousers (impeccably creased), a white jacket (impeccably ironed) and white tennis shoes (impeccably clean).

'This is for Mrs Leigh,' she said shortly, thrusting the tray into his waiting hands, then turned back, retrieved and deposited a huge bowl of steaming porridge onto the tray. 'And this is for Mr Olney. Cream is already on the table.'

Francis didn't bother to even nod, but turned silently and left. Jenny angrily dismissed the man from her thoughts. He was simply too pesky to be bothered with.

She checked her sausages, put the bread in to fry, and squeezed some more oranges. She added ice to the jug, and put it to one side. It wouldn't be long before Francis discovered it and bore it away to table. In fact, she was rather glad that she wouldn't have to serve at table. Jenny felt far happier in her kitchen. So even Francis had his uses, she reminded herself philosophically, and warned herself not to start making mountains out of molehills. There was no reason why they shouldn't all have a perfectly pleasant river cruise.

The men chose to have both porridge and the full English breakfast, and after dishing these out, Jenny heaped a plate up for the captain, adding to his tray a mug of tea and some cutlery.

Since the galley was just to the left of the bridge (which was situated right at the front of the boat, on the lower deck), Jenny had the perfect excuse to take a look at it. It was the only part of the boat she hadn't yet seen.

A tiny door in one corner led to the all-important room, and she knocked and opened it rather timidly.

Tobias Lester looked up, his face breaking into a smile at the sight of the steaming food. He was sitting in the room's sole chair, which was at that moment tucked behind a tiny desk in one corner.

Jenny handed over the tray, then stood back and looked around. The room was much smaller than she'd thought, but it had a large, wrap-around window, giving the captain a splendid 180 degree view of his surroundings. Which could only be a good thing, she guessed. She supposed a lot of the smaller river craft and narrow boats that also used the river would find the *Swan* somewhat intimidating – especially if the owners thought the man steering the big paddle steamer couldn't even see them! But as far as she could tell, there were no side mirrors like in a car to give him a view of what was behind him, and wondered if that ever worried him.

It would certainly worry *her*!

In the centre of the small wooden room was a small ship's wheel. It was entirely made of wood, and was beautifully carved, with the typical large wooden handles that could spin it all the way around. And into her mind flashed all the sea-faring pictures she had ever seen, where gallant ships' captains spun the wheel helplessly as their ship battled the storm. She had to resist the infantile urge to mutter 'hard to starboard mate' or 'splice the mizzen mast'.

Not that she had the faintest idea what a mizzen mast was, or how to splice it.

'Hmm, lovely,' Tobias said appreciatively, dunking a sausage into the yolk of an egg. He had the tray balanced on his lap with all the ease of someone used to eating this way. 'They all aboard then?' he asked, looking amiably to the back of the boat, and the cook nodded.

'Yes. All present and correct.'

Tobias smiled at the phrase, and then sighed. 'Mind you, I don't expect it will be all that jolly a jaunt,' he muttered, more or less to himself, although he didn't sound particularly concerned.

Jenny looked at him quickly. 'Oh? No. I must say I thought they seemed a rather unlikely group.'

Tobias smiled but rather annoyingly merely shook his head, refusing to be drawn further.

But Jenny was not about to be put off so easily. 'Mrs Olney in particular seemed rather out of place,' she probed as delicately as she could, and Tobias gave her another quick, assessing look.

'You don't miss much, do you, Miss Starling?' he said, but it was more of a statement than an accusation. 'I noticed it about you yesterday. I said to Brian this morning, I did, that this new cook knew her onions in more ways than one.'

Jenny obligingly smiled at the weak joke, but said nothing.

Tobias picked up a piece of fried bread, bit into it, caught the cook's patiently waiting eye, and sighed.

'Thing is, Mrs Olney's a bit of a ... well ... a bit of ... Anyway. The word is that she keeps a chap down in London,' he finally coughed up.

Jenny delicately raised an eyebrow. 'I imagine she goes there to shop,' she said, determined to be fair. First impressions could be so misleading sometimes.

Tobias smiled, and resigned himself happily to a good gossip. 'When I say that she keeps a chap down in London, I mean, she actually *keeps* a man down there. Pays the rent on a little flat, apparently. It seems that one of her bitchy friends from up Oxford way actually heard from another friend who was looking for a flat of her own, that Jasmine had, on the sly, rented out a bedsit in the West End. And, of course, she simply had to call in to look it over, and ask Jasmine for advice on getting her own flat set up.'

'Of course she did,' Jenny acknowledged drolly.

'And who should answer the bell but this big dark Adonis – the friend's choice of word, that, not mine. Well, of course, the word got round.'

Jenny smiled wryly. 'I bet it did! But surely, her husband...?'

Tobias Lester suddenly became very reticent about 'the husband'. He shrugged, muttered something about a man's married life being his own affair, and set about attacking his bacon.

Jenny promptly took the hint and left.

But afterwards, back in the galley, as she set about creating a mountain of toast and testing Mrs Jessop's homemade marmalade (and adding just a touch of much-needed lime juice), she wondered why Tobias Lester would be willing to gossip about Jasmine Olney, but not about her husband.

And then she promptly reminded herself that it was none of her business, after all, and began to industriously chop some spring onions.

This was, after all, her holiday too.

She had no idea then that, in her other role as a reluctant but effective amateur detective, it was going to become something of a busman's holiday before the weekend was over.

FOUR

JENNY HEARD THE engines throb into life and quickly finished the washing up. She left the crockery to drain and wiped her soapy hands on a towel as she went. She left the galley, moving through the main salon, and then stepped out onto the starboard side deck. There she walked to the rails and watched in pleasurable satisfaction as the riverbank began to fall away.

There was nothing quite like that first moment when a boat left the dock, be it an ocean liner about to cross the mighty Atlantic, or a river boat about to cruise through the English countryside. There was always that little tingle of anticipation, that atavistic sense of more than mere physical movement. You were afloat, and who knew where the tides of fate might take you?

Slowly, virtually silently, and with a smoothness that rivalled silk, the *Stillwater Swan* took to the centre of the River Thames, her course heading due east, towards the dreaming spires of Oxford. And with the sun facing her bridge, both of the *Swan*'s side decks were darkened in a comfortable shade. As this fact had been noted by others than herself, Jenny could just faintly hear the other guests on the port side, chattering in excitement.

The houses and cottages of Buscot were slowly left behind, and rows of willows, weeping willows and ash began to crowd down to the banks. A pair of mute swans watched their namesake with unimpressed dark avian eyes and ruffled their feathers slightly.

Jenny pulled a wooden but comfortable and – more importantly, *substantial* – deckchair nearer to the railings and sat down. A touch gingerly, it was true. In the past, she'd had some rather unfortunate dealings with deckchairs. It was a sad indictment of the new millennium, she'd always thought, that more than a decade into it, nobody had yet learned how to make proper garden furniture.

A pleasant, cooling breeze rippled across the water. At the side of the river, and well out of the main current, lime-green river reed swayed gently with the passing movement of the boat, whilst yellow-flowering native water irises grew in rich profusion in the margins at the banks. Water crowsfoot, rife with tiny white flowers, flowed past the boat just below the surface of the water, like the adorned hair of some fabulous water maiden. The turquoise and orange flash of a kingfisher darted into a bank, no doubt with an offering of food for hungry chicks.

Every now and then, on the bank, tall, amethyst plumes of a native wildflower Jenny couldn't put a name to pointed proudly to the sky. And in the open meadows, cattle that had come down to drink shied nervously away from the large, white boat, with its turning wheels and strange, melodious whistle, watching it go past with liquid brown velvet eyes.

In a world of traffic-jammed motorways, mobile phones, email, computers and stress, it was like taking a step back into the past. Jenny could have stayed there all morning. It was one of the very rare times when she could almost wish she didn't have food to prepare.

Behind her, through the open French doors that led into the salon, she heard voices, however, and sighed deeply. She got reluctantly to her feet, giving the passing scenery a last wistful glance. They were, she knew, due to stop near the village of Kelmscott for lunch, which was not that many hours away.

Time to work.

Besides, Jenny had no wish to overhear anybody's conversation. She still had vivid memories of a birthday party that she had been hired to cater, and the murder that had followed. The family concerned, as she recalled, had all had the unfortunate habit of talking about something confidential just when it was impossible *not* to overhear them!

So she coughed loudly as she stepped into the main salon to announce her presence, nodded pleasantly at David and Dorothy Leigh, who were the first to forsake the open air and were currently engaged in reading the morning papers, and returned to her galley.

There, she quickly set about making celery sauce, along with some egg cutlets, an asparagus dip, and a french bean and endive salad. To round off the snack (Jenny had never been able to think of a cold lunch as anything but) she made some cheese fingers and cheese and tomato ramekins. To go with it, she baked some milk loaves, as well as some wholemeal baps. All in all, a nice way to spend the morning.

It was just as well, perhaps, that she hadn't stayed on the deck for, in the main salon, David and Dorothy Leigh were not particularly happy bunnies.

David restlessly tossed a copy of *The Times* onto the table, and glanced uneasily over his shoulder. It was the result of a guilty conscience, he supposed, but he couldn't shake the eerie feeling that he was always being watched. As if the others had somehow been able to pick up on his dark thoughts and had taken to keeping an eye on him, perpetually on the lookout for any tell-tale signs of imminent criminal behaviour.

But in spite of his fears, Lucas, Gabriel and his wife were all still on the port deck, playing their silly game of quoits and taking no notice of him whatsoever.

David's hand went automatically to his breast pocket and then just as quickly moved away again. But it was proving impossible to ignore the simple, square piece of folded paper he kept there. He could have sworn he could feel it scraping his skin and, even more alarmingly, that it was creating a warmer patch over his heart. It was all psychosomatic, of course. That, and a severe case of the jitters. In fact, he felt physically sick whenever he contemplated what was to come, and as a consequence was desperately seeking some sort of distraction to keep his mind off it.

He sighed heavily and then frowned as Dorothy's fair head turned alertly at the sound. The eyes that met his were the colour of jade and, at that precise moment, cloudy with worry.

'Are you all right, David?' she asked anxiously, for about the fifth time that morning.

David Leigh forced himself to smile happily. 'I'm perfectly fine. I don't know why you keep asking. Naturally, I'd be a lot happier if you didn't flirt with that silly creature, Olney.'

He had to make a concerted effort not to swear roundly at the mere mention of the man's name, but he'd never thought it possible that a human being could hate so much. He'd certainly never thought that he, David Leigh, would have such a capacity for rage. He'd always thought of himself as a modest, fairly normal sort of a man.

Funny how you never really knew yourself.

Dorothy flushed. 'I'm not flirting with him,' she denied vehemently, feeling more and more sensitive on this matter. Ever since they'd come on board, Gabriel had been making a perfect nuisance of himself. 'It's just that no matter what I say, he twists it around, making it sound … oh, I don't know. Smutty somehow.' She nodded her bright head briefly in satisfaction. 'Yes, that's the word exactly. Smutty.' She produced the word with a triumphant but disgusted sigh.

David snorted. 'The man's an animal – no, worse than that. He's a joke.' Once again he bit back the more ugly expletive he'd have liked to use, and forced himself to relax.

His hand lifted to check, once again, that the square piece of writing paper was still safely ensconced in his pocket. Then he suddenly realized that his wife was watching, and quickly carried on the movement upwards, determinedly lifting his hand past his chest to go on to rub the back of his neck. It was not a wholly disguising move, for his nape did indeed feel hardened with knots, and his back fairly ached with tension. He'd be glad when this was all over with. He only wished he had a more *definite* plan.

'Have you noticed the way he's been acting?' he fumed. Like a man with a bad tooth who felt compelled to keep biting down on it, he couldn't seem to keep off the subject of his simmering rage. 'Buttonholing poor old Captain Lester, demanding to know how everything works, and then having the damned cheek to ask Lucas about the boat's running costs and so forth. None of his damned business, if you ask me. I could tell Lucas didn't like it.' David scowled at the newspaper, unaware that his wife was becoming ever more agitated. 'And he keeps running his hand across the deck rails, almost patting the damned thing! Anyone would think that *he* owned the *Stillwater Swan*. He was all but caressing that brass bell Lucas has had fixed on the outer wall to the bridge.'

Dorothy watched her husband, her eyes darkening anxiously. 'You look tired, sweetheart,' she said softly. 'You shouldn't work so hard. I know it's all these extra clients you're taking on, and I know we could do with the extra money. But you're wearing yourself down to a frazzle – it's no wonder things are getting on your nerves a bit.' She moved to stand behind him, running her fingers gently through his hair. 'You know you'll make partner one day,' she coaxed, ever the sweet, perfect wife. 'Old Soames will ...' She paused delicately, searching for the right words that didn't sound too mercenary, then gave a soft sigh. 'Well, he is getting on a bit, and Barry Pringle and old Mr Ford both know that they need new blood.'

David sighed angrily. 'It's not that,' he said, then could have kicked himself. If Dotty thought it was the pressures of work getting to him, why on earth hadn't he let her go on thinking it? Instead he'd opened his mouth before thinking. If that was an example of how he was going to carry on, he was probably going to get caught. And then what would happen to Dotty and the baby?

'Damn that man!' he suddenly burst out, slamming one fist into the palm of his other hand, and feeling the shock of it tingle all the way up his arm.

Dorothy jumped back instinctively at the hard 'whack', and her lower lip began to tremble. She moved around to stand in front of him, needing to see his face.

'It's all about him, isn't it?' she said, her voice tiny. 'Gabriel Olney.'

For just over a month now, David had stiffened whenever the other man's name was mentioned. And she couldn't understand why. Olney had been a client of her husband's firm of solicitors for years, and David hadn't seemed to mind before.

At those quiet, almost whispered words, David shot a quick look up at her that thoroughly alarmed his wife.

Dorothy stared down at him for a moment in utter amazement, which quickly turned to a sickly kind of fear. For a moment, she thought, dazed, David had looked – well – almost *afraid*.

But why? Unless … She crouched down in front of him with a quick, subtle agility that took her husband's breath away. In spite of her ethereal appearance, Dorothy Leigh was, in fact, a very fit young woman. She'd been a walker for all her life, and still enjoyed taking Josie, their collie, for five-mile rambles. She'd always had a hearty appetite, and she was, as her doctor had robustly reassured her, absolutely in top shape. No need to cut out the walks – in fact, the GP had told her, exercise was good for her in her condition. When told that she was going on a cruise and would like to take the opportunity for a long swim, he'd happily agreed that it was a good idea, just so long as she didn't strain herself.

Now, Dorothy bent lithely down by her husband's side, anxiously reaching out for his hands that were fluttering in a rather distressing and aimless sort of way in his lap.

'David,' she said firmly, but her lower lip was beginning to tremble just a little. 'Darling, it's *all right*. That ridiculous old man means nothing to me – nothing at all. Just because he keeps ogling me all the time, and dropping his awful hints and things, it doesn't mean that I find him in the least little bit *attractive!*'

She dropped her pretty silver head onto her husband's lap, just missing the half-astounded, half-impatient look he gave her.

David stared down at her bent head thoughtfully and then absently began to stroke her hair. Of course he didn't believe for one instant that Dotty, his loyal, devoted Dotty, felt anything at all for that odious bastard. Once again, she had misinterpreted his feelings. But this time, he didn't disabuse her of the fact.

If she thought it was all down to simple jealousy, so much the better. It would keep her safe. She must never learn the truth, for if she did, and suspected something after it was all over, that *he* had actually … He shuddered suddenly, causing Dorothy to clasp his hand so hard it turned his fingers numb. No, ignorance was the best thing for her, David reasoned to himself.

So he sighed, and tried to ignore the piece of paper burning a hole in his chest, and turned his feverish mind once more to working out a plan.

A really good, first-class plan.

'I just can't stand to see him touch you, that's all,' he murmured absently. His voice lent a certain, convincing hardness, since he also happened to be speaking the truth. David hated everything Olney did. He hated the way he walked. The way he talked. The way he stroked that moustache of his.

He hated the way he continued to breathe.

Dorothy lifted her head, and her lovely green eyes were misty now. 'Oh David, you know I love you more than anyone or anything else in the world. More than my own life, in fact.

Even …' She touched her still-flat belly tentatively. 'Even more than our baby.'

David looked down into her trusting, adoring eyes, and groaned. 'Oh Dot! I couldn't bear to lose you,' he said, and meant it. Dotty was the only thing that had been keeping him sane.

Ever since that research he'd done for General Wainwright.

Ever since he'd learned what Olney had done.

'I think I'd die if you left me,' he added, but his mind was once again on the piece of paper in his pocket. And the plan. He simply *had* to think of a really good plan. And he didn't have much more time in which to do it, either.

Jasmine Olney lost the game of quoits with such skill that neither Lucas nor her husband could possibly have guessed at it. She had changed into a pair of white shorts that showed off her tanned legs to perfection, and wore a scarlet top that contrasted wonderfully with her short cap of dark hair.

Lucas could see why old Olney had married her. Not too young to make him look ridiculous, but stylish enough to grace any man's life. Pity she was such a little man-eater. He watched her with unambiguous lasciviousness as she laughed and stood with her hands on her hips. She was panting a little too hard for it to be genuine, which of course drew attention to her firm breasts, and she waved a hand in front of her face.

'Phew, it's warm. I think I'll leave you two men to battle it out,' she said, reaching for a long glass of the cook's home-made, delicious lemonade, and rattled the ice cubes thoughtfully. It could do with a drop of gin, Jasmine mused, but knew better than to indulge.

Gabby could be such an old-fashioned sod when it came to drinking in the mornings.

'Are you up for it then, Lucas?' Gabriel asked, and eyed the deck thoughtfully. 'I suppose you could set up quite a few things out here? Bowls, even?' He was rather partial to bowls.

Jasmine looked at the greedy glitter in her husband's eye and smiled grimly. She knew exactly what his little game was, of course. But she would spike *that*, make no mistake about it. She flapped her hands in front of her face again, making a great show of it, and said petulantly, 'It really *is* hot. I think I'll go upstairs and take a shower.' She smiled vaguely in their direction and left, confident that neither man thought her departure in any way connived.

But she might have thought differently if she'd glanced back casually over her shoulder and seen the way her husband watched her go, his dark eyes glimmering with amused malice. But she was too self-absorbed to do so, and thus went blithely on.

On the rail, the macaw also watched her go, and then flew across the deck to land on a round, white and orange lifesaver. It began to nonchalantly preen itself.

'Bugger me, Gab old son, but I envy you that wife of yours,' Lucas said jovially. He was in a good mood. He was always willing to be generous to his guests when the *Stillwater Swan* was gliding across the water.

Gabriel Olney merely grunted.

Jasmine went straight to the stairs, genuinely glad to be out of the heat, and walked swiftly to their room.

Lucas had the master suite, of course, facing the prow, but she was quite happy with the bedroom they'd been allotted, which looked out over the port and rear of the boat. Once inside, however, she abandoned all thoughts of ablutions and walked instead to the chair by her husband's side of the bed.

He had changed into casual clothes for the deck games, and she went straight to the navy blue jacket that he had, typically, arranged with an almost obsessive neatness over the back of the chair. Her hand slipped into the breast pocket and removed the wallet. She ignored the large wad of paper money, and instead rooted through the side pockets, with all the concentration of a pig hunting out truffles. She gave a slight gasp of triumph as she withdrew a stiff piece of paper. It was obviously a cheque, and as she opened it, her eye fell to the written-in amount and she gasped once more. Louder, this time.

The sum, as she had suspected, was almost large enough to wipe out their entire savings. Or, to be strictly accurate, Gabby's entire savings, since Jasmine hadn't a bean to her name.

She had married Gabby solely for his money, of course, and the lifestyle of ease and plenty that came with it. He had married her to have an attractive wife and a bed mate whenever he felt the urge. It had been, as far as she'd been concerned, a perfect arrangement.

Trust Gabby to try and renege on it.

She'd suspected the way his mind had been working for some time now, ever since Lucas Finch had first invited them onto the paddle steamer last year. Gabby's eyes had simply lit up at the sight of it.

Jasmine took the cheque firmly between her fingers and tore it in half, then put them together, and tore again. She dropped the four fragments of paper into the pretty copper wastepaper bin nestled neatly under the side table and nodded.

She jumped as a slow hand clap started up behind her, and spun around, her face a picture of fury and angst at the sight of her husband.

'Well done, m'dear,' Gabriel Olney said, and brought the mocking applause to an end. 'Unfortunately, I can easily write out another one.'

Jasmine bit her lip furiously.

'And, needless to say,' Gabriel continued, looking eminently amused, 'I will do so.'

Jasmine tossed her head back. She was not defeated yet – not by a long shot. 'Lucas will never sell to you. You know he won't. You can wave twenty cheques under his nose and carry on doing it until your grasping, greedy little fingers fall off.'

Gabriel smiled, somewhat grimly. 'And that's just where you're wrong for once. Oh, he'll sell all right.'

There was something so confident in her husband's tone that Jasmine felt a small trickle of very real fear shiver down her back.

'Hah!' she snorted with a bravado that she hoped didn't sound as false as it felt. 'He told you flat out the last time – I heard him. The *Stillwater Swan* is not for sale.'

Gabriel smiled and inclined his head. He was enjoying this game. 'So he did. But—' His smile widened '—that was then, and this is now. Things have a way of changing. And this time, I think he'll have a change of heart.'

Jasmine's eyes narrowed. 'Just why did you go up to London last month?' she asked suddenly, her voice sharp.

Gabriel laughed. He had to hand it to Jasmine, she was as smart as a whip. 'I told you. Just to visit my club.'

Which was, in a way, strictly true. He *had* gone to the Regiment Club, a club whose membership – as its name might have suggested – consisted entirely of retired officers of the British army. What he hadn't told her was *what* he had gone to find *out*. And succeeded in finding out, beyond even his wildest dreams.

Jasmine narrowed her eyes. 'I'm not going to let you waste all our money on this floating heap, Gabby,' she warned, her voice lowering ominously. Her dark eyes flashed, reminding her husband of a tigress he'd once seen in London Zoo, pacing furiously in her enclosure and watching the human visitors with repressed feline fury.

She had looked at him just as Jasmine looked at him now.

He glanced at her hands, almost expecting her elegantly painted red nails to turn into sharp claws. She was such a cat. She looked like one, and she had the morals of one. An alleycat!

'My dear Jasmine, you can't possibly stop me from spending *my* money,' he stressed insultingly, 'in any way that I want.'

Jasmine stamped her foot. It was a ridiculous habit, she knew, and one left over from her rather spoilt childhood, but she had never managed to break it. 'I'm warning you, Gabby,' she said, her voice lowering to a hiss. 'I need that money. I like buying clothes and jewellery. I like going to Ascot, and Stratford for the Shakespeare. I like taking holidays in France and the Caribbean, and I won't give it all up just so that you can go and play captain.'

Gabriel smiled. 'I don't intend to "play" at all. Once the *Swan* is mine, I intend to learn to navigate her and overhaul her myself. No namby-pamby crew for me. This is a man's boat. It needs a man who can appreciate her, nuts and bolts and all. Lucas is no man. He just plays at being her master. He doesn't deserve a queen like this.'

He laughed openly at the look of chagrin that crossed his wife's face. 'What's the matter, Jasmine?' he scoffed softly, his voice becoming deliberately cruel now. 'Afraid that that young lad of yours will leave you if you can no longer afford to keep him in the manner to which you've allowed him to become accustomed? After all, there are plenty of other women around who can afford to buy him fancy watches and little runabouts, aren't there?'

Jasmine felt the breath leave her lungs in a quick 'whoosh'. She hadn't thought Gabby knew about Matthew. 'You … you …' she spluttered, and then couldn't think of anything suitably scathing to tack onto the end of it.

Gabriel threw back his head and laughed. 'It's your own fault, Jasmine,' he said at last, his face settling into a harsh, unyielding mask. 'You reneged on our agreement first. There was nothing in our "understanding" that allowed you to be unfaithful. I never agreed to being made a laughing stock!' he all but roared. 'If the good life wasn't good enough for you, then you've got no one else to blame now that I'm taking it all away again.'

Jasmine's hands clenched into fists. She could feel her nails digging into her palms, threatening to draw blood, but she continued to stare at her husband helplessly, with her smouldering, tiger eyes.

'Never mind, darling,' Gabriel commiserated with patent insincerity. 'It won't be so bad living on the *Swan*. Oh, I'm going to sell the house, didn't I tell you?' he added, seeing her look of astonishment. 'I'll need the capital to keep the *Swan* running. The old gal needs a lot of money to keep her looking her best. A bit like you, in that respect.'

Jasmine drew in a deep shaky breath. 'If you think I'm going to let you ruin my life ...' she said, then abruptly clamped her lips together to prevent herself from saying something she might have cause to regret later. Instead, she turned and, walking on legs that felt distinctly unsteady, crossed the room and slammed the door shut viciously behind her.

Down in the galley, Jenny heard the bang, but was too busy stuffing tomato cases with chives and cheese to wonder about it.

Later, of course, she would wonder about that, and so much more. Later, she would minutely ponder on everything, in fact, that anybody on the *Stillwater Swan* that day did, said or arranged.

Simply because it was about to become so very, very important.

FIVE

J ENNY PILED UP a plate of salads and bread and took it to the boiler room. The cruise had not stopped at the village of Kelmscott, as they'd originally planned, since the *Stillwater Swan* had made such excellent time, but had carried on instead to a lock near Radcot.

Once safely moored, Brian O'Keefe had turned off the engines, but had not emerged from the boiler room. Jenny, who had a phobia about anybody in her vicinity not being properly fed, had reminded herself of the old adage about Mohammed and the mountain, and promptly made like a waitress.

With the rest of the guests in the dining room, imbibing chilled white wine as if it was going out of fashion, the cook felt perfectly safe in taking a loaded plate out onto the port deck and down to the boiler-room door. Besides, if any little dining crisis did arise, she had no doubt at all that Lucas Finch's silent manservant would be more than capable of dealing with it. He was the kind of individual you could imagine dealing with any situation – from a social faux pas to nuclear war.

Brian O'Keefe answered the smartly rapped knock at once. He glanced once at the cook, then at the plate, and smiled. It was one of those smiles that transformed a face. Instantly the dour, brooding Irishman was gone, and a happy-go-lucky charmer took his place, as if by magic.

'Thanks, missus,' he said. He took the plate and backed back into the room, like a tortoise retreating into its shell.

The door closed firmly in her face.

Jenny looked at the wooden planks, barely an inch from her nose, and slowly raised one eyebrow. Then she shrugged. So long as he cleared his plates, the rest of his manners could go hang, as far as she was concerned. She wandered slowly along the rear decking, glad of the lightly freshening breeze.

The flight of stairs that led to the upper floor was located on the rear deck, as was the outdoor games area, with a small corridor leading to the starboard deck, and doors off it into the games room and main salon. The port deck that ran the entire length of that side of the boat doubled as a curling deck.

Jenny wandered over to the railings and looked out across the river, thinking what a very well designed boat the *Stillwater Swan* truly was. She could quite see why Lucas Finch loved it so.

Just then her sharp ears heard the faint but unmistakable sound of quacking ducks. She quickly craned her neck and looked both ways, but there were no birds in sight. Being fairly close – well, as the bird flew – to Aylesbury, was it too much to hope that some of those famous white birds had migrated this far?

The progression of her thoughts was as natural as it was habitual. Roast duck pieces, she mused, with orange sauce (naturally) would make a very good starter. Or, if she was lucky enough to catch two or possibly even three of this year's prime fledglings, she could even have them for a main course.

She quickly made her way to the games room, found a cupboard full of fishing equipment, selected a sturdy landing net, and made her way back to the rear deck. Her guests, she knew, would be eating for a good hour, and it had been made clear that serving and overseeing the actual table dining was strictly the province of Francis, whom she had no intention of crossing. And after lunch, Lucas's itinerary called for another hour's mooring, to allow anyone who wanted to take a pleasant country stroll to help their lunch go down.

So she had plenty of time.

Jenny stepped onto the soft grassy bank and set off determinedly in the direction of the quacking.

At the table, Lucas Finch tucked happily into a lobster patty and smacked his lips loudly. The parrot on his shoulder eyed a grape from the artfully arranged and appealing centre bowl of fruit with an avaricious gleam to his eye. He too smacked his lips – which was quite a feat, considering that he didn't have any.

'That lovely Amazon of a woman knows how to cook, you've got to give her that,' Lucas said happily, his cockney twang twanging, and his lips smacking once again as the sauce spurted pleasingly to the back of his throat. He detected prawns and tomatoes and something else particularly delicious but that he couldn't quite place.

'Hmm, I'll willingly second that,' Jasmine Olney said, eyeing her own heaped plate of salad leaves. 'The dressing on this is just divine.'

Her husband gave her an arch look. 'I didn't know you were up on things heavenly, m'dear.'

David Leigh shot Gabriel a killing look. Lucas, intercepting it, offered a basket of delicious bread loaves his way. 'Try some of this, David, my old china. It'll put lead in your pencil.'

'My old china,' prompted the parrot, just in case David had failed to get the point.

David accepted a piece of bread. 'Dorothy, my lovey?' Lucas asked.

Dorothy shook her head. 'No thanks, Lucas. I want to take a short swim after lunch and don't want to get too loaded down with heavy food.'

'You shouldn't do that,' Lucas said, aghast, 'it's dangerous. Or so my old mum used to say,' he added a shade shamefacedly, feeling just a little chided by the amused look Dorothy gave him.

'That's why I don't want a big meal now,' Dorothy reiterated patiently. Really, there was nothing wrong with Lucas. He was a good sort, more or less. Not at all the big bad black sheep that most people made him out to be. 'Don't worry, I'll wait a good hour before going in the water, I promise.' She raised her hand in a cheeky boy-scouts pledge. 'But I simply couldn't resist bringing my swimming suit. Who knows for how much longer it will fit me?' she giggled and Lucas almost melted.

After all, what woman didn't feel that way when they were going to have a young 'un, he mused fondly.

'And it's so hot,' Dorothy added, in the rather odd, tense silence that followed.

She glanced at her husband, wondering why he was so quiet. She could usually count on David to be both witty and fluent at social gatherings. He was always much more at ease at parties than she was. It was probably due to his job, she supposed. David was always so good with people. She just didn't have the knack. She never quite knew when someone was teasing her, or making a joke. Sometimes she worried that her husband needed a much more intelligent woman by his side, and she felt a sudden wave of inadequacy sweep over her.

'I'd join you, m'dear,' Gabriel said, 'but alas, I didn't think to bring my swimming trunks. I suppose I could always try it *au naturale*?' He smiled and fingered his moustache as Dorothy flushed beetroot.

Jasmine shot him a half-furious, half-amused look.

Lucas Finch thought about the skinny and ageing Gabriel Olney in his birthday suit, trying to impress the beauteous Dorothy, and burst out laughing. On his shoulder the parrot promptly did the same. It really was a superb mimic, and it sounded as if Lucas's laughter was echoing mockingly around the room.

Gabriel looked first at the bird, then at the man, a darkening flush coming up under his own skin.

Under the table, David Leigh held his knife so hard it almost snapped.

Lucas, belatedly aware that, as a host, he really shouldn't be laughing at a guest, coughed into his napkin. 'More wine, Gabriel?' he asked, and poured him another glass. Then he noticed David's tight, white face, and hastily refilled his glass too.

On his shoulder, the parrot considered how best to purloin one of the grapes.

An hour later, Jenny returned to the *Stillwater Swan*, luckless and duckless.

She put the landing net away, humming happily as she did so, and noticed in passing that the dining room was now empty. The table had been cleared. No doubt thanks to that paragon, Francis, she mused sourly, and returned to her galley.

There, the dirty plates and things awaited her. Obviously Francis and duty departed at the galley door. Not that she really minded. Jenny disliked having anyone lurking about in her kitchen anyway – especially after that shocking incident with Professor Mawwinney's pet rattlesnake. But was it her fault that reptiles liked to seek out warm places? Besides, it hadn't been her that had loaded the dishwasher that day.

She quickly washed and wiped, and walked to the full-length food cupboard to inspect the shelves and quickly gather together the ingredients she needed, then began heaping them in related piles onto the table.

But a quick glance at her watch reassured her that she had hours yet, and so she left the spick-and-span galley and made her way to the starboard deck. Since the port deck was the centre of all the activities, Jenny had come to regard the starboard deck as her own. She took her old deckchair of this morning and put it in her favourite spot, and settled back with a happy sigh.

As she did so, a fine pair of two-month-old mallards floated past the side, on the lookout for bread scraps. Jenny eyed them with a jaundiced eye, then returned to the galley. She came back with the leftover bread rolls and tossed them over the side.

The ducks gobbled them up, then promptly showed her their tail feathers.

Jenny smiled.

Just then, she saw a human-shaped shadow appear on the deck and looked up automatically. Above her were the bedroom balconies, and on the one nearest the prow of the ship, she saw a pair of milky-white arms appear, and then some wisps of silver-gold hair.

Dorothy Leigh looked out over the side, cautiously and sensibly eyeing the river to check on the density of the weeds. Seeing that the river was clearest on the right-hand side of the boat, she grabbed a towel and skipped lightly down the stairs. She was glad of a few moments to herself. Between them – but for vastly different reasons – her husband and Gabriel Olney were beginning to make her feel acutely miserable.

She walked to the rear deck and opened the boarding gate, which now opened out into the middle of the river, and with a slight gasp – for no matter how hot the summers were, the rivers in England always felt icy – she slipped lithely into the clear water. It wouldn't have done to do so when the majestic paddles were turning, obviously, but with the boat stationary she felt perfectly safe.

Jenny heard a slow steady splash, and opened one eye. If those ducks had returned for more bread, she'd … She opened the other eye as the silver head of Dorothy Leigh came into sight. She began to open her mouth to call out that it was dangerous to swim after a big meal, and then shut it again.

After all, it was none of her business.

Besides, the cook had to acknowledge to herself a few minutes later, Dorothy Leigh was obviously not about to get into difficulties. She swam several hundred yards in an excellent overarm crawl, then swam back in a more leisurely but strong breaststroke.

She was obviously a very fit young woman. It was a good sign, Jenny thought with satisfaction, for both the baby's sake and the mother's. The general medical view nowadays had it that cosseting pregnant women, as a rule, did them far more harm than good. Or so she'd read. She herself had no immediate plans on motherhood, no matter how much her divorced parents might collectively wheedle and moan about the lack of grandchildren to spoil.

Jenny closed her eyes again, but contrary to appearances she didn't doze. Jenny Starling never dozed on the job. She thought instead of the evening meal that she was going to prepare, and was happily imagining the looks of stunned and happy amazement on the faces of the guests as they took their first mouthful.

It was a very pleasant daydream with which to pass the afternoon away.

A pity, really, that it was the last moment of real contentment that Jenny Starling was going to enjoy on that particular trip.

The cook was just going down the corridor that ran between the walls of the salon and the engine room, when she saw Jasmine Olney cross the open space at the far end.

Jenny had been heading for the games room. She'd noticed that it also doubled as a library, and had shelves of books of the thriller, murder mystery and more salubrious kind. And she was rather partial to the classic whodunnit era of British literature. Seeing Jasmine, though, she hesitated.

She didn't like being too conspicuous to the guests, but on a ship of this size (not to mention being of a rather noticeable size herself) it wasn't always possible to be invisible.

The boat was once more under way, heading for its overnight stop near the quaintly named village of Chimney. The three o'clock sun was at its highest, and Jenny was seeking a cooler spot where she could read for an hour or two in peace before the controlled panic that always precluded a big, complicated dinner.

When she stepped out onto the rear deck, however, it was deserted. Which was decidedly odd, since the only way to get off the rear deck was to go along the port deck, or enter the salon or games room, both of which led off in the opposite direction from that which she'd seen Jasmine go.

Then she heard a throaty feminine laugh, more like a purr than any sound a human being might make, and it was definitely coming from the engine room. Jenny very quickly walked into the games room and selected a book. She most definitely did not want to know what Jasmine Olney found to laugh about with Brian O'Keefe in the privacy of the boiler room.

No siree. In Jenny's vast experience, it didn't pay to mind anybody's business but your own. And if only more people observed that rule, she thought grimly as she selected a Patricia Wentworth novel, then she might not have been called upon to help 'solve' such a depressingly large number of murders.

She took the novel and headed very firmly away from the engine room to her own galley, where it was safe.

Gabriel watched Lucas saunter to the railings on the port deck and glanced around. Dorothy and David were busily engaged in a game of draughts, his wife had had the good sense to make herself scarce, and now was the perfect time to have it out with Lucas.

Gabriel was still smarting over the way Lucas had laughed at him at lunch. Well, he thought, stepping out onto the deck and carefully shutting the sliding glass doors behind him, now it was his turn to have a really good laugh. Being as he was the one who was going to laugh last, as it were.

It all started off reasonably enough.

'Lucas,' Gabriel said, nodding amicably.

On the rail, the parrot scratched himself vigorously behind one ear. A small scarlet feather disengaged itself and floated on the breeze to settle on the water. No doubt it would puzzle quite a few anglers before the day was out.

Lucas turned, his smile widening innocently. 'Gab,' he said, and nodded back.

Gabriel leaned his back against the sturdy white-painted wooden rails, which came up almost to the lowest point of his shoulder blades. 'Great trip,' he said, feeling his way into it. He'd waited so long for this moment that he wanted to savour it. Besides, he never had been the kind of man to rush into things.

Lucas just caught something in his tone of voice, though, and his smile began to falter. He looked at his guest with a slightly quizzical air. 'It always is,' Lucas boasted. And it was no idle boast, either. Gabriel had taken four trips on the *Stillwater Swan*, and all four had been magnificent.

'I was wondering if you ever took her to London?' Gabriel said, studying his fingernails. But his eyes glittered with glee. 'I think I will, you know. Perhaps this autumn.'

Lucas felt himself stiffening. 'Not still singing that same old song, are yer, me old china?' he said, and turned to face sideways. There was something about the way old Gabby was smiling that Lucas didn't much like. 'I'm getting a bit tired of telling you the *Swan* ain't for sale. I'm thinking of getting some cards made up, saying just that, so that I can just hand one out whenever you bang on about it. Save my breath, like.'

Lucas had invited the Olneys on so many trips just because, like most people, he appreciated having his possessions coveted. And old Gabby had wanted the *Swan* from the moment he'd clapped eyes on her. All very gratifying, of course, but now the old sod was beginning to get on his nerves a bit with this bee he had in his bonnet.

Lucas made up his mind then and there that this was the last time he'd invite him on board.

'Hmm.' Gabriel continued to study his fingernails with exaggerated care. 'I bought a cheque to exchange for this magnificent lady along with me, but the wife found it, you know, and tore it up. Jasmine doesn't appreciate quality like I do. Can't expect it of her, I suppose,' he sighed. 'She's so typically middle class. It takes the upper classes, or, oddly enough, the lower classes—' And he paused here to give Lucas a telling look '—to really appreciate quality.'

Lucas was too thick-skinned to be insulted. Instead of blowing up, as Gabriel had half expected, Lucas merely laughed.

'Poor old Jasmine,' he said, not altogether insincerely. Who could envy anyone married to a boring lech like Gabriel? 'Still, it was just as well that she did tear the cheque up, you know. As I told you last time, and the time before that, the *Swan* isn't for sale.' Aand Lucas gave the wide, white rail-top an affectionate pat.

'Ahh, but that was before,' Gabriel said, and reached into his top, voluminous pocket to withdraw a rather chunky set of papers.

'Before what?' Lucas asked cautiously, his cockney twang becoming more pronounced as he began to feel decidedly uneasy.

'Before I got a friend of mine from the MOD to copy me these,' Gabriel said, and handed them over.

In the games room, Dorothy jumped the last of her husband's pieces. 'There. I knew you weren't paying attention,' she teased. 'You can usually beat me hands down.'

She'd showered and washed her hair after her swim, and now her long locks fell around her shoulders like a gossamer cloud. She was wearing a periwinkle blue summer frock and David, for a moment pushing his troubles to one side, looked at her with appreciative eyes.

But before he could reply, they both nearly jumped out of their skins.

Out on the deck, Lucas Finch roared something so loudly and so furiously that he was all but incoherent. In the summer heat, every door, window and porthole on the *Swan* had been left open, allowing the outraged bellow to be heard in every room.

In the galley, Jenny dropped an onion, nearly cutting her finger into the bargain, and cursed rather roundly. She'd learned a rather interesting vocabulary of swear words from an admiral she'd once worked for. What curse or scandalous epithet that man hadn't known hadn't been worth hearing. He could even have taught Lucas's parrot a thing or two.

She stooped down and picked up the fallen vegetable, put it in the sink to wash, and then wandered to the door of the galley. Outside, the main salon was empty, but the door to the games room stood open.

She could clearly see Dorothy and David Leigh, their mouths dropped comically open, staring out onto the port deck.

There, Jenny saw, Lucas Finch had Gabriel Olney by the throat.

Literally.

The cook firmed her lips grimly. She wanted none of *that* on *this* trip. She marched briskly across the games room, bypassing the Leighs, who seemed rooted to the spot in shock, and quick-stepped to the French windows.

By now, Gabriel Olney was turning rather purple. Rather like the shade of a good Victoria plum, Jenny thought inconsequentially.

She pulled open the door, just as Lucas Finch snarled.

'Where did you get it, Olney?' the cockney asked, all but shaking the older man, like a terrier might shake a rat.

Even his own parrot obviously thought this was a bit too much, for he was pacing agitatedly up and down the rail, saying 'Who rattled your cage then? Aye, aye?' over and over again, at a rather hysterical pitch.

'Mr Finch, put that man down at once!' Jenny barked, her voice cutting across the air like a schoolmistress's voice cutting across a classroom of naughty children. It made Lucas drop his man in shock.

Gabriel began to gasp like a beached fish. His hand went automatically to his throat, and his eyes began to lose that rather distressingly bulged look.

'I will not have that sort of thing,' Jenny added, aware that she was sounding like an escapee from a rather bad British film, but not caring much. Her eyes glittered angrily. All too often in the past, she'd been minding her own business, just doing her job and cooking good food, when somebody decided to bump somebody else off. And the worst of it was, it was usually left to her to find out the who and why of it! Well, she was getting heartily sick of it.

'Now, behave yourself,' she finished, eyeing first the slack-jawed Lucas Finch, and then the fast-beginning-to-rally Gabriel Olney.

'Finch, you ... you ...' he spluttered, and Jenny turned on him with a gimlet gaze.

She raised one finger in his direction. 'Mr Olney,' she said. Just that. Nothing more. Gabriel Olney stared at her, then fumed at Finch, then began to stroke his moustache.

The parrot coughed and began to thoroughly inspect his claws for dirt.

Jenny, once assured that peace had been resumed, nodded, turned and left, glancing curiously at the Leighs as she did so. She couldn't help but notice that both of them looked delighted at Gabriel Olney's obvious physical discomfort.

She walked to the galley, poured a glass of lemonade and returned with it. Without a word she handed it to the now silent Gabriel, who, after a startled pause, took it and tentatively swallowed, wincing at the soreness of his throat. He managed to croak rather desultory thanks.

She once more bypassed the quiet but gleeful Leighs, and returned to her galley and the basting lamb.

And that, she thoroughly hoped, was the end of that.

It was, of course, something of a forlorn hope.

Jenny sprinkled some thyme onto the top of the dishes of cold cucumber and watercress soup, and handed the tray across to Francis.

Francis carried it solemnly to the sideboard in the dining room, and glanced poker-faced at the guests.

The table had been covered with a pristine white cloth. In the centre rested sparkling silver candlesticks with tall, elegantly tapering green candles. Around the base was a froth of pink, red and white carnations. Deep red napkins rested beside places set with green Worcester plates. Even if he said it himself, Francis thought smugly, he had done a wonderful job with the table. Small crystal finger bowls filled with scented water matched the pattern of the crystal goblets.

It was a lovely scene, and the guests sat around it were as elegant as the table. The ladies, catching the spirit of the cruise, had all changed into their best finery.

Dorothy Leigh, of course, would look stunning in a sack, but was wearing a silver and gold lamé evening dress and radiated beauty and health. In a different way, the scarlet-garbed and dark-headed Jasmine Olney looked equally eye-catching, but was aided by a stunning diamond necklace, which she wore with undeniable panache.

The men, including Lucas, were all dressed in tuxedos.

It was a pity, Francis thought, that none of them were talking.

Only the gentle 'clink' of Francis's soup plates being distributed, broke the silence.

Dorothy Leigh was the first brave soul to attempt to do anything about it.

'I had a wonderful swim this afternoon,' she said, to nobody in particular, and lifted her spoon for a tentative sip of soup. She wasn't quite sure what she thought about cold soups – she could only ever think of soup and imagine steaming broth – but this was delicious. It had a lovely flavour – not cloying, but not wishy-washy either. It was clear and deliciously tangy. 'Mmm, this is lovely,' she said, prompting Lucas to half-heartedly reach for his own spoon.

Only Gabriel ate with a hearty appetite, and if he occasionally winced when swallowing, it didn't seem to annoy him too much. In fact, he was looking almost unbearably smug. Not that he was openly grinning. Nor had he yet said a word. But everyone, especially David Leigh (who seemed to have particularly sensitive antennae as far as Olney was concerned) sensed a very strong feeling of *gloating* emanating from the man. It seemed to waft from him in a particularly noxious but invisible cloud. It was almost unbearable for him to sit still for it, when all he wanted to do was launch himself across the table and smash his fist into that oily face. Smash and smash and smash….

Francis turned, glanced once at Lucas, and almost paused at the expression on his employer's face. He recovered at once though and carried on, walking back to the galley in soft-footed silence, but a long, almost telepathic look had already passed between them.

Dorothy noticed it especially.

She'd remarked to her husband on their earlier trip on the *Stillwater Swan* that Francis and Lucas made a very odd pair. Lucas was just so cockney, and Francis was so proper. They should have been oil and water, but weren't. They seemed to *conspire* against the world in some odd sort of way. It was almost spooky.

Now she took another sip of soup, and tried again to break the deadlock.

'I must say, I really do like this,' she said stiltedly. 'You wouldn't have thought our cook would have had such a subtle hand, would you? Not to look at her, I mean,' she laughed. 'When I went for my swim this afternoon, I saw her sitting out on the deck, and I could have sworn she was asleep.'

'Probably stuffed herself on all the leftovers from lunch,' Jasmine said cattily, and totally inaccurately.

Jenny always prepared a plate of food for herself at the same time as she prepared the plates for the guests.

Jenny was no mug.

In the galley, Francis returned, his face thoughtful.

Something was up, that was for sure. He'd never seen Lucas look so upset and uneasy before.

Just then, Captain Lester came through from the bridge. The *Swan* was moored not a mile from Chimney, and he accepted the plate of soup the cook gave him with a somewhat distracted air. He looked at Francis.

'Any idea why Lucas wants me and Brian to join them—' He nodded in the salon's direction '—after dinner, for drinks?'

Francis frowned. First of all, he had no idea what Lucas intended, which was a normally totally unheard of development. Lucas always told him everything. *But everything.* And secondly, Lucas never asked the captain or O'Keefe to mingle with the guests at dinner time. During the day, yes. But never during the more formal evening meal. It broke the atmosphere of elegance and olde-worlde dining that Lucas strove to create, and which he himself enjoyed so much.

'It must be something unusual,' Tobias Lester added – a shade uneasily, Jenny thought. 'I said as much to Brian when he asked us.'

'When was this?' she asked automatically, then could have kicked herself for asking. After all, it was none of her business.

'About five.'

After the scene with Gabriel Olney then, she thought, before she could stop herself.

She sighed as she watched Francis depart then return with hardly touched soup bowls. She stared at the bowls grimly and handed over stuffed crabs on a bed of rice.

Even Tobias, usually a hearty eater, couldn't do the crab she handed him justice. She made up a tray for the engineer, intending to take it to him later. Perhaps *he*, at least, would appreciate it.

The cook became grimmer and grimmer as the evening wore on, and the plates kept returning, barely picked at.

What was wrong with these people? she fumed. She went to all the trouble of creating a multi-course masterpiece of contrasting tastes, textures, sights and smells, all of which were culinary delights, and they didn't even have the good manners to eat them.

It was enough to make her spit tin-tacks.

Well, she'd see they ate the baked Alaska, if she had to ladle it out herself and spoon feed the lot of them!

So it was that Jenny Starling herself brought in the towering, impressive dessert and put it on the sideboard for Francis to serve.

Tobias Lester was asked to send for the engineer, and Lucas Finch, looking curiously stiff-faced and unnaturally silent, poured a dozen glasses of champagne. David and Dorothy Leigh accepted their glasses, looking merely bewildered. Jasmine took hers, and peered over the rim of it at the sour-faced Brian O'Keefe, giving him an openly and blatantly smouldering look. Lucas's hands shook as he held his own glass.

Only Gabriel Olney looked at ease.

As well he might.

'I've called you all here to join me in a toast to the new master of the *Stillwater Swan*,' he said, dropping the bombshell in a voice so monotone that it was obvious he had been rehearsing the simple stark line for a long time.

Jasmine Olney gasped audibly.

Tobias Lester looked as if he'd been poleaxed.

Brian O'Keefe went as pale as his swarthy colouring would let him – which was surprisingly pale indeed.

Francis almost dropped his glass. His eyes flew to those of his master.

Lucas's left eye twitched as he raised his glass. 'To Gabby,' he said, and swigged the finest Grende as if it were cyanide.

SIX

I T WAS JUST beginning to turn dark – that lovely deepening of lavender into something more nocturnal. A warm breeze played like velvet over the skin, whilst a more than three-quarters moon celebrated by turning from the colour of milk to the more emphatic colour of a mature cheese.

The last of the aerial patrols of swooping swifts peeled off high overheard, their screeching and screaming calls piercing the night air in a last hurrah. A rarely seen soft-winged, ghostly barn owl set off on his night's hunting, whilst the sky steadily turned to sapphire and the stars began to twinkle like an accompaniment of diamonds.

Jenny rested against the deck rails on the port deck, glad that the evening meal was over and the debris from it all cleared away, and she could now mourn it in a dignified silence. Tomorrow, for lunch, she would have to do something clever with all the leftovers. She refused, but simply *refused*, to let good food go to waste.

She heard a soft footfall behind her and half turned, seeing the leonine head of Tobias Lester as he crossed the rear decking and pushed open the engine room door. 'All settled down for the night?' she heard his voice, dull and flat, echo easily across in the stillness of the night.

Brian O'Keefe's reply was a terse affirmative. Both men sounded tense, and little wonder, Jenny mused. And as the captain and the engineer talked together quietly, she strained to catch their words, but couldn't quite manage it. They sounded friendly enough though, as if adversity had bonded them together with a far stronger cement than the mere shared duties of keeping the *Swan* in good working order.

In fact, the more they talked, the more conspiratorial their tone seemed to become – as if they were plotting some scheme, and thus needed to whisper.

The thought made her feel uneasy.

Jenny sighed, knowing she had to get away from the murmur of masculine voices, otherwise she was going to become downright paranoid. On the other hand, she had no wish to retire early. Her bedroom was a cramped space in which she could hardly turn around, and she was still roiling and simmering with righteous indignation over the fate of her feast. Perhaps a moonlit stroll along the banks of the Thames would calm her and bring about a return of her equilibrium.

As a large person, with a large personality to match, Jenny Starling cherished her equilibrium. She liked to feel centred and balanced.

She left the boat, glad of the light from the nearly full moon, and found a well-worn path that meandered through the open meadows. Buttercups had closed up their business for the night, their petals furled tightly into pale orbs. Every now and then, the perfume of clover wafted on the warm night breeze, and moths and bats winged by in a mutual, potentially fatal, ballet. After a while, Chimney's church clock tolled out the hour of eleven. Jenny paused to listen, then, somewhat reluctantly, turned back towards the *Stillwater Swan*.

She wasn't happy with the way things were going. What on earth had induced Lucas Finch to sell the boat to Gabriel Olney of all people? That afternoon's rumpus between the two men had obviously played a big part in it – it hardly took a genius to come to that conclusion! And if she had figured out as much, so had everyone else.

One thing was for certain – no one but Gabriel himself seemed at all happy about it. Even his wife had been shooting daggers at him all evening, which was faintly surprising. She'd have thought a woman like Jasmine Olney would have relished being the mistress of such a prestigious acquisition as the swan. She could easily see the chic and stylish Jasmine holding soirees and playing the gracious hostess to a party of B-list celebs. Obviously, there was something else going on in the Olney marriage that was causing friction.

And something was seriously biting David Leigh. Every time she went near him, she could feel him practically vibrating with angst. It was scaring his sweet and devoted wife too, and that couldn't be good for her.

Jenny sighed deeply and wearily. Things were becoming nasty, and no doubt about it. And although she'd only known them a short time, the passengers and crew of the *Stillwater Swan* were beginning to exert their influence over her. She'd be glad to get back to the security of Oxford, before she became even more embroiled. Still, she cheered herself up with the thought that there was only one more day to go – and a Sunday, the traditional day of peace and rest, at that.

Hah! A little voice sneered at the back of her mind, and she determinedly ignored it.

They had a long stretch of river to negotiate tomorrow, with no further villages in which to moor before their final destination of Swinford. There she would spend the night at the local pub then catch the first bus back to Wainscott House and collect her trusty little van.

Perhaps, next year, she really *would* take a holiday. Oh, not to the seaside, but inland somewhere. Scotland, perhaps. She could learn how to make a proper haggis.

As she approached the river, she heard the low murmur of voices from the riverbank, and stopped, in some amazement, to watch Tobias and Brian put up a fairly large tent.

As Brian rolled out some sleeping bags, the cook suddenly

realized that, with all the rooms on the *Swan* currently occupied, the crew had no other choice but to camp out on the
shore. She glanced to the right and, sure enough, pitched a
good few yards away was a slightly smaller but very neat little
tent.

The good Francis, no doubt, preferred not to kip down with
mere engineers and a glorified – if nautical – chauffeur. Jenny
coughed, just to alert all concerned that she was about, and
then stepped out from the shadows of the trees.

'Good evening, Captain,' she said pleasantly, and saw Tobias
turn her way briefly. In the darkness she couldn't make out the
expression on his face.

'Hello there ... er ... Cook,' he said, his voice still stuck in a
flat, dreary monotone. No doubt, in the aftermath of Lucas
Finch's announcement, he had forgotten her given name, but
Jenny didn't mind. Being called by her title was more gratifying
anyway.

She walked to the wide plank that connected the *Swan* safely
with the bank and stepped onto the deck, almost bumping into
somebody coming the opposite way. It was, of course, the other
person who rebounded off her girth, and had to take a few stag-
gering steps backwards. 'Sorry,' Jenny said automatically.

'That's all right, dear lady,' came back the unmistakable
voice of Gabriel Olney. 'I should have been looking where you
were going,' he added with what he supposed was a dry wit.
His voice, unlike that of the captain, was rich with feeling. Too
much feeling, in fact. Jenny didn't appreciate being patronized.

'Yes, perhaps you should,' she said, somewhat coolly. 'I am,
after all, big enough to be seen,' she added, totally flooring the
old ex-soldier, who stared after her as she left, his mouth falling
open in surprise.

Jenny, about to carry on and stomp off to her bedroom in
high dudgeon, suddenly remembered the cramped proportions
of said bedroom, and did an abrupt turn in the direction of the

railings instead. A few more breaths of air before turning in would do her no harm, after all.

She heard Gabriel's footsteps on the plank, and a moment later saw his dark shape silently make its way towards the large tent.

'Ah, chaps, I was hoping to catch you alone for a few minutes,' she heard him say jovially. 'I thought it best to tell you straight-away, so there would be no misunderstandings, so to speak.'

Jenny, who had already guessed exactly what it was that Gabriel Olney wished to say – namely 'you're both fired' – hastily decided she'd had enough air for one night, and stepped through into the games room.

Although most of the lights had been turned off now that the Swan's engines were idle (the bulk of the electricity coming via a generator that the turning paddle wheels kept charged up), she easily made her way into the salon. She'd gone through the room so often, her mind had memorized the layout of it without her conscious thought. From there she went through the galley and into her own little cubbyhole of a bedroom. There she brushed her teeth at a tiny washbasin, donned her nightgown and crawled into the tiny bed.

It squeaked and groaned like a tub of trampled mice.

Jenny gave a grunt, turned off the puny overhead light, and rolled onto her side. She only just managed to stop herself falling off the narrow mattress, and gave a long, tremulous sigh.

Then she closed her eyes and went to sleep.

Breakfast next morning was an odd affair. Lucas Finch was determinedly jovial. It was almost as if he was trying to fool himself into thinking that he didn't really care that the Swan was lost to him. He helped himself to huge amounts of food, and ate it with every outward appearance of pleasure.

Francis watched him with blank eyes that Lucas would catch now and then, and ignore.

Jasmine simply sat and glowered, at her husband, at Lucas, and at the parrot.

The parrot, sensitive soul that he was, was very much aware of her acrimonious gaze and paced nervously across the sideboard. So intent was he on keeping an eye on Jasmine that, when he reached the end, he kept on walking, and with a squawk of utter surprise, fell off the other end.

Jasmine laughed nastily.

Lucas looked down at the parrot, which turned and looked up at him, and said mildly, 'What a pillock.'

He returned his attention back to his eggs and bacon, and beamed at Dorothy Leigh, who was half-heartedly picking her way through some deliciously fragrant scrambled eggs with herbs.

'Do you have any pets, love?' he asked, and nodded at the parrot, which had flown back to the sideboard, and was eyeing his dish of nuts and fruit with a somewhat bilious eye.

Dorothy smiled. She was rather fond of the parrot. 'I have a dog. She's a Collie, actually. I have a devil of a job keeping her coat in top condition. I seem to spend hours grooming her.'

Lucas cast the parrot an amiable look, and then reached for a piece of peach with which to tempt him. 'The things you do, hey?' he said softly, watching the bird eat with a crinkle-eyed smile.

Dorothy gave him a rather tender look. She thought Lucas was being a really good sport about all this, and she liked that in a man. She had no idea what Gabriel had done to him to make him part with the boat, but she knew it must be breaking his heart. Yet here he was the next morning, acting as right as rain, and trying to make sure that all his guests were having a good time. He might be a diamond in the rough, but at least he was acting like a real man should.

When he turned back from feeding his bird, she gave him a dazzling smile.

Gabriel watched her, his lips twisting into a malicious grin.

Let old Lucas have his moment of glory. He could afford to be magnanimous, now that he had what he wanted. Now, all he had to do was get rid of Jasmine.

David Leigh suddenly pushed his plate away. 'If you don't mind, I think I'll just ... er ... go and change. I was hoping to take a walk before we started off.'

Lucas glanced at the young solicitor. He had difficulty in focusing his thoughts. All he could think about was the *Swan*. His lovely, elegant and beloved *Swan*. 'What? Oh, yes, that's fine. We won't set off until ten o'clock or so. Take your time, me old china,' he said heartily.

David nodded. Dorothy tried to catch his eye, but he studiously avoided looking at her as he rose. She gnawed on her lower lip worriedly as she watched him go. He'd said nothing about her joining him for this walk of his. Should she go up to their room and invite herself along? Or was he desperate for some time alone? Oh, if only Gabriel wasn't aboard this trip. She was sure that all of this tension was his fault. Poor Lucas. Poor Jasmine. And poor, poor David.

She stabbed her mound of eggs viciously with her fork.

But she was not the only one who'd be glad when this trip was over. Jasmine Olney, for one, was desperate to get to the bank. If only she could withdraw some money before the second cheque Gabby had written out could be cleared, she might yet still be able to salvage something. Better still, if she could only think of some way of getting her hands on *all* their money! She'd be off like a shot. Let Gabriel divorce her if he couldn't find her!

Lucas was finding it harder and harder to carry on playing the role of genial host. All he could think about was what happened once they docked. For as soon as David Leigh had drawn up the papers, and they'd been signed and processed, the *Swan* would glide out of his life forever.

With Gabriel Olney at the wheel.

It was a thought that left a gaping hole in his soul. He

couldn't bring himself to look across at the gloating ex-solider. If he did …. His hands curled so hard around the knife he was using that his fingers ached.

Jenny, knowing that everyone was at breakfast, had taken the opportunity to use the bathroom. She had luxuriated in a ten-minute soak in the tub, and now, powdered and glowing a healthy pink, she opened the door, dressed in a fresh summer dress of pansy purple.

As she shut the door behind her, she heard a second, echoing click, and stared at the door handle blankly for a moment. Then she quickly turned around and saw David Leigh coming through the open door opposite. She made a rapid show of rooting about in her toiletries bag, checking that her soap and flannel were present, and not even glancing up as David Leigh passed her.

If she had done so, she might have noticed the rather pensive glance he gave her. Only when she heard his light steps going quickly down the stairs did she close the bath bag and look up thoughtfully.

The bathroom was on the port side of the boat, at the rear.

That meant that the bedroom opposite her, the bedroom that David Leigh had just exited, was on the rear side of the starboard deck. But yesterday she'd clearly seen Dorothy Leigh lean on the balcony of the bedroom nearest the *prow* – the front end of the boat. Or the pointed end, as her father had been wont to call it. So either Dorothy had been in Gabriel Olney's bedroom yesterday – a patently absurd thought – or David Leigh had just emerged from the Olneys' room just now.

Now what, Jenny thought grimly, had he been up to in there?

She frowned, then sighed, and went slowly down the stairs. Just a few more hours, she thought encouragingly. A few more hours and she'd be free and clear. There was no need to be so pessimistic. After all, what could happen in just a few hours? Unfortunately, as Jenny knew only too well from past and bitter experience, an awful lot *could* happen. But that, surely, wasn't going to happen here? No. She gave a mental head shake and told herself not to worry.

She was beginning to let this paranoia where murder was concerned get the better of her, she thought grimly.

She made her way, with determined optimism, towards the galley via the starboard deck, and glanced in the window to the dining room as she did so.

David Leigh had reappeared, and was tucking into his sausages with every appearance of appetite. Opposite him, Gabriel Olney reached for some more toast.

Well, at least it appeared that *this* meal was going to be consumed, she noted with a satisfied nod. In a much better frame of mind now, the uneasy cook stepped into her domain, and awaited the arrival of the dirty dishes.

Using the block and tackle, Brian O'Keefe hauled the heavier logs he'd chopped up on the riverbank earlier that morning and winched them on board, placing them onto a trolley. It was an old porter's trolley, exactly like the kind they used in railway stations, with long upward handles and four tiny wheels attached to a low wooden base. He pushed the trolley towards the storeroom, and upended the wood onto the floor. He'd chop them into more manageable logs later. Lucas liked to raise steam the old-fashioned way. The sun was rising, and they'd be setting off soon. He'd have to start hauling in some more coal soon. Then he'd need to wash up, because bloody coal dust got every-where.

He moved down the small corridor to the starboard deck, and once there, turned towards the rear. He walked to the very end and lifted the lid off a wooden box, where the non-essen-tial equipment was habitually stored. He had, at that point, no idea that he had an audience.

He dropped in the block and tackle and let the lid drop with a small thud. His shirt was already beginning to stick to his back, so he pulled it off, turning to the fresh-water butt stored at a right angle to the trunk. It was about four feet high, a foot or so wide, and was full of blessedly cool water. It was used as a backup, in case the boat ran out of water for domestic use.

Brian scooped a large handful in his cupped hands and sluiced it over his face, shivering happily as he did so. He felt it run over his chest and down his nape, and sighed loudly. He put the lid back on, mindful of how easy it was for water to evaporate in this heat, and turned.

Then stopped dead in his tracks.

The large and oddly attractive cook, and the pretty blonde woman, were sitting on chairs at the other end of the deck, openly watching him. He smiled at them, gave a slight nod, and with a rather wry twist of his lips, headed back down the corridor towards his engine room.

He hoped they'd enjoyed the show.

Now it was time to work up some steam.

Jenny (who had indeed thoroughly enjoyed the show) turned back to her contemplation of the river whilst also reviewing the tempting display of rippling, masculine muscle she'd just seen.

She'd been a little surprised to be joined by Dorothy Leigh, just ten minutes earlier, but she could quite understand why. With her husband off on a lone walk, she hadn't felt like joining the others on the port deck. With the mouse away, the cat in Gabriel would have been apt to play.

A few minutes later the engines began to throb, so presumably David had returned from his walk. That he seemed to be in no hurry to seek out his wife, however, was soon obvious, for, as the *Swan* began to move out into mid-stream, they remained alone on the deck.

'Really, I do wish Lucas hadn't invited Mr Olney along on this trip,' Dorothy said suddenly, as if she'd uncannily read the cook's thoughts. 'He can be so … well …' She fumbled in vain for the right words. 'I don't think he realizes how people can misinterpret his teasing.' She had eventually settled for something of an understatement, and glanced at her companion awkwardly.

Jenny cast her a quick, thoughtful look. She herself had seen the way Gabriel had openly pursued Dorothy, and was a little surprised by the married woman's naiveté.

'I don't think that he is teasing, is he?' she said, but very mildly. 'A man like that, a man who's so obviously dissatisfied with his marriage, is always on the lookout for a good excuse to break away from it. And what better excuse is there than to find another woman?'

Dorothy stared at her aghast. 'But I've done nothing, I've said nothing to make him think that I....' Her voice spluttered out in an appalled whisper, and Jenny cursed herself for her lack of tact, and quickly shook her head.

'No, Mrs Leigh, I didn't mean to suggest that you had,' she said, gently but firmly. 'I'm merely pointing out that, to a man like Gabriel Olney, you make a very good target.'

Jenny, in fact, doubted that Gabriel *was* serious in his pursuit of the pretty blonde. Apart from his natural and somewhat loathsome method of flirting, he was probably only trying to push Jasmine to the limit, thus forcing her to seek a divorce.

The very fact that Dorothy was pregnant, not to mention happily married, had probably made Gabriel feel very safe indeed. After all, what man wanted a pregnant woman for a mistress? No, Jenny was mostly convinced that he was just using Dorothy as a convenience.

A quick flirtation, a good excuse to give to a judge in a divorce hearing, and he'd be free of Jasmine once and for all. What would it matter to a man of Gabriel's unfeeling arrogance if he ruined Dorothy's marriage in the process? So long as he got what he wanted. Then it would be just himself, and the *Stillwater Swan*.

Jenny felt a ludicrous surge of sympathy for the boat. It was as if she was beginning to think of the elegant white vessel as a living creature!

On the bank, a party of girl guides shouted and pointed in excitement as they caught sight of the steamer. Their group leader impulsively waved, which, of course, immediately set the rest of the gang off. On the bridge, Tobias Lester must have spotted them, for the next instant the melodious, haunting tone of the *Swan*'s steam whistle rent the air, letting off a cloud of steam as it did so.

The girls on the bank became frantic with excitement, jumping up and down, and making Jenny smile.

Beside her, Dorothy Leigh did not smile. In fact, Dorothy Leigh looked very near to tears.

Knowing she could do nothing to help her, Jenny left Dorothy to her thoughts and returned to the galley. Noon was fast approaching, and she wanted to make some chestnut forcemeat to wrap in cold chicken, to go with the salad. Whilst she was at it, she supposed, she could also make some devilled butter and some tomato cream butter. It went so well with the cold meats and garlic bread she had prepared.

On the port deck, an energetic game of some sort was being played, and from time to time the cook could hear the odd shout of triumph or groan of displeasure.

Dorothy, drawn by the same sounds, made her way to the other side of the boat, and immediately spotted her husband sitting in a deckchair and observing the activity with a brooding air.

Lucas and Jasmine were teamed up against himself and Gabriel. It was an odd arrangement and one that made David want to laugh out loud. If only they knew.

Lucas rattled about, sweeping a highly polished round piece of wood along the smooth planking, bringing it to within only inches of the target. It was a sort of curling-cum-bowls game that went so well with life on board a boat. Jasmine applauded his accuracy. 'Well done, partner,' she squealed theatrically, throwing her arms around his neck and giving him a kiss.

Lucas smiled at her, somewhat bleakly. He was having a hard time of it. He wanted nothing more than to go somewhere and shout and scream.

In fact, he wanted to kill.

The *Swan* was lost. This might be the last time he ever cruised aboard her. And the wife of the man who'd taken her away from him was kissing him, playing her own damned silly little games.

'Your turn, Leigh,' Gabriel prompted, from where he was watching at the side of the rails.

David, who from the dark circles under his eyes obviously hadn't slept well, got up tiredly and with some difficulty from the chair and walked towards his own 'stone'. As he did so, Gabriel moved over to his spot, taking his place in the chair.

Dorothy, who had been leaning on the back of the chair, quickly straightened and went to take a step away, but before she could move, Gabriel grabbed her wrist.

'Stay, and keep me company, Dotty. Your husband and I are partners, after all,' he laughed, and indicated the improvized game under way.

Dorothy swallowed hard. Her throat felt suddenly dry.

'I don't think …' she said, then gasped to a halt as, with deliberate insouciance, Gabriel took her hand, which he was still holding, and raised it to his lips. As well as being old-fashioned, the gesture was also curiously intimate.

She cast an agonized glance at her husband's back. Luckily, he was too busy concentrating on aiming his stone to look behind him at what was going on. But Gabriel *was* looking at his wife, his eyes glittering with amused animosity.

Jasmine returned the compliment, staring at him with hard, hating eyes.

'You know, m'dear, you really shouldn't be so standoffish,' Gabriel purred as Dorothy snatched her hand away, her furious scowl making Jasmine laugh scornfully. Olney flushed an ugly red.

David, hearing the laugh, turned, saw the direction of Jasmine's gaze, and looked over his shoulder. He saw Dorothy's scowl and Gabriel's sudden smirk, and the wooden ball in his hand twitched as a spasm of uncontrolled rage washed over him. His fingers curled tight around the wooden stone.

And then David looked down at the smooth, hard, wooden ball, as if seeing it properly for the first time, and began to smile.

A few yards away, Gabriel lowered his voice to a husky whisper. 'You really shouldn't antagonize clients of your husband's firm, m'dear,' he chided her gently, studying Dorothy's mutinous face with a half-angry, half-amused smile. Really, the woman was such a child. 'After all, if I were suddenly to withdraw my business from the venerable offices of Pringle, Ford and Soames, they'd be somewhat concerned. And if I should tell them that it was because I wasn't happy with the performance of one of their juniors....' He shrugged eloquently.

He knew that baiting Dorothy was rather unsporting, a bit like shooting fish in a barrel, in fact, but he was in a fey kind of mood. Jasmine was wearing on his nerves like a bad-fitting uniform, and he was in just the right frame of mind to curse all women.

Dorothy gasped and went pale. 'You wouldn't,' she said.

The very way she said it, with such an appalled air, made Gabriel feel even more vicious.

'I just might,' he said, keeping his voice deliberately light. 'Why don't you try being nice to me for a change, hmm?' he goaded, his eyes on his wife, who was watching them with narrow-lidded alertness. 'After all, it's not much to ask, is it?' he murmured, recapturing her hand, and pressing the back of it to his lips.

Dorothy could feel his moustache, like hairy bristles, on the back of her hand, and shuddered. The touch reminded her of the bristles on a pig's back.

Jasmine's eyes became glued to those of her husband. So, he was angling for a divorce, was he? Leaving her out in the cold, with precious little money and no security. She felt a lance of fear hit her. Although wild horses wouldn't have made her admit it out loud, she knew that she was well past the first flush of her youth. Finding another rich husband, when you were a poor, middle-aged divorcee, would be no picnic.

She had to put a stop to it. And she had to put a stop to this ridiculous boat business as well. Her nails curled into her palms so hard it made her wince.

Gabriel fiddled with Dorothy's cold fingers. He kept a wary eye on Leigh, but the solicitor seemed to be staring off into the distance in some sort of trance.

'When a person's in a much stronger position than you are, my dear little Dotty,' Gabriel mused, thoroughly enjoying himself now, 'you really do have to be careful. I mean, what would your husband say if I were to infer that the child you carry might not be his, for example? Now wouldn't that create a stir? And all because you couldn't take a compliment or two.'

He twisted his neck to look up at Dorothy, who stood as if turned to stone. 'Now, it wouldn't be so hard, would it, to play along a little? To help me play a little game with Jasmine? She's been rather naughty, you know, and deserves to be taught a lesson.'

But Dorothy was hardly listening. She was thinking how odd and tense David had been lately. But surely he didn't think.... He *couldn't* have got it into his silly head that she might have been unfaithful.

Gabriel turned, satisfied that he and the lovely Dorothy now had an understanding, and turned to glance once more at his wife.

His smile was wide as he kissed one of Dorothy's cold finger-tips.

It was at that precise moment that David Leigh turned to look at him. He had his plan now, his precious plan, firmly completed in his mind. And there was nothing to stop him going ahead with it.

Nothing at all.

SEVEN

JENNY GLANCED INTO the main salon, checking for the arrival of hungry lunch guests. So far, only the Leighs were hovering around, David looking casual in a light, fawn-coloured pair of slacks and a dazzlingly white shirt. His face, however, had a curiously shuttered look – as if he were trying to hide some kind of strong emotion.

He made Jenny feel instantly uneasy, because instead of emanating waves of angst and anger, he seemed to be on some sort of a high. When he glanced at her, and then quickly away again, she thought she caught glimpses of both relief and resolve, in equal measures, flash across his face.

It should have made a nice change from his usual glowering, gloomy countenance, but somehow it didn't. Instantly, the statuesque cook wondered what he was up to. Or, perhaps to be more precise, she wondered what had occurred to him to put that different look on his face.

In spite of the heat, Jenny felt herself shiver.

Dorothy Leigh looked extremely fetching in a light summer dress, a lovely shade of powder blue. It contrasted wonderfully with her silvery gold hair. Jenny thought how pretty the colour was – the same colour as meadow blue butterflies. It was a rather more soothing exercise, after witnessing the husband's volte-face, to contemplate the pretty wife. She was so obviously in love with her husband, and had a baby on the way. In many ways, she looked the picture of contentment. But in that moment, Jenny didn't envy Dorothy Leigh at all.

With a mental shrug, the cook returned to the galley and checked that the bread was just the right temperature, and glanced around, expecting Francis to appear at any minute.

But Francis, most unusually, was a few minutes late, and lunch didn't begin until nearly a quarter past one. Not that it mattered, but Jenny was already counting off the hours. She'd asked Tobias Lester that morning what time he expected them to dock at Swinford, and was told it would probably be at any time between six and seven o'clock that evening.

So just six more hours to go.

But the cruise wasn't over until the final evening meal, of course, and for that the cook intended to excel herself. In fact, she was beginning to feel quite cheerful again just thinking about it.

What was said between the guests over lunch Jenny had no idea, nor did she care. It was because of these moody, squabbling people that her little cruise had been quite ruined. Some people could be so damned thoughtless, she fumed crossly, as she added shredded chocolate to her coconut and chocolate trifle.

As soon as lunch was over, and the debris had been cleared, cleaned and put away, Jenny took herself off for a nice leisurely stroll. It felt good to get away from the boat for an hour or so but as much as she enjoyed her 'me' time, and watched the antics of a pair of kingfishers with chicks with pleased delight, much later Jenny was going to wish that she had stayed firmly put on the boat.

Or maybe not.

Dorothy felt keyed up and nervous. She paced in the games room, casting anxious glances at her husband every now and then and sighing morosely. But, as is sometimes the way with things, in direct contrast to his spouse David now seemed almost happy. It was as if whatever bogeyman had been pursuing him these last few months had suddenly taken a sabbatical. She was glad of that, of course. David had always been her rock and her anchor, and she felt lost whenever he was upset. In these modern days, Dorothy knew she was considered by many of her friends to be something of a throwback, being content as she was to be simply a wife and, soon now, a mother. It made her sick with worry whenever she contemplated the thought that she might lose him.

David was unaware of his wife's tender eyes upon him. As he leaned back in his chair, his thumbs lazily twirling in his lap, his eyes slowly wandered over in Gabriel's direction. It was all set. He had everything planned at last. It had all seemed to fall into place, as if it was meant to be. Never a religious man, or even a particularly superstitious one, he now felt as if there might be something to this fate malarkey after all. It certainly felt as if something or somebody was on his side all at once, lining all the dominoes up in a neat row, just waiting for him to topple the first one. All he needed now was the right opportunity. And surely it would come. With his newfound belief in providence, how could it not?

On the sofa, Jasmine Olney lazed with all the instinctive, sybaritic indolence of a cat. Every now and then she turned a page of her fashion magazine, and cooed or sneered at the pictures revealed.

Tobias Lester looked in tentatively from the French doors that led out onto the port deck and coughed discreetly. 'The cook's not back yet, Lucas,' he said quietly, and glanced at his watch. But he was not angry. In fact, it suited the captain of the *Stillwater Swan* very well to have a slight delay before starting off.

It would give them more time.

Lucas, who was sitting in a big, black leather armchair, staring at nothing in particular, shrugged lethargically at this news, nearly up-tilting the parrot, which squawked indignantly on his shoulder.

'It won't make much difference if we wait another hour,' he said drearily, and Tobias nodded. His thoughts exactly. He scratched the back of his neck, finding the hairs there to be stiff and cold. He was getting too old for this sort of thing. He was beginning to wonder if he should have let Brian talk him into it.

By the drinks cabinet, Gabriel, who was busy pouring himself a whisky and soda, stifled a sneer. Such slipshod timetables would not be permitted once *he* took over.

'I know,' Dorothy said quickly, as if she could bear the simmering tensions no longer, and must do something – *anything* – to make things more lively and friendly, a bit more … well … *normal*. 'Why don't we hold a darts tournament?' she asked hopefully.

Lucas glanced at the full-sized dartboard attached to one wall, his blank gaze altering not a whit. Then he looked at Dorothy's pretty, unhappy face, and silently cursed. He made a valiant effort to rouse himself.

'Well, we haven't played yet,' he agreed, and glanced at Gabriel. 'Olney?' he asked curtly.

Gabriel shrugged. 'Why not?'

'David?' Lucas glanced at the young solicitor, who shrugged without much enthusiasm but without any undue reluctance either.

'Suits me.'

'Tobias, perhaps you'd join us?' Lucas asked, looking a shade guiltily at the captain. Tobias loved the *Swan* almost as much as himself. And the captain had told him just this morning that Olney had informed both himself and Brian O'Keefe that their services would no longer be required once the papers transferring ownership were signed. So a final afternoon's get-together could surely do no harm.

Tobias stepped fully – not to mention eagerly – into the games room. Everything was going better than he could have hoped. Nevertheless, the smile he gave seemed rather wooden. He glanced slyly at his watch, then forced the smile on his face into a fully fledged beam. He had to be careful. 'Sure. I used to be a bit of a player once,' he laughed and rubbed his hands together. 'Perhaps we can give the ladies a run for their money.'

Lucas gave him a rather curious look.

'Oh, count me out,' Jasmine Olney said at once. 'I never learned to play.'

Nobody was surprised. Anybody in the room would have bet money that Jasmine Olney wouldn't know a double top from a dart feather.

'And I don't mind just watching,' Dorothy said firmly, in a show of feminine solidarity, and settled herself onto the nearest chair, arranging her pretty powder-blue skirts around her.

Jasmine yawned mightily and flipped over another page of her magazine. She'd only brought one magazine with her – a French fashion magazine – and she was already thoroughly bored with it. But really, what else was there to do in a dead-end hole like this? she thought savagely. The thought of living here permanently, endlessly cruising through the boring countryside, was enough to send a visible shudder running through her.

'What about Brian?' Lucas asked, bringing out the dart sets from the top drawer of a short bureau. 'That is, if you can get the surly bugger to come out of the engine room.'

'He's chopping wood,' Tobias said quickly. 'We need it for later on. It'll take him a while.'

Lucas nodded, then glanced at David. 'You and me, then, me old china?'

David nodded, more than happy with that arrangement. Tobias cast Gabriel a brief, angry look, and quickly turned away, ostensibly to inspect his darts. The last thing he wanted was Olney for a partner. On the other hand, it was rather ironic, when you thought about it.

And so the game began.

Lucas, to nobody's surprise, was a rather good darts player, and achieved a double with his first throw.

Jasmine turned another page of her magazine and blinked. There, tucked in the pages, was a single piece of neatly folded white notepaper. It said a lot about Jasmine Olney's personality that she didn't gasp, start or so much as cast a quick guilty look around her. Instead she merely ran a finger along the edge of her page in masterly nonchalance, and took a slow look up.

The men were all gathered around the darts board, and little Dorothy-goody-two-shoes was watching her husband with wide, adoring eyes.

Jasmine slowly unfolded the notepaper. It was in a writing she didn't recognize, written in black ink and with bold upsweeping lines.

Jasmine,
Meet me upstairs, in your room, at two o'clock. Keep near the door and keep a sharp eye out, just in case your husband comes a-calling.
I can't wait to touch you. You've been driving me crazy ever since you stepped on board.
But then, I expect you already know that.
B.O'K.

B.O'K, Jasmine thought, her lips curling into a whimsical, highly self-satisfied smile. Brian O'Keefe. So, the engineer had been playing little games with her all along, had he? Pretending not to notice whenever she looked his way, giving her those arrogantly knowing little smiles. She had begun to feel a bit put out about the engineer. She wasn't used to men not reacting to her the way she expected.

Now, though, she almost purred.

Not that she'd allow anything to happen, of course. Not now, and certainly not here, aboard this damned boat. Gabriel might catch them out, and that really wouldn't do. Giving him any ammunition in the divorce courts – even in these days of so-called fault-free divorces – wouldn't do her chances of a hefty alimony settlement any good. Especially if the case got assigned to some silly old fart with old-fashioned views.

Jasmine's eyes narrowed to slits. No, that wouldn't do at all.

Still, it would be interesting to see what the swarthy engineer had to say for himself. How he handled himself. A few passionate kisses on a slow, Sunday afternoon – no harm in that, surely. A little heavy petting too, if he played his cards right.

Jasmine carefully re-folded the paper and took a surreptitious look around, and was mollified, for once, to find that nobody was paying her the slightest bit of attention.

David Leigh was at the oche now, and still struggling to get his first double to allow him to start accumulating his own score. She turned a page of her magazine, checked her watch – which said nearly ten past two – and smiled.

She was already late. Perhaps he was waiting for her upstairs even now? She gave a pleasurable shiver, then yawned widely and stood up. 'Well, I'm going to take a little nap in my room,' she said, her voice dripping ennui.

Her husband barely gave her a look. It was not hard to see why. Gabriel was already forty points down on Lucas. Jasmine could have crowed over her good luck. Her husband was a competitive man in everything he did – even a silly game of darts would keep him riveted until he had won.

Of course, it also meant that if he lost, he'd be impossible to live with for days. Jasmine shrugged, smiled at Dorothy, who asked her if she had a headache or needed some aspirin, shook her head 'no' and sauntered away.

Her room was empty, but as she'd walked towards the closed door she could have sworn she'd heard something – some kind of noise coming from inside. Obviously, though, it had been wishful thinking, for the bedroom was deserted. Even the windows had been closed, and not so much as a lace curtain moved in the still air.

But she didn't really mind her would-be lover's tardiness.

The captain had said he had a lot of wood to chop. He'd probably be all sweaty and callus-palmed when he came.

The thought brought a happy, feline smile to her face. She picked up a chair and set it about a foot from the door, where she was sure to be able to hear anyone coming up the stairs in plenty of time.

Downstairs, Dorothy slowly began to go pale. She leaned back in her chair and breathed deeply, but it didn't take her husband long to notice her distress.

'Dotty, are you all right?' he asked sharply, and quickly came across to take her hand. Behind him, both Lucas and Gabriel looked around curiously.

Dorothy smiled, a shade unconvincingly. 'I'm feeling a bit … iffy, really,' she said, a shade embarrassed. 'I expect it's morning sickness. Although the doctor didn't say anything about getting it in the middle of the afternoon!' She tried to make a weak joke out of it, making Lucas's heart swell in pride for her pluckiness.

He abruptly put down his darts and walked across. 'Can I get you anything, love?' he asked anxiously. 'You really do look dicky. I can ask Francis if there's anything in the medicine cabinet for jippy tummies.'

'I don't think that she should take any medication that hasn't been specifically prescribed for her by a doctor, not in her condition,' David said sharply, and Lucas, to do him justice, looked suitably appalled.

'What? Oh, right you are. No, of course she mustn't. You can tell I'm a bachelor boy, can't yer, born and bred. Got no sense, 'ave I, aye, girl?' He guffawed and winked at Dorothy, who managed a rather wan smile in return.

'I think I'd better go upstairs to the … er … bathroom,' Dorothy said, her eyes assuming a wild, helpless look.

David quickly took her by the arm and helped her upstairs.

After that, the darts match was naturally abandoned.

Having no wish to stay in the same room as Gabriel Olney,

Tobias quickly excused himself to go to the bridge. He went smartly along the port deck and shut the door firmly behind him. There he looked at his watch. He was sweating now. He would be glad when it all was over.

Blast that cook! Where was she? Suddenly he had the intense desire to be on the move again.

Upstairs, Jasmine Olney stiffened as she heard footsteps and voices but, opening the bedroom door a crack and peeking out, she saw only the Leighs.

Dorothy paused outside the bathroom. 'David, why don't you go to our room and finish up those papers you brought with you? I know you wanted to get them done before we docked,' she urged him, with typical patience and understanding.

David shook his head stubbornly. 'They can wait.'

Dorothy put a hand to her stomach and swallowed hard. Her eyes became very wide and appealing. 'Please, David, I'd rather you didn't hang around out here. It's … well … so *embarrassing*, being sick and everything. I'd rather you didn't, well, have to hear me, and so on. Besides, I think I'll be here for quite some time. And it's nice and cool inside. There's no point in you hanging around out here – it's not as if there's anything you can do, you know, darling,' she added, cupping his face in her palm. 'I'll be all right, you'll see. And I'll come straight to our room as soon as I'm sure this bout of sickness has passed.'

She gave his hand a squeeze.

David nodded at once, sympathetic and anxious to please, and gave her a quick peck on the forehead. He turned, still obviously rather reluctant to leave her, but after a moment's hesitation, walked on into their room.

Jasmine, afraid of being spotted, quickly pulled the door shut. She heard the bathroom door open and close, and breathed easier. It wouldn't have done for the sickeningly cooing couple to notice when the engineer came to her bedroom door!

Downstairs, Gabriel wandered out onto the starboard deck. It was the first time he'd been on that side of the ship for quite some time. He stood watching the view of the deserted river-bank with a pleased smile on his face.

All was peaceful and quiet on the *Stillwater Swan*.

Jenny looked a little guiltily at her watch, and knew she must have held the boat up a little. It was nearly three o'clock. She stepped on board, made her way to the bridge, told the some-what disgruntled Tobias Lester that she was back, and made for her galley.

There she found the parrot raiding her bag of raisins.

She eyed the bird, which had been caught red-handed. Or rather, red-clawed, with one bit of fruit already in his beak, and the split bag open at his feet.

Jenny walked forward, left the spilled raisins on the side – after all, she could hardly use *those* now – and folded the bag back into some semblance of order.

The parrot watched her, head cocked to one side. ''Ere, what's your game then?' he demanded, in Lucas's wide, cockney drawl.

Jenny paused, looked at the bird, and fed it another raisin.

Really, it was extraordinarily uncanny the way the bird could come out with apt phrases at just the right time. You could almost be fooled into thinking you could hold a normal conver-sation with it.

She removed the various meats from the fridge and set them, in various sauces, to cook in the oven. She took a veritable mountain of vegetables from the tiny cold cupboard next to the fridge and set about chopping, peeling, dicing, mincing and shelling. It was a task that would have daunted many a lesser person but only served to fill the cook with a sense of peace.

Upstairs, Jasmine Olney still waited in vain for Brian O'Keefe. She was beginning to get right royally angry. When she heard the engines turn over, and she knew it would be impossible for the engineer to leave the engine room now, she left her post by the door, yanked the handle open, and marched out onto the landing. Although she could hardly go straight to the engine room and tell the oaf off, she would certainly think of a way to make her displeasure felt.

When she thought of him, sniggering away in his cubbyhole, imagining her waiting for him up here, all hot and bothered under the collar, she felt like she could literally kill him.

She was just in the mood for it.

As she passed the bathroom, the door opened and Dorothy Leigh emerged. She looked, even to Jasmine's unsympathetic eye, a little pale and tremulous. It must be horrible feeling sick all the time, she acknowledged vaguely. It was one of the many reasons why she herself had always refused to have children.

Hearing the two women exchange greetings, David opened the door to his bedroom, spotted his wife, and stepped out.

'What you need is a nice cup of tea, darling,' he said soothingly. 'Let's find Francis and get you one.'

Somewhat reluctantly, Jasmine thought, Dorothy allowed herself to be led back downstairs.

Poor Dotty, she thought, with a savage twist of her lips. No doubt if she started to feel sick again she'd have to make a dive for one of the side decks. Really, men could be such inconsiderate pigs at times. Why couldn't her husband have just let her go back to their room and lie down, as she so obviously wanted to do?

Even as her husband led her away, Dorothy cast a forlorn and longing look over her shoulder at the door to their bedroom.

But Jasmine had no sympathy for women who couldn't stick up for themselves. And with a shrug, she followed them down the stairs.

*

Jenny sluiced some cold water over her face and let her wrists run under the cold tap. It was hellishly hot in her cramped little galley.

She glanced at her watch. It was now nearly 4.15. Time for a breath of air in her favourite spot. To her surprise, the main salon was empty when she walked through it. In fact the whole boat, she noticed for the first time, seemed to have an almost deserted air.

It felt like being aboard the *Marie Celeste*.

But as she stepped out onto the starboard deck with a sigh of pleasure, she realized just how misleading this feeling was, and she stopped, just a little miffed to find that her 'territory' had been invaded.

David Leigh turned warily as he sensed another presence, but visibly relaxed on seeing who it was. Beside him, sitting in the cook's favourite deckchair, Dorothy watched the passing scenery with apathetic eyes. She looked rather pale, Jenny thought, and guessed instantly that the curse of the dreaded morning sickness had hit. 'I think some dry toast and tea might be in order, don't you?' she murmured.

Her husband looked at her gratefully. 'Just what I thought, but I couldn't find Francis to ask him.'

Jenny shrugged, retreated back to her galley, and emerged five minutes later with the unappetizing but tummy-settling food.

She nodded in satisfaction as Dorothy took a sip of weak, milky tea. She looked really washed out, poor thing, the cook noted in some concern; her hair seemed to have lost some of its lustre, and her cheeks were sallow and her neck was drooping. Even her pretty powder-blue dress looked less like a meadow blue butterfly in colour and more like a limp delphinium. She really shouldn't wear that dress in a shady place, Jenny thought inconsequentially – it obviously needed the sun to bring out its best. Then Jenny glanced at Dorothy's miserable face, and realized that being in the sunshine was probably the last thing on her mind.

Far better to leave her out here, where it was at least cool and a bit of breeze was to be had.

'Well, I'd best get on.' Jenny backed away, thinking somewhat glumly that it would have to be to the port deck or rear deck after all.

The games room, too, was oddly deserted when she passed through it.

Out on the port deck, only Lucas Finch stood at the railings, watching the passing riverbanks with a glum air. He looked odd, almost undressed, Jenny thought, and then suddenly understood why. He was without his ubiquitous bird. The perfidious parrot had momentarily deserted him for the lure of raisins.

Jenny walked slowly away from him, not wishing to interrupt his solitude, but noticing as she did so that the planking, just a few yards from his left foot, was wet.

Very wet indeed.

She felt a surge of alarm, and hoped that they weren't sinking!

Then common sense quickly took over from a landlubber's (and non-swimmer's) natural momentary panic. Of course they weren't sinking! The ship was as steady as a rock.

But *something* had made that big pool of water on the port deck. Perhaps the engineer had had to bring on some water for something or other. Her ignorance of the workings of the boat's steam mechanism wasn't something that concerned her.

She shrugged the thought aside and revelled in the cool river breeze as she took a slow turn on the rear deck. There she watched Brian O'Keefe stow away a rather vicious-looking axe, and then pondered the great paddles as they slowly and hypnotically turned, churning the clear water up into a wide, white, frothy path in the *Swan*'s wake.

Where was everybody?

Then she remembered her kidneys, which were soaking in red wine. Not her own kidneys, of course – Jenny seldom drank to excess – but the kidneys that were going to go into the little individual steak and kidney puddings, which were due to be served as a starter, and she rapidly headed back to her galley.

Too much red wine was bad for kidneys.

The parrot saw her enter and quickly scoffed the last of the raisins, just in case she felt inclined to pinch one or two for herself. The parrot obviously understood Jenny Starling far better than any of her fellow humans, and proceeded to whistle a fairly passable rendition of 'Colonel Bogey' as he watched her work.

She chopped some chives, checked the single cream was still fresh and usable, and then jumped a little as she felt a slight scratch on her shoulder.

By turning her head just a little to one side, she could see nothing but scarlet and blue.

She felt rather flattered that the bird, on such short acquaintance, should trust her enough to choose to sit on her shoulder, but she wasn't any too happy about the possible hygienic repercussions.

She'd have to shoo him off, she supposed, glumly.

But first she could gather all the jars, tins, cans and glass bottles she might need from the supply cupboard. There was no harm in that, after all, with everything being hermetically sealed.

So it was that when Jenny opened the door to the supply cupboard, she did so as Long John Silver might have done, with a smile on her face and a parrot on her shoulder.

She pulled the simple wooden door open, her mind on chutney and pickles. And Gabriel Olney stared back at her, his eyes wide open, his moustache rather droopy. Jenny, stunned to find an interloper amongst her comestibles, had just opened her mouth to ask him what the bloody hell he thought he was doing lurking about in her cupboard, when he began to fall forward.

More instinctively than anything else, she smartly stepped to one side and out of the way. And Gabriel Olney, with a rather squelchy 'whoomp', fell flat on his face at her feet.

He was, of course, exceedingly dead.

'Well, bugger me,' said the parrot.

EIGHT

FOR SEVERAL SECONDS Jenny stood rigid in surprise, staring down at the back of Gabriel Olney.

After a few more seconds, and very, very slowly, her brain began to function again, receiving messages from her eyes that she noted without really realizing that she was doing it.

Gabriel Olney was wet. His shirt was wrinkled and clinging to his skin, as only wet cotton can. There was no blood. At least, none as far as she could see, and she couldn't remember seeing any on his chest either, for that scant second that he had been stood upright in the cupboard, facing her.

He was missing one elegant boot. Funny, she'd never noticed his boots before. They were just above ankle-high, made with fine black leather, and had rather thick, soft soles. For a moment she was puzzled by those soles, and then realized that they'd probably been made specifically for people who lived or worked on boats. It was typical of Olney's personality that he had gone the whole hog and bought a complete new wardrobe to go with *Stillwater Swan*.

She seemed to stare at his left foot for a long while. It was completely bare. He hadn't even a sock on.

His back was not moving. There was no reassuring rise and fall of a man who was breathing. But Jenny already knew that it would be pointless to check to see if he was still alive. In her heart of hearts she knew he was dead and probably had been for – well, who knew how long?

113

It was at that point that she herself took a long, deep, shuddering breath, unaware until she did so that she'd been holding it in all this time. She felt a dizzy wave hit her and quickly moved back, so as to avoid touching Gabriel. The parrot on her shoulder lurched a little, unused to her way of moving, and his long scarlet and blue tail flattened against her back for balance.

Jenny walked the short distance to the galley door, opened it, went through, and then firmly shut it behind her, all still in a state of blissfully numb shock. She couldn't feel her legs beneath her. She had the distressing sensation of seeing and hearing things as if from a great distance.

But she couldn't give in to that sort of thing. Dimly, she began to recall the routine from past, bitter experiences with sudden death.

No one must be allowed into the room. No one must disturb the body or any possible evidence. She had to call the police.

It was this last imperative that finally washed away the last vestiges of her numbness, forcing her to think. How *could* she phone the police? They were on a boat, in the middle of the River Thames, cruising sedately through the deserted Oxfordshire countryside. But surely someone on board had a mobile phone? She'd left hers behind in Oxford, not wanting to risk losing it on the river. But the others would have one. Or would they? Mobile phones were just the sort of thing you deliberately left behind on a getting-away-from-it-all river cruise.

'I must see the captain,' she thought, and the sound of her own voice surprised her. Talking to herself out loud simply would not do. She must pull herself together. But Tobias Lester represented, if nothing else, an authority figure, one who had always struck her as level-headed and competent beneath that avuncular exterior. And right now she felt in need of some friendly, human company that she could rely on.

Moreover, he was in charge of the boat, and they'd have to dock somewhere, wouldn't they? She gave a quick, brisk shake of her head again, as if the movement could somehow physically kick-start her sluggish brain into working order again.

She checked the galley door but quickly discovered that it had no locking system. So she dragged one of the main salon's ladder-back chairs to stand in front of it. It was hardly ideal. Anybody could remove it, of course, and go in, whilst she was informing Tobias Lester of their circumstances, but there was nothing else for it.

Besides, nobody but Francis, perhaps, would have any reason for wanting to go into the galley.

Except the murderer.

Jenny shook her head, angry at herself. She really must pull herself together. *Why* would the murderer *want* to go back there? He or she was safely away to some other point on the boat by now, and the last thing on their mind would be to come back and incriminate themselves by riffling through the scene of the crime. And that old chestnut about the criminal always returning to the scene of the crime had gone out with the ark!

Jenny, very well aware that she had spent valuable minutes thinking all this through, and was consequently dithering like somebody's idea of a dotty maiden aunt, firmly marched out through the games room and onto the port deck and from there made her way forwards to the bridge. She knocked firmly and opened the door, not waiting for a summons.

By the wheel, Tobias looked around in surprise. He looked disconcerted at her abrupt entrance, but nothing more than that, as far as Jenny could tell.

But the murderer must know that it was bound to be the *Swan's* cook who discovered the body, and would therefore be prepared, when first spotting her, to act as if nothing out of the ordinary was happening.

'Cook, I don't think Lucas would like—'

'You have to dock at once,' Jenny interrupted rudely, 'and send someone, Brian O'Keefe, I suppose, to the nearest village to telephone for the police. Unless you know if there's a phone on board?'

Tobias stared at her as if she'd suddenly acquired several bats in her belfry.

'Dock? Here?' He glanced automatically towards both banks, his trained eye instinctively looking for the best place to berth, even as he shook his head. 'There's no phone on board – Lucas insists on it. And we're down in the valley here, in a bad reception area. Most mobiles wouldn't work anyway. But—'

'Gabriel Olney is dead,' Jenny said shortly, and was very careful to state nothing more than the bare truth. She'd watched a lot of police activity around murder cases in her time, and one thing she'd noted was that they never gave information away. And it was, she had always thought, a very good policy to mimic.

Tobias's leonine head abruptly swung her way. His eyes went wide. He went just a touch pale. 'Dead?' he echoed blankly.

Jenny nodded. 'We must dock and send for the police. At once.' She repeated it all patiently, knowing that – if genuine – shock could momentarily befuddle the clearest of brains.

It had befuddled hers. But never for long.

Tobias nodded, seeming to grasp the seriousness of the situation at last, and began to push and twiddle various levers and knobs, slowing the vessel down and heading her towards the right-hand bank. Satisfied that he was doing as he'd been told, Jenny nodded and left, determined to stand guard in front of the galley door.

Just in case.

In the main salon, Lucas Finch stepped in from the direction of the rear corridor. 'Hello, love. The boat's stopping, did you notice? I wonder what Toby's up to.'

The parrot on her shoulder, spotting his master, gave a little wriggle and was quickly airborne, and flying back to Lucas. It settled on his shoulder and began, very gently, to gnaw on a claw.

Jenny walked steadily to the chair in front of her galley and very firmly sat down on it. It would take a better man than Lucas Finch to shift her now.

'I told Captain Lester to dock,' she admitted coolly. 'Gabriel Olney is dead. Do you have a map of the immediate area?'

Lucas stared at her. His face seemed to shut down – only his eyes glittered. And in that moment, Jenny could clearly see the man who profited from war. The man who'd earned himself (by fair means or foul) a considerable fortune. He didn't say anything for quite some time. When he did, it was to ask a question.

'Why do you want a map?'

'You must send Brian O'Keefe to the nearest village to ring for the police. To do that, we need to know where the nearest telephone is likely to be. I understand mobiles don't work here, and that you don't allow any on board anyway?'

Lucas looked at her levelly, perhaps a little surprised by her cool-headed logic, but nodded acquiescently. 'I have a full-length map of the River Thames in the drawer somewhere.'

He turned to a large, all-purpose set of drawers set flush to one wall, and riffled through the top one for a map. Once it was found, he carefully unfolded it and spread it out on the dining table. 'I'll have to go and get Tobias. He'll know best what our position is, exactly.'

Jenny nodded. By now, the boat was almost at a complete standstill.

Out on the starboard deck, although they must have noticed that they were docking, David and Dorothy Leigh never came to investigate. Outside, on the rear decking, Jenny heard rapid footsteps and saw the engineer heading quickly towards the bridge. No doubt he too wanted to know the reason behind the unscheduled delay.

As he passed the French windows that led to the games room, Jenny clearly saw, through the open inner door, Jasmine Olney suddenly rear up from her position on a deckchair and grab Brian's arm. What she might have been about to say to him, however, was never uttered as Lucas and Tobias chose that moment to step out of the wheelhouse.

'Ah, Brian, secure the boat then come into the salon will you?' Tobias ordered, making Jenny blink a little in surprise, for he had assumed command with an ease and natural affinity that halfway stunned her. And yet she knew that it shouldn't have done: Lester was a very competent man. Very competent indeed – hadn't she herself instinctively gone to him when times had got tough? Somehow, she seemed to have forgotten that. He was such a modestly unassuming man, he made it very easy to forget how very capable he must be. It must be a trait that could come in very handy.

Had Gabriel Olney, too, forgotten that?

Jenny shook her head, telling herself it was useless to speculate. Besides, the police would be here soon. It would be up to them to find out who'd killed the ex-soldier.

Jasmine, perhaps sensing that now was not the time to pick a fight with the engineer, subsided reluctantly back onto her deckchair. Lucas paused, looked at her, seemed about to say something, then shook his head.

The two men quickly joined Jenny, Tobias Lester efficiently checking the map. He glanced at his watch, did his mental arithmetic, and put his finger firmly on one point.

'I'd say we are here, give or take half a mile or so. That makes the nearest village Carswell Marsh, which is about three miles south of here. It's all cross-fields so Brian should make good time.'

'Good time for what?' Brian asked, catching the last sentence as he came in. He nodded at Tobias. 'I've got her well secured. What's going on?'

'Gabriel Olney's dead. You have to go and get the rozzers.' It was Lucas who answered, but Brian O'Keefe stared at Tobias Lester for a long, hard time. Then he finally nodded. 'Right,' he agreed curtly.

Jenny had the strong feeling that, whatever his immediate thoughts, Brian O'Keefe would never utter them now.

'Once you've phoned them,' Jenny spoke up, her voice quite steady and firm now, 'you'll have to wait for them and then lead them back here to the boat. Especially if there's no road for them to follow.'

Brian glanced at her curiously, saw her strange seating arrangement for the first time, and cast a curious look at the closed galley door. Then he checked the map for himself, saw where he had to go, and shook his head. 'There are no roads near here indicated on the map.'

'Right, then you'd best set off fairish, like,' Lucas said, and rubbed his nose. 'Think you can find the village all right?'

Brian O'Keefe smiled wryly. 'I can smell a pub from five miles away. I'll find the nearest one to me, no trouble.'

The three of them watched him go in silence. He was young, fit and set off across the fields like a hare.

Lucas slowly swivelled his eyes through the open door of the games room and out towards the port deck. His eyes moved quickly away again from the beautiful dark-haired woman sat sunning herself, and moved apprehensively to those of his captain.

'Someone should tell Jasmine,' he said heavily.

Tobias looked appalled. 'Not me.'

As one, both men turned towards Jenny.

Jenny said, very firmly, 'I'm not leaving this room.'

Lucas opened his mouth to say something, then glanced at the door behind her. As if sensing the tension in the air, the parrot on his shoulder bobbed his head up and down uneasily.

'He's in there then, is he?' Lucas finally asked. Rather pointlessly, she thought. Jenny nodded. 'And you don't want anyone going in there?' Lucas carried on the theme, his suspicious, thoughtful tone of voice making Tobias suddenly jerk his head towards the cook, a questioning look on his face.

'You said he was dead,' Tobias said, almost accusingly. 'You didn't say how.' He chose his words with an odd kind of care, almost as if he was afraid of the answer.

'I'm not sure how he died,' Jenny said, quite truthfully. 'And it's useless to speculate. We'll just have to sit quietly until the police come. And I think it will be a good idea to tell Mrs Olney nothing, for the moment. Unless she asks, of course.'

Naturally, both men agreed, and sincerely hoped that she wouldn't.

The police arrived in a surprisingly short time. Brian must have run all the way to the village, and the nearest police station must have been close by, for barely an hour had passed when O'Keefe returned to the *Stillwater Swan* with what looked like a herd of constables and plain clothes detectives.

Jasmine, who'd never left her seat in the sun, looked up with every apparent evidence of bewilderment as strange men began to file into the main salon, and she took off her sunglasses to follow their progress inside with her eyes.

Jenny slowly rose from her chair, trying to sort the men out. The tall, stoop-shouldered man with glasses and carrying a black bag was the easiest man to allot, since this had to be the police surgeon or medical examiner. Two other, rather cherubic-faced men carried what looked like briefcases. From past experience, she knew that these had to be the forensics experts. But they were both looking at the oddest little man Jenny Starling had ever seen. (And in her time, she'd seen very odd-looking men indeed.)

He couldn't have been more than five feet in height, for a start, which made her wonder how many powerful people he must have known in the police department to allow him to get around the minimum height restriction rules. Or did they even still exist?

But it was not just his height (or rather lack thereof) that made her goggle at him. He was, without doubt, quite simply the most ugly individual Jenny had ever seen. His eyes were tiny, button black and set deep in his face. His chin was non-existent, his mouth a rather lipless gash. But it was the turned-up nature of his nose, which the cook suddenly saw as he turned and looked directly at her, that made him look most like a human variety of a pug dog. It was so squashed up it looked almost comical. And the nostrils ... yes, they were almost pointing upwards.

If he ever got caught out in the rain he'd surely drown, Jenny thought inconsequentially, and suddenly became aware of the hysteria behind that thought. Not to mention the unintentional unkindness. She mentally apologized, stepped to one side, and pointed into the galley. 'He's in there,' she said quietly, and the small man gave her a single, sharp glance, nodded and led the way briskly inside.

The surgeon was close on his heels. The two forensics men, and the final man of the group, a big, solid, blond individual who was presumably a sergeant, stayed by the door, awaiting orders.

Jasmine said, rather loudly, 'What on earth is going on?'

'If you please, madam,' the sergeant said in a deep, pleasant bass. 'Take a seat. We'll know more shortly.'

Hearing sudden and unexpected voices, David and Dorothy Leigh at last appeared in the doorway leading from the starboard deck and stared at the strangers in disbelief.

Inside, Inspector Neil Rycroft, he of the pug face, stared at the dead man on the floor and watched the police surgeon give his usual thorough but of necessity brief examination.

'Dead no more than four hours, no less than one. No outward signs of violence. No cuts, bumps, contusions or entry marks that I can see. No signs of strangulation.'

'He's wet,' Rycroft said. His voice was high-pitched, almost child like in tone, but curiously expressionless. He didn't seem to be accusing the surgeon of missing the obvious, nor did he seem to be coming to any conclusions himself. That voice had misled many a criminal – and many a criminal's solicitor – into thinking that Neil Rycroft was a bit of a simpleton.

Which he most definitely wasn't.

The surgeon obviously knew Rycroft's ways well, for he merely responded, just as impassively, with a single 'yes'.

'Drowning would seem to be the obvious cause of death,' Rycroft added thoughtfully.

The surgeon grunted and stood up. 'I'll let you know as soon as I've completed an autopsy. We're a bit stacked up at the moment though. A lot of those train-crash victims from Richester way have been sent down to our labs. It'll be a few days before I can give you any details.'

Rycroft sighed. 'Right. But you think he drowned?'

The surgeon turned the corpse over, did some rather disgusting-type medical things and then nodded.

'I'd say, unofficially, there was little doubt of it,' the surgeon said, then added cautiously, 'but don't quote me just yet. And certainly don't put anything down on paper until I can confirm it.'

The inspector nodded, showed the surgeon out, and beckoned his forensic boys in. He shut the door carefully behind them, then stood looking at the group scattered throughout the main salon.

'Who discovered the body?' Rycroft asked, looking automatically at Tobias Lester.

It was odd, Jenny thought, just a shade miffed, how men of authority seemed to naturally seek out another of their kind.

Tobias nodded at Jenny. 'Our cook did.'

The inspector and his sergeant glanced at the large, calm woman, their eyes assessing. She looked like an avenging goddess from some long-forgotten mythology – six feet tall, voluptuous and rather beautiful, in an odd way.

The parrot, which had returned to his perch on her shoulder, gave them pause, but not for long. No doubt, in the course of their professional life, they came across all sorts.

'You found him like that?' Rycroft jerked his head towards the galley.

Jenny shook her head. 'No.'

Rycroft stiffened. It was a rather absurd gesture in one so small and ugly, confronting one of Jenny Starling's girth and six-feet-tall frame. 'You really shouldn't interfere with a body, you know,' he said crisply, disapproval now rife in his high voice.

'I *do* know, as a matter of fact,' Jenny shot back just as crisply. 'When I went into the galley at about half past four, everything was perfectly in order. It was only when I opened the door to the cupboard that Mr Olney fell out. I left him where he lay. I touched nothing, immediately put a chair in front of the door, left to tell the captain to dock the boat and send someone for the police, then sat in the chair in front of the door until you came. Nobody went in or came out of the galley, unless they did so during the brief minute I left to inform the captain what had happened.'

She stated the facts in a calm, unassertive manner, but she noticed both policemen's eyes sharpen on her in sudden, avid interest. She could almost read their minds.

Very calm. Very cool. Very correct. All very praiseworthy but totally unnatural. We'll have to keep our eye on this one.

Jenny had seen that look before in a policeman's eye. Alas, all too often. She was dreading the time when they finally got around to taking down names and details. For her name had to be mud in the vast majority of police stations in and around Oxfordshire and the home counties.

'I see. Very commendable,' Inspector Rycroft said dryly. 'Since you seem to have such a good grasp of events, perhaps you could give Sergeant Graves here a list of all the people on board? I'd also like a run-down of the ship's itinerary.'

Tobias winced at the term 'ship'.

Lucas stirred, thinking that he, as host, should be the one to do the talking, then suddenly remembered that these were rozzers – and Lucas Finch and rozzers had never mixed – and just as quickly subsided again, more than happy to leave the dirty work to the cook.

123

Jenny glanced at the sergeant who was waiting, pencil in hand, hovering over his ever-ready notebook.

Jenny knew all about policemen's notebooks too.

'The mur— the dead man is Mr Gabriel Olney,' she said. 'I'm not sure where he lives but I'm sure that Mrs Olney, Mrs Jasmine Olney, will be able to tell you,' she began, getting off to a thoroughly disastrous start.

First of all, she'd almost said 'the murdered man' when, in reality, she really had no reason to believe it was murder. But she'd have bet her last penny that the inspector hadn't missed the tell-tale slip. And secondly (and much worse) she'd boldly stated the fact that it was Gabriel Olney who was dead when his widow, who was standing not more than ten yards away, had not been given a shred of warning.

It just went to show, Jenny thought sourly, that practice hardly made perfect.

Jasmine abruptly sat down, and blinked.

At this point, Rycroft and Sergeant Graves glanced at her curiously. Rycroft said, reasonably softly, 'Mrs Olney? You had no idea of your husband's death?'

Jasmine shook her head. Then she blinked again. She seemed to be unable to find a thing to say. Eventually she licked her dry lips and said, somewhat unsteadily, 'No one told me.'

'We thought it best not to,' Jenny said quickly, but inside she could have kicked herself for her thoughtlessness.

But then again, a suspicious little voice would insist on piping up in the back of her mind, Jasmine might have known all along about her husband – if she was the one who'd put him in her cupboard in the first place.

Rycroft glanced back to the cook, obviously puzzled. He thought that either the cook was the most cold-hearted woman he'd ever met, or the shrewdest.

He would soon learn which.

'Carry on, please,' he said, his disconcertingly high-pitched voice once again as bland as milk.

'There's Dorothy and David Leigh.' She nodded to the young couple, who were still standing transfixed in the doorway to the starboard deck. 'They live in the village of Buscot, the same as Mr Lucas Finch, the owner of the boat.' She hesitated over the word 'owner', not sure of her ground. Had Gabriel Olney already legally bought the *Stillwater Swan*?

If he noticed her sudden stumble, Rycroft didn't mention it. 'Go on.'

'There's the engineer....'

'We know all about Mr O'Keefe, madam,' the sergeant said helpfully, and Jenny nodded. Of course, they'd have questioned him thoroughly on the way here.

Again Rycroft wondered at the statuesque cook's apparent understanding of the way the police mind worked. He began to feel distinctly uneasy. There was something about her that looked familiar, now that he thought about it. Not that he'd ever met her before – Rycroft had an excellent memory, and someone as noticeable as the cook would have stuck in his mind like a rose thorn.

Nevertheless....

'Who else is on board?' he prompted crisply.

'Captain Tobias Lester.' She nodded at the captain. 'He lives in a cottage on Mr Finch's estate at Buscot. And then there's Francis ... er Grey,' she said, for the briefest of moments having forgotten his surname. It was not, perhaps, surprising. Francis had a way of making himself seem almost non-existent.

Which reminded her. Just where *was* Francis?

'Mr Grey is Mr Finch's manservant. The Leighs and Olneys are Mr Finch's guests. I was hired to cook for the weekend. We set off from Buscot yesterday morning about ... ten o'clock?' She glanced questioningly at the captain, who nodded.

At that point, Tobias took over, very competently giving the police the *Stillwater Swan*'s timetable and docking points over the past two days. When he'd finished, Rycroft nodded, turned back to the cook and said smoothly, 'You've left yourself out, madam.'

Jenny sighed. 'My name,' she said heavily, 'is Miss Jenny Starling.'

And waited for it.

She didn't have to wait long.

Opposite her, Sergeant Graves started to write it down, and mumbled automatically, 'Do you have any other Christian names, please,' before his head shot up comically. 'Did you say *Starling*?'

Jenny, who considered her parents to have gone rather mad in the first names department, saddling her with two other totally unusable ones, was glad not to have to say what the rest of them were in front of witnesses.

'Yes. Starling,' she repeated heavily.

Rycroft was staring at her, his face falling into a look of utter dismay. It was most unfortunate. Folds of skin suddenly seemed to mould themselves into the semblance of a chow, and a rather sick-looking chow at that.

'Sir, we've finished.' The two forensic experts chose that moment to emerge from the galley. Rycroft glanced at them, eyebrows raised. They shook their heads. 'Plenty of finger-prints – probably all legitimate. We'll have to take samples from everyone present. Nothing much else – or rather, too much of everything else to be of use, I'm afraid. It's a storage cupboard after all. It'll take days to identify and sort out all the trace elements in there. But we've all the photographs we need.'

Which meant, Jenny thought, no obvious murder weapon, no traces yet or fibres. Someone, she thought grimly, had been very clever. Very clever indeed.

And that someone was on this boat now.

Rycroft sighed. 'Take a thorough look over the rest of the boat, will you?' he said curtly, and resumed his scowling contemplation of the cook.

Tobias and Lucas cast first the policemen, then the cook,

curious looks. 'Is something wrong?' Lucas asked, rather absurdly, given the circumstances.

But both policemen ignored him. They were both staring at the cook as if at a rather unusual specimen in a zoo.

'So you're Jenny Starling,' Rycroft said, his voice flat and yet very much aggrieved.

'Yes,' she agreed flatly. 'I'm *Miss* Starling.'

'And you're at it again,' Rycroft sighed. 'In my patch, this time.'

'I've not been at *anything* again,' Jenny denied hotly. 'All I do is mind my own business and cook good food. If people around me will go around kill—' She abruptly bit off her angry words as Jasmine Olney suddenly raised her dark head and looked at her speculatively.

What Rycroft might have said to that they never knew, for at that moment one of the forensics boys came running in, his cherubic face flushed with excitement. 'Sir! Sir, come and see this.'

Naturally, after that, *everybody* rushed outside to the port deck, where the second forensics man waited. He was stood, more or less, in the exact same spot that Lucas had been standing in, just a short while before.

Jenny saw again the same wet planking as everyone – the Leighs, Jasmine, the captain, Lucas and Brian – jostled around her. What she *hadn't* noticed before was the piece of rope that was tied from the bottom of the railings, and that disappeared over the side to dangle in the river below.

As Rycroft walked carefully around the wet decking, the forensics man pulled up on the rope.

And revealed at the other end, sopping wet and dripping river water, was Gabriel Olney's missing boot.

NINE

FOR A WHILE, Inspector Rycroft simply stared at the boot, a totally unreadable expression on his remarkable face. He had not, of course, missed the fact that Gabriel Olney's corpse had been minus one of its boots, but until now he hadn't really come to any significant conclusion to account for its absence. Murder victims, in his experience, were apt to struggle, and in a struggle, all kinds of things could go astray, including items of clothing. Now, though, the salutary sight brought an obvious inference with it, and one that made his blood run cold.

He leaned over the rail and glanced down into the river below. The rope was thick and sturdy, and ropes, he imagined, were probably plentiful in the storeroom of a boat such as the *Stillwater Swan*. So, no mystery as to where the murderer might have acquired the murder weapon then. For now there could be no doubt that it *was* murder they were dealing with.

He examined the knot closely and hopefully, but it looked simple enough. Not a complicated, nautical knot certainly. Which meant that if Tobias Lester was in any way involved, then he'd been clever enough – and cool-headed enough – to remember to tie a knot that any other landlubber might have used.

He glanced down the side of the boat once more, his brow furrowed in thought. The river surface was nearly two feet from the bottom of the railing, where the rope had been securely tied.

So if someone had knocked out Olney, tied the rope round his foot and then hefted him over the side to watch him drown, it would have taken a person of considerable strength to pull him back up again. The victim was not particularly fat, it was true, but still, he was an adult, well-nourished male. And would have been – literally – a dead weight.

He certainly couldn't see any of the ladies involved being capable of such physical manoeuvrings. Except for Jenny Starling, perhaps. She looked big enough to throw *anybody* around. But then again, a generously curvaceous hourglass figure didn't necessarily mean that she had superior upper-arm strength or muscles like Jean-Claude Van Damme.

And in any case, he thought with an inner wince, Jenny Starling, as everyone on the local force knew only too well, had a reputation for *solving* murders. Not for committing them.

Worse luck.

Rycroft would have been delighted to be the copper to rid the force of the pesky presence of the successful but strictly amateur sleuth but no matter how tempting the thought, Rycroft just couldn't see the phlegmatic cook suddenly turning into a deranged killer.

No, he had to be looking for a man.

He nodded to the forensics team, knowing without having to tell them that they'd give the rope, boot and the rest of the boat a meticulous going-over, and turned to observe the faces of the others.

Lucas Finch was staring at the rope as if it were a snake. The parrot, perhaps out of instinctive or simply because of avian loyalty, suddenly snuggled closer to Lucas's neck and suddenly began to croak/croon a very swing-time rendition of 'Stranger On the Shore'.

It made everybody feel, for some reason, abruptly uncomfortable.

The handsome young couple, the Leighs, were furthest away, and he noticed them begin to back off, the pretty blonde whispering something into her husband's ear. The pair then rapidly disappeared back into the games room. Brian O'Keefe looked implacable. If he recognized the rope specifically, he gave no indication of it. But he shot the skipper a quick, thoughtful look that was more puzzled than anything else.

Jasmine was still staring at her husband's boot as if spellbound.

'I'll have to ask you all to assemble in the salon and give me an account of your individual movements for this afternoon,' Rycroft began crisply, ushering them backwards like a farmer's wife shooing a flock of recalcitrant chickens.

Jenny led the way, selecting a large, black leather armchair for herself. She knew full well just how time-consuming these things could be. You might just as well make yourself comfortable as not.

Sergeant Graves brought out his notebook yet again.

Rycroft fixed Jenny with a gimlet eye. 'Right, Miss Starling, we'll begin with you, shall we?' he asked, somewhat maliciously.

Jenny inclined her head. 'I prepared lunch for one o'clock as usual. It started a little late, as Francis didn't come to the galley to start serving until about a quarter past. Mr Olney ate, I believe, the same dishes as everyone else.'

Sergeant Graves' lips twitched. She certainly wanted to make it clear that there was nothing suspect about her food.

'After I'd cleared away the dishes, I decided to take a long walk. It was hot in the galley, it was our last day out, and I wanted to stretch my legs.'

Sergeant Graves, for one, didn't doubt it. A woman the size of the cook would no doubt find the tiny galley something of a trial.

'I returned about three o'clock and informed the captain. I started preparing the vegetables and various other edible items for the dinner this evening. I did not, at that point, go to the cupboard,' she added quickly, seeing that Rycroft was about to ask just that.

'At about a quarter past four, I went out for some air on the starboard deck, and found Dorothy and David Leigh already out there. Mrs Leigh looked unwell, so I returned to the galley to make her some weak tea and some toast. I then took it out to her. I took a short turn around the boat, going on down the deck, through the back corridor, out onto the rear deck and, lastly, along the port deck. Mr Finch was stood on the port deck, alone. I noticed at that point that the planking next to him was wet. I then returned to the galley. I had been gone only five minutes or so. When I returned, I opened the cupboard door to get some pickled vegetables and discovered the body.'

Lucas had stirred a little angrily at her mention of himself and the wet planking, and then sighed wearily. It was no good blaming the cook for merely stating facts. The rozzers, he knew, would ferret about asking questions and no doubt unearthing all sorts of unsavoury titbits about himself and his guests before all this was over.

'Thank you, Miss Starling,' Rycroft said. 'Very succinct,' he added a touch dryly. 'Mr Finch?'

Lucas stuck out his long, spindly legs and closed his eyes for a moment. He seemed to have aged somewhat in the past few hours.

'Let's see. We all had lunch together. And yes, Gabby did eat the same as the rest of us. It was all very tasty.' He bowed to the cook.

Sergeant Graves' lips twitched again.

Jenny – who noticed everything – thought somewhat inconsequentially that the sergeant's personality did not match his name very well. He seemed to be brimming over with repressed good humour.

'After lunch, we all sort of moped around for a few minutes, then Dorothy – Dorothy Leigh, that is – proposed a game of darts. Er … let's see. The captain had come in at that point to say that the cook hadn't yet returned, so I dragged him in on the game. David Leigh and myself played Gabby and Tobias.

Or was it the other way round? Buggered if I can remember now.'

'What time was this?' Rycroft asked quickly.

'About twoish? Somewhere round then. Mrs Olney said she couldn't play, and Dorothy said she didn't mind just watching. So we played for … I don't know, twenty minutes. Maybe less. Then Dorothy became rather ill, and her husband took her upstairs. After that, the match was abandoned, of course, and we all dispersed. I think Gabby went out there—' He pointed '—onto the starboard deck. I don't know how long he stayed out there, of course, or where he went afterwards. I myself went out onto the rear deck to snooze for an hour or so. Then I sort of wandered around the boat for a bit. I'd only just stepped onto the port deck a few seconds before I spotted Miss Starling. I too noticed that the deck was wet, but I assumed Brian had been taking on some river water.'

'What time was this?' Rycroft asked again.

But Lucas wasn't so sure. He thought it was sometime after four.

'Then I took a turn round the end of the boat, checked that everything was OK and all that. Then I noticed the boat was slowing and turning into the bank and wondered why. It wasn't a scheduled stop, and nobody had come to tell me about it. I was just going to the bridge to find out what was going on, and as I came into the salon, I found the cook sitting in the chair by the galley door. She told me what had happened. Then we arranged for you lot to come and….' He shrugged. 'That was that.'

'So the last time you saw Mr Olney alive was at about half past two, when the darts match broke up?'

Lucas nodded.

'Captain Lester?' Rycroft glanced at the captain.

'I had lunch, as usual, on a tray in the bridge. The cook brings it to me, or I go into the galley for it. I think I went to the galley to collect it today. We were due to sail at two, but I knew the cook had gone for a walk, and hadn't reported back, so I went to tell Lucas we'd be delayed. Then we played darts, as he said, until poor little Dorothy got so sick. Then I went back to the wheelhouse.' He paused and took a breath, obviously considering his words carefully. Once again there was that air of calm competence about him. 'Sometime near ... three o'clock, I should think it was, Miss Starling reported back and I took the *Swan* out. I was in the bridge until Miss Starling came in, about half past four, to tell me we had to stop and get the police. And that's about all I can tell you.'

Sergeant Graves licked the end of his pencil and turned another page. So far, everybody seemed to be singing from the same hymn sheet, he thought sourly. If anybody knew anything, nobody seemed in any hurry to speak up.

It was all very prosaic, but even as the laborious process of establishing everybody's alibis went on, Jenny knew, arrangements were probably being made to collect Gabriel Olney's body. And back at the local station, she was also sure that a veritable army of policemen were busily checking into the backgrounds of all those concerned.

The murder of a man of Gabriel Olney's status would almost certainly be given top priority. She wondered what the diligent sergeants and constables would unearth about all of them. And any skeletons in the cupboard, she warned her fellow shipmates silently, had better get ready to be thoroughly rattled.

'Mrs Olney, I know that this is a hard time for you, but if you could just tell me what happened this afternoon?' Rycroft asked, a little less curtly, of the dark-haired woman.

Jasmine Olney took a deep breath. She'd seemed to be genuinely bewildered throughout the whole experience, but now she could clearly be seen to pull herself together somewhat.

'I'm afraid I can't help you much there, Inspector,' she said, her voice composed but a little husky. 'Like the others, I had lunch, then followed them into the games room. I can't play darts, so I read a magazine for a while and then, while the game was still going on, I left to take a nap in my room. Mrs Leigh – she's very sweet – asked me if I was all right, or wanted an aspirin, but I said no. I wasn't ill, just sleepy. I took a nap for … oh, I don't know, about an hour or so. When I came back down it must have been about ten past three or thereabouts. I met the Leighs on the upstairs landing and we all came down together. I thought I'd get some sun, so I took a chair on the port deck and sunbathed. I stayed there until you policemen came. Oh, no, wait a moment, I think the engineer passed me about an hour or so before that. And that's all I know.'

Jenny kept her mouth firmly shut. No doubt either she or the police would find out sooner or later just what all that fuss had been about between Brian O'Keefe and the newly created widow. Although it wasn't hard to guess. Some serious flirting had been going on, and somebody had probably overstepped the mark, or misjudged the mood. On the whole, she thought it was far more likely to be the more volatile Jasmine at fault than the cocky engineer.

'You didn't see your husband at all in that time?' Rycroft asked, his voice openly surprised now.

Jasmine started. 'Well … er … no, actually I didn't. I assumed he was reading out on the rear or starboard deck. He is a very avid reader … *was* a very avid reader, I suppose I should say,' she corrected herself, her voice beginning to wobble just slightly. She reached for a tissue and leaned back in her chair, her pretty dark eyes filling with tears.

Rycroft coughed uncomfortably, and muttered squeakily, 'Er, yes, quite so, madam.'

He looked up then, and saw, for the first time, that the Leighs were not present. Had not, in fact, been present since the group had returned from inspecting the dripping boot.

'Sergeant, I think you'd better go upstairs and ask the Leighs to come down,' he snapped, his voice dripping disapproval. 'I don't remember giving them permission to leave.'

'Mrs Leigh is pregnant, Inspector,' Jenny explained helpfully. 'I think she's been suffering from morning sickness rather badly this trip, poor thing. A shock like this probably made her feel even more ill, and I imagine her husband insisted that she lie down.'

Rycroft, unbelievably, blushed beetroot. 'Oh? Yes, well … er … We'll still have to take a statement from them. And this Francis fellow. Where the hell is he?'

As the sergeant left to fetch the Leighs, Lucas shifted himself from the chair. 'I think you'll find he's in the small room off the galley. That's usually where he skulks off to, if he wants some time alone. I'll go get him,' he offered helpfully.

Jenny opened her mouth to say what a damn cheek it was for Francis to use her bedroom in such a way, then subsided. To be fair, she could hardly call it 'her' bedroom. All it contained was her still largely unpacked suitcase.

Francis, in due course, reappeared with Lucas, but could add nothing to the proceedings. He'd served lunch, and apologized for being late about it. After lunch, he'd made sure drinks were served, then took himself off to the small bedroom for a bit of a lie down. He had, he confessed shamefacedly, fallen asleep and hadn't awakened until right this minute. He apologized profusely to Lucas, who looked more amused than anything else.

At this point, the sergeant led the way back down the stairs and into the salon, with a somewhat chastened husband and wife close on his heels.

Dorothy Leigh did indeed look pale. She was wearing one of those very fluffy, long-haired jumpers in a pretty pink shade, and a long, warm-looking caramel-coloured skirt. On a hot day such as this one, it was clear she must be suffering from shock to feel so cold. She sat down in the chair that Inspector Rycroft hastily pulled out for her, rubbing her hands together for warmth, and her husband pulled up his own chair, deliberately close to her. He took her hand in his and met the inspector's gaze clearly.

'Now, Mr Leigh. You're a solicitor, I believe?'

David nodded.

'Then you'll understand why we need a full statement from both yourself and your wife as to your movements this afternoon?' Rycroft pressed.

Again, David nodded. And started first. He spoke in a sure, confident, not-quite-but-almost-challenging tone of voice, as if he dared the police to disbelieve what he was about to say.

'We all had lunch, then went into the games room. Dorothy asked if anybody was interested in a game of darts. We played for a while, then I noticed that Dorothy looked ill. My wife is expecting our first child, Inspector, so I hope that you will be rather considerate of her?'

Rycroft assured him hastily that, most likely, apart from getting her statement, Mrs Leigh need not be bothered any further.

'Right. Well, I noticed she was ill, and took her upstairs. I left her in the bathroom. She insisted I leave. She wasn't well, you understand, and didn't want to be … er … disturbed.'

Rycroft assured him hastily, and with more blushes, that it was all very understandable.

'I went on into our room to work on some paperwork that I'd brought along with me. I know it was unusual, and probably rude, to bring work on board, but it was a last will and testament that simply had to be done and handed in on Monday, and I knew Lucas wouldn't mind.'

Lucas, at this point, waved a hand in a vague sign of agreement. 'Business is business,' he muttered magnanimously.

'I worked on the will for about … oh, three quarters of an hour or so. I was worried about Dotty, so I went out to check on her, but she was just coming back out of the bathroom at that point. I think Mrs Olney came out of her own room just then, and we all came downstairs together. Dotty and I went to sit out on the starboard deck. It's quieter out there – all the games and things are played on the port side. And I thought Dotty could do with some peace and quiet. We sat there for something like an hour, I suppose it was, just watching the countryside go by, then the cook appeared and asked Dotty if she'd like some tea and toast. It was very kind of her. She brought it out, then left. We noticed the boat was docking, but thought it might be because of something technical – you know, the engine going wrong or something.' He shrugged vaguely.

Sergeant Graves' lips twitched. It was obvious to him that the young solicitor was hardly mechanically minded. Probably the sort, Graves thought mildly, to send his car to the mechanic to have a flat tyre changed.

'Anyway, we stayed on the deck until we heard strange voices. It was you and your men. And that's all I know.'

'Hmm. And you didn't see Mr Olney after the darts match broke up?'

David shook his head firmly. 'No.'

'Hmm. Nobody seems to have seen Mr Olney at all after the darts match, until his body was discovered. That's nearly two hours or so. Unless you saw him, Mrs Leigh?'

Dorothy tucked her cold hands under her armpits in a touching, vulnerable gesture, and shook her head. Her pale hair shimmered in the sunlight.

'No. After David and I left the darts match, I stayed in the bathroom for what seemed like ages. Well … I was a bit afraid to leave, actually. I do so hate to make a fuss, and it was all rather embarrassing. After I went downstairs with David to the deck, we just stayed there all afternoon. The cook brought me some tea and toast, and I ate it, and felt a bit better. And now all this! I'm sorry, but I really do think I should go back upstairs. I'm feeling a bit queasy again.'

She did, in fact, look very ill, and she had begun shivering. How much of it could be put down to shock, her timid nature or to her condition, it was hard to say. Jenny, who knew little about pregnancy, watched her with some concern.

Inspector Rycroft hastily assured her that this would be all right, and the Leighs once more departed, David's arms firmly around his wife's shoulders. But, presumably, Dorothy Leigh once again wanted no witnesses to her illness, for he came back down again after just a few minutes, looking restless and unhappy and muttering about sending for a doctor if she didn't look better soon.

'Now, Mr O'Keefe.' Rycroft turned to look at the engineer. 'Can we have your movements, please?'

The engineer smiled grimly. 'I was where I always am – in the engine room.'

'You must have left it from time to time, though, sir,' Sergeant Graves said mildly.

The engineer shrugged. 'Not so's you'd notice. And no, I never saw Olney.'

It wasn't much of a statement, and Jenny knew that neither of the policemen would let it stand at that, but for now Rycroft seemed disinclined to pursue it.

Instead, he got together with Sergeant Graves and painstakingly wrote out a timetable.

Glad that Leigh had returned, for he wanted everyone to hear what he had to say, he coughed as impressively as his high-pitched voice would let him, and was satisfied to see all heads once more turn in his direction.

'Right then. According to your statements, I've compiled the following list of events and times. The times, of course, are approximate only, and we can allow five to ten minutes either side of them to take into account any inaccuracies.'

Jenny, although finding him somewhat pedantic, was also glad to find him very competent. It made life so much easier when you had a policeman in charge who actually knew what he was doing.

'Right then.

'1.00 p.m. to 1.50 p.m. Lunch. All present expect for cook, Francis Grey, Captain Lester and Brian O'Keefe, who ate in separate parts of the boat.

'2.00 p.m., Mrs Leigh proposes darts match. At the same time, or thereabouts, Miss Starling leaves the boat for her stroll.

'2.10 p.m., Mrs Olney goes up to her room.

'2.30 p.m., Mr and Mrs Leigh leave the games room. One goes to the bathroom, the other to their bedroom.

'2.35 p.m., the captain goes to the bridge.

'2.35 p.m., Mr Olney goes to starboard deck, presumably alone. At the same time, Mr Finch "wanders about the boat."'.

'3.00 p.m., Miss Starling returns to the boat, and the *Swan* sets sail. Miss Starling goes to the galley.

'3.10 p.m., Mrs Olney and the Leighs come back downstairs. The Leighs go to the starboard deck (Mr Olney not present at that time) and Mrs Olney goes onto the port deck to sunbathe.

'4.15 p.m., Miss Starling notices the Leighs on the starboard deck and returns to galley.

'4.20 p.m., Miss Starling takes Mrs Leigh some tea and toast and takes a walk around the boat. She notices the port deck is wet. Mr Finch is on the deck, and notices it too.

'4.30 p.m., Miss Starling discovers the corpse in her cupboard.

'4.40 p.m., Mr O'Keefe sets off to report the matter.

'Now, does everyone agree with that timetable?'

There were a few glances cast around between members of the group, but nobody spoke up against it.

'Right. Can anybody add anything to that timetable?'

Brian O'Keefe, somewhat surprisingly, spoke up immediately. 'Yes. I can.'

All eyes swivelled in his direction.

'Yes, Mr O'Keefe?' Rycroft asked archly.

'The port deck wasn't wet at four o'clock. I know, because I was going to go to the bridge to ask the captain how we were doing for time. I needed to know if we would need any more wood cutting. Starting out later than planned had put our original time schedule out.'

'I see,' Rycroft said thoughtfully. Then, 'You didn't mention this, Captain Lester,' he added abruptly.

Tobias gave Brian a furious and – to Jenny's mind, at least – slightly surprised look, and opened his mouth to reply, but was forestalled.

'Captain Lester didn't forget,' Brian cut in quickly. 'It just so happened that I never got as far as the bridge. I could see for myself where we were, because that part of the river was particularly memorable. We were on a very straight stretch of the Thames – it goes on for very nearly a mile or so, so I knew exactly where we were and knew for myself that we were all right for fuel. I didn't notice Mrs Olney sunbathing, though, but I *did* notice, now that I think back, that the deck was perfectly dry. If it hadn't been, I'd have checked it out immediately. I knew that I hadn't taken any river water on board, and it would be my job to investigate any water spillage at once. On a boat you have to be careful,' he added firmly. 'At four o'clock that deck was dry – that I'll swear to on a stack of Bibles.'

Rycroft looked at him thoughtfully for a long time, but when he did speak, it was to Jasmine Olney.

'Mrs Olney. You said you were on the port deck all afternoon after leaving your room? How is it that Mr O'Keefe never saw you sunbathing there?'

Jasmine blinked. 'Oh but I don't … oh yes, yes, I remember now. I went upstairs to my room, briefly, to fetch my magazine. Oh, yes, and of course I changed too. Put on a little make-up in preparation for dinner. I was only gone about ten minutes – less probably. It just slipped my mind. It must have been then that Mr O'Keefe looked out.'

Rycroft nodded. An interesting omission, but perhaps perfectly innocent. It was the sort of uninteresting detail that might slip your mind – especially after receiving a shock. And becoming a widow must be something of a shock, even for someone as self-possessed as the lovely Jasmine Olney.

'I see. So. The big question is where was Mr Gabriel Olney all this time?'

But to that, nobody had any kind of an answer.

Rycroft sighed. 'Come now, ladies and gentlemen. You must realize that this death is, to say the least, suspicious. It looks, on the evidence so far, that somebody tied the rope to Mr Olney's foot, tossed him overboard, and drowned him at some time between 4 and 4.15. Then, probably whilst Miss Starling was taking Mrs Leigh her tea and toast and circumnavigating the boat, that same somebody then stashed his body in her galley cupboard. You, Mr Leigh, were on the starboard deck, yet you say you heard nothing?'

David Leigh's lips firmed. 'I'm not *saying* that I heard nothing, Inspector. I'm stating it as a fact.'

'You, Mrs Olney? You never noticed anything unusual when you returned to your deckchair?'

Jasmine bit her lip. 'I noticed the deck was wet, of course. And I think I saw Lucas just disappearing into the games room. But I didn't see Gabby.'

The inspector glanced at Brian, who merely shook his head.

It was a most unsatisfactory state of affairs.

'Well, *someone* must have killed him,' Rycroft growled.

Sergeant Graves' eyes swivelled everywhere, seemingly at once, but nobody gave so much as a guilty start.

'Couldn't somebody have swum across from the riverbank and done it?' Lucas asked, somewhat diffidently.

Rycroft snorted. 'It's possible, Mr Finch, but hardly likely, is it? You yourself were stood at that deck not a minute before it must have happened. Did you see anybody swimming back to shore?'

Lucas flushed. 'No, I didn't,' he muttered angrily. 'And it was just a thought.'

The parrot very neatly relieved himself on Lucas's shoulder. The millionaire, though, merely brushed it off without any obvious signs of distaste, as if he was used to it – as he probably was.

'So I repeat,' Rycroft said, turning away from the boat owner and his disgusting parrot with a look of chagrin on his face and a rather supercilious sneer on his ugly mouth, 'who murdered him?' He thumped a small fist onto the tabletop as he did so and made everyone jump most theatrically.

It was at this dramatic moment that one of the forensics boys stepped into the electric silence and said loudly and excitedly, 'Sir, I think you'd better come upstairs. We've found a suicide note!'

TEN

FOR A MOMENT, nobody moved. It was so unexpected, so …
impossible, that nobody seemed able to take it in.

It was at that moment that Jenny looked across at David
Leigh, and felt her whole body stiffen with shock. For David
Leigh looked appalled. Stricken. Disbelieving. He looked, in
fact, the very opposite of what Jenny had imagined he should.

That he hated Gabriel Olney was obvious. The looks he had
given the man when he'd been alive had hardly been meant to
hide the fact. And now he was dead, and if there was a possibility, no matter how fantastic, that it was not murder after all,
then surely the solicitor should be relieved? Or, at the very
least, fascinated.

Instead he looked sick at heart. It was very odd indeed.
Unless of course … Jenny's eyes became thoughtful, and then
just slightly puzzled.

Inspector Rycroft came out of shock first and uttered a soft
but very colourful exclamation, and tossed his ugly head at the
forensics man. 'It's in his bedroom?' he barked sharply.

'Yes, sir.'

'Right. Lead the way.'

Once again, everybody went after him, like a flock of curious
sheep. Once again, the policeman, rather surprisingly, made no
move to stop them. Then again, the cook thought, as she took
up the rear and climbed the stairs, perhaps it was not so

surprising after all. She'd noticed that both Graves and Rycroft had very sharp ears. And very *quick* eyes. Between them, in a matter of seconds, they could look at every face and, no doubt, fairly shrewdly gauge every mood. And as this particular case seemed determined to take on so many twists and turns, faces could reveal an awful lot about how people reacted to them. Hadn't she just seen an example with David Leigh?

No, Rycroft might be a shade unorthodox in his ways, but there was method in his madness. And she couldn't help but wonder what the policeman made of this latest twist in the case. He must surely have come across any number of suicides during his career so far. Weren't most of them supposed to leave notes? And although she was no expert, she could well imagine that different personalities would choose various different ways in which to end their lives. Women, she'd read somewhere, were supposed to choose things that didn't mar their looks – taking pills being a leading choice, as well as that old standby, putting your head in a gas oven. Men, she rather thought, didn't mind so much using a gun for a quick but messier way out, if they had access to one.

But she was willing to bet that as a method of suicide, drowning yourself in such a spectacular manner must put Gabriel Olney in a league of his own.

Much as she might applaud the investigating officer's reliance on his observance of the witnesses to help his case along, she guessed that both Rycroft and Graves had been momentarily too stunned themselves to notice the young solicitor's reaction.

Now, Jenny began to wonder about this so-called suicide note.

In fact, she wondered about it a great deal.

The Olneys' bedroom offered a mute testimony to the personalities of the two people involved. On Gabriel's side, the room was immaculately neat. His clothes were hung circumspectly in the wardrobe and all his drawers were tidily shut. His shoes were carefully aligned on the shoe tree provided, and his side of the dressing table held toiletry things in rows of pristine precision.

Jasmine's half of the room, in contrast, was in utter chaos. A scarlet silk shift lay half on, half off her side of the bed. A pair of silk stockings, looking shockingly intimate under the macabre circumstances, lay trailed across the carpeted floor. Her side of the dressing table was a riot of mess, with jars of cream with their tops removed and lipstick tubes undone, leaving greasy pink, red and purple lines on top of the wooden surface. A make-up bag was tossed haphazardly onto the bedside chair.

The forensics man led them to the top drawer of the dresser – obviously nabbed by Gabriel for it contained socks, ties, a spare shirt and a solid gold pair of cufflinks.

It also produced a single piece of folded paper.

Rycroft raised an eyebrow at the forensics man, who interpreted it easily. 'It's been dusted for prints, sir. There's only one set – belonging to the deceased.'

Rycroft grunted.

Jenny nodded. Yes. That made sense, if what she suspected had happened *had* happened. It would have been a bit touch and go as to whether only Olney's prints were on the paper, but if Jasmine's were on it too, well, it would hardly be a surprise, would it? It would all depend on the circumstances. Her thoughts were abruptly cut off as the senior investigating officer moved forward.

Rycroft very carefully unfolded the paper and read the lines aloud with quick, bland precision.

Dear All,
Sorry to do this to you. Be a bit of a shock, I suppose, but there are reasons. Aren't there always? Bury me next to the parents at Gatesham, will you? Oh, and keep the flowers down to a sensible level, Jasmine. No need to go overboard.
Gabriel.

Into the profound silence that followed, there came a half laugh, half sob, shocking in its abruptness and lack of self-control.

Jasmine Olney quickly put a hand to her mouth as everyone turned to look at her, Rycroft, at least, looking a shade guilty at his lack of tact. 'I'm sorry, Mrs Olney. That was stupid of me,' he apologized at once.

But Jasmine shook her head. 'It's not that,' she found her voice at last. 'It was just that … well, it *sounded* so like him. It had his … flavour. I could almost imagine him saying it out loud. It, well, it just took me by surprise a little, that's all.'

Rycroft nodded, but quickly sorted through all the flotsam to find the real nugget. 'In your opinion then, you think your husband probably wrote this?'

Jasmine nodded, then asked tentatively, 'May I see it? I know his writing well.'

Rycroft hesitated for a scant second, then slipped it into a clear plastic evidence 'envelope' and handed it over.

Jasmine read it, her face perfectly still. 'It looks like his writing to me,' she said at last.

'Do you have a sample of his writing with you?' Rycroft asked, but Jasmine quickly shook her head. 'Never mind. We'll send a constable over to your house to pick up a sample, and then send that, together with this note, to our experts at the Yard. We'll soon know whether this document is a forgery or the genuine article.'

Jenny hid a smile. So the policeman doubted the veracity of it. It was hardly surprising, in the circumstances. She herself had no doubts at all that it was a forgery. Nor did she have any real doubts as to who had written it. Of them all – a ship's captain, an engineer, a cockney business man, a housewife, a faithless spouse, and a solicitor – it was obvious to her, at least, that only one of them had the professional know-how to create a reasonable forgery.

She wondered, idly, how many clients David Leigh had

defended on such charges.

Rycroft handed the note to his sergeant, who quickly left to hotfoot it back to the village with the note. No doubt at Carswell Marsh they already had a small contingent of police, awaiting more orders.

'Right, carry on.' He nodded to the forensics expert. 'I want a list of all the equipment on board ship, and I want anything in any way out of the usual reported to me immediately.'

'Jenkins is already doing the inventory, sir,' the man replied smartly, and began promptly taking samples out of every toiletry item on the table. Not that they seriously suspected poison, the cook knew, but still, it paid to be thorough. And there was always the possibility, of course, that Olney had been drugged first. A woozy or unconscious man was more easily disposed of, after all. Still, a Mickey Finn applied through his aftershave lotion was just too James Bond for her to take seriously.

Rycroft turned and raised his eyebrow at the crowd, who had no trouble interpreting this silent but graphic gesture, and Tobias Lester led the exodus back out of the bedroom and downstairs to the salon.

There everyone hung about looking a trifle lost.

Jenny glanced at her watch and frowned. She approached Rycroft tentatively.

Rycroft looked up at her.

Jenny looked down at him.

'Well,' Rycroft barked, 'are you now going to tell me whodunnit, where, why and how?'

Jenny blinked. 'Actually, I was going to ask you if you still wanted me to cook dinner. I assume the sergeant will be returning, and that you will be staying the night on board, and I thought you might be hungry. And the others, of course....' She glanced across at them. 'Although they're in shock now but when it wears off, as a man of your experience probably knows, it can often leave people feeling ravenous.'

Rycroft wilted. 'Oh. Right. Er … the body's still in the galley. I'll just go and take a look before the sergeant gets back with the others. They'll have made arrangements for the removal of the corpse by now and be waiting for permission to remove it. If everything's been seen to, I can't see any reason why you can't resume your duties.'

Jenny nodded and followed him to the galley. Rycroft looked displeased, but again made no move to shoo her back. Which was probably just as well, really. When he moved through the opened door, the cook made sure to shut it firmly behind her. She didn't want any of the others – especially Jasmine – to catch a glimpse of where her husband's corpse had been found.

It was only good manners to give the widow the benefit of the doubt in a case of murder, she always thought.

'And it is murder, of course,' she murmured out loud, and then could have kicked herself. About to kneel down beside Olney's body, Rycroft suddenly looked up in mid-crouch, his eyes narrowing.

Then at last he smiled and straightened up.

'I agree. I've never known anybody yet tie a rope around their ankle, throw him or her self into a river, drown, and then get up and tidily stow their self away into a cupboard.'

Jenny sighed.

'Any idea about the note?' Rycroft asked, hating himself, and having to force out every syllable.

But Jenny surprised him. First of all, by having an answer, and second of all, by divulging it so quickly.

'Hmm. I rather think you'll find that that's the result of David Leigh's handiwork. As Olney's solicitor it would have been an easy matter for him to get Olney's fingerprints on a piece of paper. Slipped underneath or on top of other papers that needed Olney's signature, for example. Or maybe he just filched a bit from the Olneys' bureau on some social occasion – I suppose the Olneys would have entertained the Leighs in their home at some point. And of all of us, he's the most likely person to have specialist knowledge – or have access to specialist knowledge – on the subject of forgery. How to do it, and how to avoid detection.' She waved a long and rather elegant hand in the air in a vague gesture. 'You know, that sort of thing.'

'Hmm.' Rycroft, after his initial surprise, thought it over. 'But why forge a suicide note, and then put the body in a cupboard and fairly advertise the fact that it was murder?'

Jenny frowned then shrugged. 'Just because he forged the note doesn't necessarily mean he did the killing,' she pointed out reasonably.

'He was in cahoots with someone else, you mean?'

Jenny thought about it, then shook her head. 'No, that would hardly make sense either. I think, perhaps, David Leigh intended to kill Olney. Or at least had fantasized about it. But somebody else beat him to it.'

'Or else he was very clever, and planned it to look that way. A sort of double-bluff,' Rycroft said, giving the cook a fascinating glimpse into the way his convoluted brain could work. 'Any idea *why*, though? We need a motive.'

Jenny was beginning to *like* the way Rycroft's mind worked. He went right for the nubbin of a problem with the unerring instinct of a weasel going down a rabbit hole.

She liked that in a policeman.

'I have no idea, specifically,' she admitted. 'I can only say that it was obvious that David Leigh hated Gabriel Olney intensely.'

At that, Rycroft perked up. 'Oh?'

But now Jenny was staring at the body. She looked in detail at the body's shirt, now dry. Her eyes followed the clean white folds, and then moved down, over his dark blue slacks, and finally, to his bootless, pale foot.

'Can you turn him over?' she asked respectfully.

Rycroft did so, somewhat impatiently. 'So you think Leigh hated Olney? That's significant, at least.'

'Hmm?' Jenny said, distracted, still staring at the body. Rycroft looked down, but couldn't see what was so fascinating to her. Olney was beginning to dry off now. His hair was dry and clean, but his moustache, though, was still somewhat limp.

'David Leigh, Miss Starling,' Rycroft prompted with a touch of asperity.

Jenny dragged her eyes from the body, a puzzled frown still wrinkling her forehead. 'Leigh? Oh, yes, David Leigh. He hated Mr Olney certainly, but he was not the only one, I'm afraid.'

Rycroft felt his spirits sink. 'Oh? Who else was there?'

Jenny shrugged. 'Well, Mr Olney was making a very determined play for Mrs Leigh.'

'Ah,' Rycroft said. 'So that's why Leigh had a down on him,' he said, totally missing the point.

Jenny, with a slightly sinking heart, hoped that he wouldn't prove to be one of those officials who had a frustratingly one-track mind.

'I don't think so,' she said firmly, watching the man's face fall. 'I don't even think, in fact, that he noticed much. Or, if he did, it certainly didn't *worry* him. And nor should it. Dorothy Leigh is devoted to her husband – anyone with even a half-decent pair of eyes in their head can see that. She's the sort of woman whose life revolves around that of her husband and home. And, when the baby's born, around her child too. I doubt she'd even think of looking at another man.'

Rycroft nodded, obviously thinking that that was only as it should be.

Jenny was rather of the opinion, however, that too much devotion and adoration could be just as dangerous as too little.

'So Olney was after her because of the challenge, was he?' He looked down at the corpse but his face revealed neither disgust nor admiration. 'An ex-soldier, I believe. Some men are like that.'

But again the cook shook her head. 'I don't think that was it, no. Oh, it added a little piquancy, I suppose. But what he really wanted was a cat's paw.' And when Rycroft looked blank, added succinctly, 'Divorce.'

Rycroft stared at her. 'You think he wanted to divorce his wife?'

Jenny nodded. 'I do.'

'Why?'

The cook thought of Jasmine's hot and hungry look that first morning, when she'd spotted Brian O'Keefe's half-naked torso, and shrugged.

'I imagine it had something to do with a man. Mrs Olney is very attractive, as you've probably already observed, and she is twenty years or so younger than her husband.'

Rycroft grunted. 'So that's the Leighs and Mrs Olney. Anyone else who might want our chap here dead?'

Jenny sighed. 'I'm afraid so. Mr Olney and Lucas Finch had a terrible argument yesterday afternoon.'

'How terrible?'

'Mr Finch had Gabriel Olney by the throat. Quite literally, I mean. I had to insist that Lucas put him down. Mr Olney was turning a quite unbecoming shade of purple,' she said, in massive understatement.

Rycroft swore roundly. As an effort at profanity, it was well beneath the parrot's expertise, but the high squeaky voice with which he made his delivery might well have caught the bird's attention, had he been present.

'Anyone else?'

'I think you'd better talk to Captain Lester about that,' Jenny said at last. 'I don't know any of the details, but yesterday evening Mr Finch announced that he'd sold the *Stillwater Swan* to....' She nodded down at the corpse, her eyes once again lingering in a puzzled frown on the cleanly drying body at her feet.

'Sold the boat? What, this boat?' Rycroft asked doubtfully, and obviously not grasping the significance at all.

Jenny sighed. As a general rule, she would never knowingly

drop anybody in the cacky-cart, but when it was murder, you had no choice but to be a tattle-tale.

'Lucas loves this boat like … well … like Dorothy Leigh loves her husband – with a blind kind of devotion. And I have no doubt whatsoever that he was somehow coerced into parting with it.'

Rycroft considered this for some time. 'So. Our victim was blackmailing Lucas?' he mused at last.

'I can't say that for sure, of course, but there was definitely some sort of paperwork involved in the argument yesterday. I saw Mr Olney put some papers away in his pocket,' the Junoesque cook agreed.

'Right.' If he was feeling a bit battered by the relentless information being poured down on his head, Rycroft showed no sign. 'So that's—' he counted them off '—four people who wanted our chap dead?'

Again, the cook heaved a massive sigh. 'Both the captain and engineer work full-time for Lucas Finch. Both live in cottages in his grounds. Gabriel Olney was a do-it-yourself kind of man. He wanted the *Swan* to himself. I believe, although I don't actually know,' she said, determined to be scrupulously fair, 'that last night Olney told Tobias and O'Keefe that their services would no longer be required.'

Rycroft sighed. Heavily. 'So they lose their jobs and their homes as well in one fell swoop.'

Jenny shrugged. 'Lucas might have been prepared to let them stay on at the cottages, but I'm sure he would have charged them rent.'

Rycroft finally hunkered down on his knees and looked at the dead man glumly. 'Not very popular, were you, chum?' he murmured. 'Is there anybody you didn't tick off?'

Jenny also took the opportunity to stoop down beside the body, her nose twitching.

She carefully shut her lips most firmly and then took several long breaths up her finely quivering nostrils. She had a cook's delicate nose, one that was used to picking up the faintest nuances of aroma.

Rycroft watched her in amazement and fascination for a moment, and then hastily – very hastily – followed suit. Rather belatedly he remembered her fearsome reputation and felt a moment of panic. Had he missed something? It would be just too damned humiliating to have the case solved by a modern-day Miss Marple!

One moment of panic spread into more moments of panic, however, as his nose picked up nothing. No scent at all. So what the hell was she getting at?

'What can you smell, Inspector?' Jenny asked at last, that puzzled frown once more back on her face.

Rycroft made a very agitated movement with his hands and abruptly stood up. 'Nothing,' he snapped, aggrieved. 'I smell nothing at all.'

Slowly, the cook rose to her own towering height, unknowingly adding to the inspector's ire.

'No,' she finally said. 'I can't either,' she added thoughtfully, making the policeman yearn to yank out great clumps of his hair by the roots.

Mercifully for him, there was a sudden knock on the door and Sergeant Graves entered. He'd been gone such a short time, the cook surmised that the police must have rigged up some sort of transport system to and from the boat site. Probably some sort of scrambling-style motorbike or a quad bike. Something, at any rate, that was easy and safe to use over farming terrain.

She wondered what the farmer thought about having the police cross-countrying across his fields. Probably not a lot, she mused with a wry twist of her lips.

'We've got an old van outside, sir, to take the body,' Graves said respectfully.

Jenny discreetly left. Rycroft watched her go, his face gloomy. 'Everything we heard about her was spot on, you know,

Graves,' he said despondently. 'She's already onto something, but I'm damned if I know what it is. She's got David Leigh pegged as the forger of the suicide note, and I'm not willing to bet so much as a penny that she'll be proved wrong. And she's got the rundown on every blasted person on the boat.'

Briefly, Rycroft filled his sergeant in on Miss Starling's view of the suspects.

Graves whistled between his teeth. 'Still, it does make our job much easier, doesn't it?' he finally said. 'I mean, she's not known for hogging the limelight, is she?'

Rycroft reluctantly admitted that she wasn't. As far as the public was concerned, all the murders that she'd helped solve before had been put down to the credit of the various police officers involved. There was *that* to be said for her.

'But,' Rycroft said grimly, 'I want us to get there first. Have David Leigh checked out thoroughly – he had some reason (other than the victim making lovey-dovey with his wife) to hate Olney, and I want to know what it is. Also, find out what you can about the widow's socializing habits. There's a man lurking about somewhere, I'd bet my last month's wages. And I want Olney's room turned inside out. He had some papers on him that had Lucas Finch grabbing him by the gullet. I want to know exactly what they are. And have a background check run on our Mr Finch. I've got an idea I've run across that name before somewhere. I wouldn't be at all surprised if our cockney chum hasn't got form of some kind.'

Sergeant Graves nodded as he made copious notes, and left with the two sombre-suited men who had come to remove the body.

Rycroft watched Gabriel Olney being loaded onto the stretcher but still couldn't, for the life of him, see exactly what it was about the body that had so intrigued the cook.

Once the galley was cleared, Jenny proceeded to prepare dinner. It was no longer going to be such a lavish feast. For a start, it wouldn't have been appropriate. Secondly, it was getting too late in the evening, and the guests and the two policemen would need something in a hurry. And thirdly, with more people to cater for, she couldn't afford to be so lavish with the food.

She knew how these investigations could drag on. She could see them all still being on board the boat tomorrow night as well.

She put the finishing touches to a huge steak and kidney pudding and stepped outside, on the lookout for Lucas, to announce that dinner was ready.

But only Rycroft, Graves (who had returned after setting his superior's orders in motion) and the two forensics men sat around the main salon. The others, perhaps not surprisingly, had taken themselves off to less harrowing, calmer parts of the *Swan*'s interior.

She wondered if somebody had sent for a doctor, just to check over Dorothy Leigh. A woman in her condition had to take care of herself and her unborn baby.

'We've gone over everything, sir,' the chief forensics man was saying. 'Apart from the wet planking on the port deck, there's nothing else amiss.

'In the rear engineering sections, there's only the usual equipment you might expect. An axe for the wood, with a large plastic sheet covering the woodpile. It's totally dry. There's a loading trolley, a half-full coal-room and plenty of oily rags. The equipment box for odds and ends is at the rear starboard deck. Again, it contains nothing more than you'd expect. Ropes, the same kind as the one used on the deceased, a block and tackle, boxes of nails, spare gauges ... I've written it all down.' He handed the detective the list.

Rycroft scanned it without much enthusiasm. 'And the boat itself? Any irregularities or instances of cut corners that could be offences?'

But the man was already shaking his head. 'Not that I know of, sir. Of course, this isn't my field. But there's a ship's horn and a bell at the forward end. There are four life-rings, two on each side, both located at front and rear. Firmly fastened and fully inflated. The one on the rear starboard side, just above the equipment box, is on an especially large bracket. I imagine it was once used to hold something much heavier. And there's a small lifeboat, situated at the rear, enough to seat ten people at a pinch. No, I'd say that the ship's well run and as safe as houses.'

Rycroft nodded gloomily. 'I expected as much. But best to make sure. Well, that's it then. And you're sure there are no papers in Olney's room?'

The forensics man shook his head.

So they'd gone missing, Jenny mused. Interesting, that.

'And you've found nothing suspicious around the scene of the crime itself?' Rycroft pressed.

But it seemed that there wasn't. Lucas Finch's fingerprints were on the railing top, but then so were practically everyone else's. More importantly – and revealingly – there were no fingerprints at all around the bottom of the railing, where the rope had been tied.

'Humph. The killer obviously wore gloves,' Rycroft sighed. 'And, presumably, threw them away afterwards.'

By now, Jenny knew, all the rooms on the boat had been thoroughly searched, and nobody had brought a pair of gloves with them. In high summer, it was not so surprising, she thought. But surely, if somebody *had* brought gloves with them, it would mean the killing was premeditated.

Somehow, Jenny Starling had the feeling that the killing of Gabriel Olney had been anything but. Still, you didn't need gloves in order not to leave fingerprints, she quickly surmised. Any piece of cloth wrapped around the hands would do. But she didn't think it would be very politic to point that out to Inspector Rycroft right now. He was already looking considerably miffed that the killer was not in any apparent hurry to make his life easier for him.

'Dinner is ready, Inspector,' she said quietly, making the man jump and look around at her suspiciously. He wondered fleetingly how much she'd heard, then shrugged. The forensic report had hardly been important.

But, in fact, Jenny had found it fascinating. And very illuminating.

'Right. Well, go and find the others, will you, Miss Starling? We might as well all eat a decent meal together like civilized human beings. Even though one of them isn't.'

Jenny blinked at that rather unexpected statement, but followed the departing forensics team out onto the deck. This policeman certainly liked to do things differently all right. And she rather suspected he had the reputation as being a bit of a maverick, back at the old cop shop. She wondered if he was popular with his superiors, and somehow doubted it.

On the riverbank, the cook noticed two constables helping Brian O'Keefe set up the tents. She wondered where Rycroft and Graves would be spending the night.

She only knew that neither of them would be sleeping in *her* bunk. Nobody was going to filch her digs from her. No damned way!

She was just about to call out that dinner was served, and ask O'Keefe if he knew where everyone was, when she heard the sound of a motorbike.

She watched another young constable dismount and practically leap onto the boat. She wisely took a quick step back as he rushed past and then followed him in, wondering what all the excitement was about.

'Sir, Constable Wright, sir.' The young, red-faced bobby faced his superior with brightly gleaming eyes. He didn't look any older than eighteen, Jenny thought with a smile. No doubt he'd never had a murder case before, and this was the height of excitement for him.

'Slow down, Constable,' Rycroft ordered prosaically. 'You have news?'

'We do, sir. We've spent the afternoon walking the riverside route the boat had taken, searching for witnesses who might have seen anything,' he began, getting it all out on one shaky breath.

'My idea, sir,' Graves put in quietly. Obviously he was used to working on his own initiative, and was encouraged to do so, for Rycroft merely nodded.

'Well, sir, we've found a chap – a fisherman – who says he saw the *Swan* going by, and noticed some man climbing down from the top balcony of the boat onto the bottom deck.' The youngster paused, looking as pleased as punch to be able to deliver his next bit of news. 'And he swears the figure was climbing down from the top at the rear end of the boat, sir. That would make it the victim's room!'

ELEVEN

FOR A MOMENT, Inspector Rycroft merely stared at the triumphant-faced constable, his funnily ugly face splendidly inscrutable. You could almost hear his brain working, so obviously was he mulling the information around. Then he grunted.

'This fisherman,' he began. 'I hope you checked that he had the proper licences and permits?'

The constable's jaw dropped. Whatever he'd expected, it most certainly hadn't been that. Come to that, it wasn't the first thing that had leapt to Jenny Starling's mind either. But then, she wasn't as pedantic as the inspector.

'Well, no, sir. I mean, sir, it slipped my mind, sir,' he mumbled. 'I thought you should have his information urgently, sir,' he rallied. For it had suddenly occurred to the youth that there was a distinct possibility that his superior officer was having a little joke at his expense. Jenny wasn't so sure.

Whether he was a secret leg-puller or not, Rycroft merely grunted again at this explanation. But behind the somewhat laconic facade, Jenny could sense that his astute mind was still rapidly working away at this new information and what it could mean.

She herself was feeling just a bit distracted. The mere possibility that Rycroft might have a sense of humour was enough to boggle the cook's mind.

'You have this witness at the station?' Rycroft asked, to which the constable nodded so energetically his helmet nearly fell off.

'He's made a full statement?'

The constable very ceremoniously withdrew a sheet of paper. Rycroft read it, his eyebrow going up.

When he spoke, however, it was to Tobias Lester. 'I take it that there is only one man on board who fits the description of a male, between the ages of twenty to thirty, with thick black hair, and dressed in white work trousers and a white shirt?'

Tobias met the policeman's eyes for a scant second, and then looked swiftly away again. He looked, Jenny thought, almost angry. 'You know the answer to that as well as I do, Inspector,' he finally said, somewhat grimly. 'Brian O'Keefe is the only young and black-haired man aboard this boat.'

As he spoke he looked at David Leigh. But David, although brown haired, wore neither white trousers nor white shirt. Only an engineer traditionally wore white.

Rycroft nodded. He too had noticed the captain's reaction, but was less surprised by it than Jenny. As a man who had charge of subordinates himself, he knew how easy it was to feel protective of them.

The crew and guests of the *Stillwater Swan* had gathered in the main salon/dining room ostensibly for dinner, but the inspector knew that it was really curiosity that had gathered them together so rapidly. From their various positions on the boat they must have heard the motorcycle and looked out to see the excited entrance of the constable. One and all, they'd come down quickly and congregated to see what all the fuss was about, and had been richly rewarded for their efforts.

Only Jenny, alone among them, looked not so much relieved as thoughtful by this latest news.

Nobody liked to have the charge of murder hanging over their heads, and if it had to be somebody, then everyone was secretly relieved that it should be Brian O'Keefe. Brian O'Keefe, after all, was the outsider. The hired help. Brian O'Keefe, it had to be said, was not one of *them*.

The inspector looked once again at Tobias who, to give him credit, was looking exceedingly unhappy, and said quietly, 'I take it that the engineer is in the boiler room?'

The captain nodded reluctantly.

Sergeant Graves led the way to the door, then, as an after-thought, turned to wave one meaty paw at the assembly, silently indicating that he would like them to remain seated. This time, the policeman didn't want an audience.

Jenny, though, had other ideas, and nodded at Francis. 'The dinner is prepared and ready in the galley, Mr Grey,' she said briskly, then turned on her heel and firmly followed the two officers out onto the deck.

Francis Grey thinned his lips at being spoken to like a servant by what he deemed to be nothing more than another servant, then glanced at his employer to see if he too had noticed the outrage. But Lucas, who had his own views on the enigmatic cook – which didn't include getting on her bad side! – merely shrugged and said quietly, 'Well, I for one, am hungry,' and, like the good host that he was, ushered his guests to the table.

Francis took the hint with apparent magnanimity and quickly disappeared into the galley.

Out on the deck Jenny softly called Rycroft's name. Since he was by now at the rear deck he had to pause and wait for her to catch up. The sun was just setting, casting a lovely red-orange glow over the river. The solid bulk of the sergeant cast a great shadow over the tiny man, but he appeared not to notice it.

'Can I ask at what time this witness saw Mr O'Keefe climbing down onto the lower deck?' she asked, as soon as she'd drawn level with them.

Rycroft quickly consulted the witness statement again, his eyes narrowing. He looked as if he might like to let rip with a curse, but refrained himself with an effort. Unfortunately, this self-restraint made his face quiver and his eyes bulge. To Jenny's somewhat alarmed eye, he looked a bit like a frog made out of blancmange that she'd once created for a child's birthday party.

Which gave her an excellent idea to recreate the design, this time as a birthday cake. The dons at the college where she worked often called upon her to bake a cake for their offspring.

'It says here it was about a quarter past two,' Rycroft admitted grimly, snapping the cook's attention back to the matter in hand.

She sighed deeply. 'I see.'

Graves' great bulk shuddered, just once, as he too understood the full import of the timing. If the murder hadn't been committed until between 4 and 4.15, then….

'What the blazes was he up to?' Sergeant Graves muttered more to himself than to anyone else.

'I shouldn't attach too much importance to this business, Inspector Rycroft, if I were you,' Jenny said quietly. She was always reluctant to offer advice, mainly because people so seldom had the good sense to take heed of sound advice when it was offered. She did so now only because she was sure that Rycroft was the sort of man who could get very nasty if he was seen to be publicly embarrassed.

'Oh?' Rycroft said icily.

Jenny smiled. 'I think you'll find that O'Keefe was searching for the papers that Gabriel Olney was brandishing about yesterday afternoon, during the fight he had with Lucas. I think that he and probably the captain, got their heads together sometime yesterday evening and mapped out a plan of action.'

Rycroft thought for a second or so and, intrigued in spite of himself, said somewhat less coolly, 'Carry on.'

'I think they thought that if they could destroy whatever Olney was using to blackmail Mr Finch, then the plan to sell the

Swan would fall through, and their jobs and homes would be safe.'

'But surely Olney would have made copies?' Graves pointed out with reasonable logic.

Jenny shrugged. 'I imagine that occurred to them too. But it was worth a chance. After all, it wouldn't be hard. During dinner, O'Keefe was always absent, so nobody would remark on it. He could take a good long hour to meticulously search the Olneys' room. If he found the papers, well, all to the good. If it turned out that Olney could produce duplicates when the time came to hand over the deeds to the boat, well, what had they lost? I should think that to men of action like O'Keefe and Captain Lester, they would consider it a chance well worth taking. And better by far than attempting to do nothing about it at all.'

Rycroft slowly stroked his chin. 'So you don't think it has anything to do with the murder itself?'

But on that, Jenny was too wily to be drawn. She merely shrugged and said that, at the moment, she couldn't see how it could have.

Rycroft reluctantly agreed, but nevertheless proceeded to march straight into the boiler room like an invading fury.

Jenny, who'd never taken a really good look around inside the engine room before, took the opportunity to follow them in and have a good nose.

The room was more or less divided into two, with the wood and coal in one section of the room and the actual boiler and engine in the other. O'Keefe, who'd been sat on top of a fairly respectable woodpile, slowly stood up. His feet rustled a crumpled sheet of thick plastic that he'd cast aside and which now lay on the floor.

'Yeah?' he asked, not quite surly, not quite polite.

'We would like to know what you were doing in Gabriel Olney's room at two o'clock this afternoon,' Rycroft said, not quite surly, not quite polite.

O'Keefe gave him a long, slow, measuring look. No doubt he was wondering what the policeman actually knew, and how much he had merely guessed.

Rycroft smiled. It was quite a nasty smile. 'You were seen, O'Keefe,' he said shortly. 'So let's not have any fun and games, hmm?'

Brian ran a dirty hand through his dark hair, then shrugged. 'Oh. Right. Well, then, I suppose I'd better tell yer. I was looking for them papers of Olney's.'

If he thought anyone would be surprised by his answer, he was thoroughly disappointed. Rycroft merely gave a what-did-I-tell-you-about-this-damned-cook look to his sergeant, and Graves gave a there's-more-to-you-than-meets-the-eye look at Jenny Starling, and O'Keefe was left to wonder, in some frustration, just what it was that was going on.

'Did you find them?' Rycroft got on with it brusquely.

Reluctantly O'Keefe nodded.

Rycroft held out his hand.

O'Keefe stared at it for a moment, then shrugged, then smiled. It was a roguish smile. No doubt, Jenny thought with a wry twist of her lips, Jasmine would have found it very appealing, if she'd been present.

O'Keefe shook his head. 'I ain't got 'em on me. I hid 'em upstairs, in the lav.'

'Go and get them,' Rycroft ordered shortly.

O'Keefe nodded and moved forward. Just when he'd got to the door, Jenny, whose mind had wandered a little, suddenly snapped to, and said curiously, 'Is this the wood we saw you bring on board yesterday?' She nodded at the woodpile on which he'd been sitting.

The engineer, somewhat surprised by the cook's presence, not to mention the copper's tolerance of her, looked at her suspiciously. 'What's it to you then?'

'Just answer her,' Rycroft snapped, although he too wondered why the infuriatingly useful woman wanted to know. He also wondered just where she could possibly be headed with the seemingly irrelevant question.

'Yeah, it is,' O'Keefe said slowly.

'Is it dry?'

'Yeah, it is.'

Jenny nodded. 'So why did you cover it with plastic?'

Rycroft, who'd been becoming impatient with the cook's continued questions, suddenly began to look alert.

O'Keefe, too, stared at her. 'I didn't,' he said at last. 'I found it on the wood this afternoon. I was the one that took it off – it can make the wood sweat, see, in this kind of heat. Which is the last thing I need.'

'What time this afternoon?' Rycroft cut in, not because he thought the answer important, and not because he could see any significance in it. He just wanted to get the question in before the cook could.

But Brian shrugged. 'I dunno. After lunch sometime. Before we started off. Just gone three, summat like that.' He shrugged in obvious indifference. Or was he just faking it?

Jenny felt her heartbeat quicken. So, she was right! But knowing how a murder was done was not the same thing as knowing who had done it.

Rycroft, sensing that the cook was now way ahead of him, as usual, snarled at O'Keefe to get going, then stared at the wood-pile and the sheet of innocuous plastic. But try as he might, he couldn't see what wood, plastic and the engineer had to do with anything.

Jenny, rather wisely, chose that moment to excuse herself and check that her fruit tarts weren't burning.

Rycroft made no move to stop her. Only when they were safely alone did he turn to Graves, one eyebrow lifted.

'Well?'

But Graves couldn't see what the cook had been getting at either. It left both men feeling rather frustrated, not to mention nervous. So far, no policeman had out-thought the cook. Both of them were anxious to be the first, and thus restore honour to the Oxfordshire constabulary. But they were beginning to lose their previous self-confidence.

Which went part of the way, at least, to explaining why they were so hard on Lucas Finch when they returned to the dining room some ten minutes later.

By then, the soup had been mostly consumed, and Jenny put two servings of the main course into the oven to keep hot, for the policemen to enjoy later. When they stepped back into the dining room, she was just emerging from the galley with a large, shortcrust pasty tart, filled with apricots, raspberries, blackcurrants and plums, in an apricot-brandy jelly. This she put onto the side table to come to room temperature, which is when it should be served to be at its best, and noticed the pinched and disapproving look on Rycroft's face. Graves, she noticed, for once *did* look grave.

The parrot on Lucas's shoulder dipped its head from side to side. 'What's up with you, shortarse?' it asked, rather loudly.

Rycroft went beetroot.

Lucas, for once, could have throttled the bird. 'Don't mind him, Inspector,' he said hastily. 'It's what I'm always saying to him. First thing in the morning, I open up his cage – he always sleeps in one at night – give him a raisin and say, "What's up with you, shortarse?"' He trailed off miserably as he became aware that his explanations and apologies were falling on deaf ears.

Rycroft, with the manner of a magician pulling a rabbit out of a hat, took a fairly thick wad of papers from out of his suit breast pocket and said grimly, 'Do you recognize these, Mr Finch?'

It was immediately apparent, to Jenny at least, that Jasmine Olney certainly recognized them. She watched them pass across the table, from policeman to her host, her eyes widening.

She'd seen her husband reading them several times over the past week. If only she'd known that they were so important!

Her look of vexation made Jenny wonder what else Jasmine Olney might have overlooked.

Lucas went white, then grey, then back to white again. He swallowed hard. 'Yes, I recognize them,' he croaked.

David Leigh glanced at Lucas, his solicitor's instincts coming to the fore. His firm was courting Lucas Finch and his accounts assiduously. If he could leap into the breech now and come to the rescue, who could say how grateful Lucas might not be? But before he could open his mouth to reassure Lucas that he needn't answer any of the inspector's questions, Rycroft was steaming ahead.

'Are they accurate?'

Lucas flinched. 'They're accurate,' he agreed. 'In as far as they go.'

Dorothy Leigh pushed her untouched plate of food away, and gave Lucas a sympathetic look. She touched her husband's arm, silently urging him to step in.

But David had had time to think things through, and was, as a consequence, somewhat more cautious than he might have been just a few moments earlier. 'Lucas, if you need legal representation, then you can hire me now, on the spot. At least then you'll be covered by legal privilege if—'

But Lucas held up his hand. 'I don't need a solicitor, thanks, Dave. What the inspector has there are army records of an old court martial. A court martial in which I was cleared of any wrong-doing. Isn't that so, Inspector?' Lucas raised his voice, and his chin.

Obviously, Rycroft thought, he intends to bluff it out. But then, what other course was left open to him, he mused, with an ugly sneer.

'The military court hardly cleared you, Finch,' Rycroft bit out. 'It merely had to conclude that there was not enough evidence to convict you.'

Dorothy Leigh gasped, but Tobias Lester, Jenny saw, was not looking at all surprised.

No doubt O'Keefe and he had already read the document. Tobias had been present at the darts match, Jenny instantly surmised, knowing all the time that O'Keefe was searching Olney's room. She wondered, idly, if maybe O'Keefe and the captain had planned to do a little blackmailing of their own, just to ensure that they kept their cottages, at least. And their jobs, too, if the *Stillwater Swan* had somehow stayed in Lucas's possession.

Of course, since the court martial was a matter of record, whether or not Olney *had* kept copies was irrelevant. In which case, something more drastic would have to be done. And the obvious solution was to make sure that Olney didn't live to wrest the boat away from Lucas. It could have happened that way, Jenny mused. Two strong men of action – what chance would Olney have had against the both of them?

But she was getting well into the realms of guesswork now, which was something that she didn't like to do. It was far too easy to come up with beautifully crafted theories that fizzled out in the light of more solid proofs. Besides, it was far easier to concentrate on one thing at a time.

Which meant Lucas Finch and his court martial.

'But what was the court martial about?' she asked out loud, knowing that it was the thought on everyone's mind.

Lucas gave her an *Et tu Brute?* look and the parrot blew a raspberry.

It was a very good raspberry, and it set Graves' lips to twitching once more.

'It appears that our friend Mr Finch here commandeered medical supplies during the Falklands war,' Rycroft grated. 'Medical supplies that proved to be very lucrative for certain suppliers of the street drugs trade. It must have made you a lot of money too, Finch,' he finished disdainfully.

But by now Lucas had had time to rally, and he merely smiled grimly. 'If you've read those documents thoroughly, Inspector, you'll know that nothing was ever proved.'

'But it put the wind up you enough to make you agree to sell this boat though, didn't it … *sir*,' Graves put in, his voice dripping with disgust. 'No doubt if your friends in the drugs gangs learned that you and your past dealings with them were about to become public knowledge, they might have got a little worried about your continuing ability to keep your mouth shut, hmm? Is that why you knuckled under? It certainly wasn't because you cared about your reputation, was it, Mr Finch?' he sneered.

Lucas returned to a dull grey colour, all but admitting that the sergeant had hit the nail right on the head.

But he said nothing.

Rycroft turned away in disgust. Then he glanced across at the assembled company, who were all being very careful not to look Lucas in the eye.

'I want everyone to spend the night on board,' he said heavily, half expecting to be the brunt of the usual grumbling that such an order might be expected to generate. But, somewhat to his surprise, nobody demurred. Obviously they had been expecting such an order, and none of them seemed inclined to rail against it.

It was an odd reaction, Rycroft thought. And their meek acceptance unnerved him somewhat. He even wondered, for a brief, wild, insane moment, whether it was possible that they were *all* in on it together. Each and every one of them had their own reasons for wanting Gabriel Olney dead.

Was that sort of thing even possible, he wondered, breaking out into a cold sweat. He'd never had to deal with a fairly large-scale conspiracy case before. And they were absolute sods to prove.

Then sanity overtook him again. He'd been at work all day, rushing about in the heat, and getting nowhere. He was just overtired, that was all.

'Have the lads set up our tents for the night?' he asked his sergeant, his weariness very apparent now.

Graves nodded.

'Then I think I'll turn in.'

'Don't you want any dinner, Inspector?' Jenny said, her voice rife with disapproval. 'I've kept some hot for you. And for you, too, of course, Sergeant Graves,' the cook added cunningly. 'I was just about to ask Francis to serve the main course anyway.'

Nor had she misread her man. Sergeant Graves hadn't grown up to be such a strapping lad by nibbling on lettuce leaves. His big face lit up and his stomach growled, quite audibly. The parrot cocked his head to one side, the better to hear this intriguing new noise.

Rycroft, admitting defeat, sat down in a vacant chair, a rather amused gleam in his eye as his sergeant quickly did the same. But a scant minute later he was forced to admit that he was glad he had, as an extremely appetizing dinner was put down in front of him. The smell coming off the meat alone had his mouth watering.

Jenny stayed only long enough to watch the sergeant begin to wolf down his dinner, before taking a plateful to the engineer, who, rather wisely, had returned to the boiler room to keep his head down.

She came straight back, however, appeasing Rycroft somewhat. If she'd stayed behind to question the engineer further, he might just have been tempted to order her off the boat and back to Oxford, just to get her out from under his feet.

But he was too good a policeman not to admit that she had proved helpful so far, and might do so again. And as much as he wanted to beat the cook to the punchline, so to speak, he wanted to apprehend the killer more.

Rycroft hated murder. He hated civil disobedience of any kind.

Perhaps not surprisingly, the rest of the dinner was a quiet affair, and quickly over. Lucas had lost his appetite for his fruit tart, though the parrot had been a gentleman about it, and had helped him to clear his plate, much to Graves' amusement and Rycroft's finicky disgust.

Jasmine suggested a game of cards, and cast a look of silent appeal across the table at Dorothy, who, with typical feminine intuition, picked up on it at once and plucked at her husband's sleeve in gentle persuasion.

All three disappeared into the games room. Lucas said, somewhat grimly, that he wanted a word with O'Keefe, and quickly left. No doubt, over dinner, he'd been figuring out who had removed the papers from Olney's room, and why. He must have been both astonished and relieved when the police search had failed to turn them up in Olney's room.

Jenny wouldn't want to be in the engineer's shoes at that moment. Not that Lucas could fire him, of course. Not with what O'Keefe now knew. And that led her onto another line of thought.

Had Olney been killed because of what he knew? Lucas was now, in anybody's book, looking to be the prime suspect. And a man with such a ruthless nature had to be top of Rycroft's list.

She cleared away the dishes, with the help, of course, of the silent, heavily disapproving Francis. Jenny was glad when the silent servant did his usual disappearing act. There was something very nerve-wracking about Francis. Perhaps it was because she was never sure just what he was thinking.

She even went so far as to watch him leave the *Stillwater Swan* and enter his neat little tent on the riverbank. The thought of him sleeping the afternoon away on her bed gave her the shivers.

If he had slept the afternoon away at all, that is.

She had seen for herself how oddly devoted Francis Grey was to his employer. She'd also noticed, during the revelation about Lucas's ugly past, that Francis had never so much as winced. That he already knew about Lucas's evil deeds during the seventies and eighties was, to her mind at least, beyond doubt. And yet still Francis was happy to carry on working for Finch. Finch, a lowly cockney. Finch, the very antithesis of a gentleman.

And yet Francis was so very much a gentleman's gentleman.

What was going on there?

No, Jenny didn't appreciate having Francis around, but that didn't necessarily mean he would commit murder, just on his employer's say-so. When all was said and done, Francis had no real motive for killing Gabriel. His position as valet was safe, whether the *Swan* was sold or not.

Besides, Jenny couldn't help thinking that now she knew *how* the murder had been committed, she should know *who* had committed it.

In the back of her mind, she knew that she had seen something important that afternoon. Something very important. And somebody, much earlier on, had said something that kept haunting the fringes of her memory, but refused to surface. And, like a bad sense of déjà vu, there was something else that somebody had said still later on that kept niggling at her. Something Jasmine Olney had said.

But what?

Jenny sighed and checked her food supplies for possible breakfast dishes. She made up a short mental menu for tomorrow morning then decided to take a slow stroll around the decks to clear her head.

She, like Rycroft, was beginning to get overtired. A good night's rest and who knew what the morning might bring?

She stepped through the French doors onto the starboard deck.

The night was beautiful. There was a full moon and the first few twinklings of evening stars. The sky was just turning that lovely soft sapphire shade before full darkness descended.

She folded up and put her favourite chair back against the deck wall, and did the same with a second one, frowning a little as she did so. Two chairs? Then her puzzlement cleared. Of course – the Leighs had been sitting out here earlier. She must be even more tired than she thought, to have forgotten that.

She continued on to the end of the side deck, glanced at the equipment box and the round, red and white inflated life ring that was hung above it, then turned down the corridor to the rear deck.

She glanced at the boiler room, her ears pricked. It was quiet, however, so presumably Lucas Finch had given the engineer his rollicking and left. Nevertheless, she didn't go in. She'd seen all she needed to see in there.

She took her time strolling along the port deck but when she got to the front of the boat, the decking was now dry. The rope and boot were gone – obviously with the forensics team.

That boot had been clever. Very clever.

She sighed and stepped into the games room.

Jasmine had apparently just lost her game of gin rummy, for she tossed down her cards with a softly muttered 'damn' and stood up. 'I need a drink,' she added, and walked over to the drinks cabinet.

Lucas, sat on a sofa and ostensibly reading a book, glanced up when Jenny entered, but said nothing.

Even to Jasmine, he could see that he was *persona non grata*.

Jenny wondered how long it would take for fresh rumours to start circulating about Lucas around the village of Buscot, and supposed it wouldn't take long. This time, however, the rumours would have rather more substance to them.

She found it hard to feel sorry for him. But at least he had his faithful bird for company.

The parrot, as if in agreement, proceeded to preen itself and cast tiny, scarlet feathers all over his master's shirt.

Dorothy stood up slowly but shooed her husband back into his seat as he rose to join her. 'Miss Starling, do you think I might have a milky drink to take to bed with me?' she asked, and Jenny instantly beamed approval.

'Of course you can. Would cocoa be all right?'

Dorothy nodded. 'I haven't had cocoa in years,' she said wistfully and followed her through into the main salon to stand, hovering by the galley door as the cook quickly set about making her the hot drink.

Hearing a rustle behind her, Dorothy half turned in surprise as Inspector Rycroft, who'd gone unnoticed on a large sofa, suddenly rose.

This time he was going to hit the sack. He only hoped that Graves didn't snore. As if on cue, the burly sergeant also rose from the depths of a shadow, where he'd been putting his feet up on a recliner chair in one corner.

Dorothy quickly glanced through the door to the games room, and gently coughed.

Jenny heard it first, and walked to the door. 'Inspector,' Jenny said quietly yet firmly.

Rycroft rounded on her. 'What is it now?'

Jenny, however, didn't take offence. Instead she merely nodded to the woman stood beside her.

'I think Mrs Leigh has something to say to you,' she hazarded gently.

Dorothy Leigh gave her a rather surprised look, then quickly glanced at the inspector, then once more cast the games room a rather anxious look.

Graves and Rycroft stiffened like dogs picking up a scent.

'Yes, Mrs Leigh?' Rycroft said softly, instinctively moving away from the games room and closer to the pretty, fair-haired woman who chewed her lower lip in a becoming, if indecisive, manner.

'Well, it might be nothing,' Dorothy said, a touch nervously, 'but I suppose I really *should* mention it....'

'Anything can be important, Mrs Leigh,' Rycroft agreed firmly.

Dorothy nodded. 'Well ... it has to do with Mrs Olney.'

TWELVE

RYCROFT'S EYES BRIEFLY flickered at the name of the grieving widow, but other than that he merely raised his expressive eyebrows. This silent demand, designed no doubt to intimidate more information from its recipient, wasn't really necessary on this particular witness, Jenny thought, but supposed it had become something of a habit of his, and one that must have served him well in the past.

As it was, Dorothy quickly wrung her hands together and glanced yet again towards the games room, as if fearing that the woman in question had super-sensitive hearing and could somehow listen in on her near-whispered words.

'It was during the darts match,' Dorothy began reluctantly, her pretty blue eyes creasing into a frown. 'I don't know *what* it was, exactly,' she admitted, confusingly, 'but I'm sure it was the real reason why she suddenly left the room.'

Rycroft smiled politely. 'Yes, Mrs Leigh. Now, could you tell me exactly what it is that you're talking about?'

Dorothy flushed. 'Oh. Sorry, aren't I making any sense? I happened to look across at Jasmine to ask her if she wanted a drink, when I saw her turn a page of her magazine.'

'Magazine,' Rycroft repeated blandly. He glanced at Graves, who merely gave an infinitesimal shrug of his mammoth shoulders.

'Yes. Her magazine,' Dorothy continued, apparently unaware that the two men were beginning to regard her as something of a featherbrain. 'And in between the pages of the magazine, I saw a white piece of paper.'

'Oh?' At this, Rycroft perked up considerably. Jenny, who was watching the both of them carefully, was struck once more at the pug-like looks and tendencies of Inspector Neil Rycroft. All he needed was a larger pair of floppier ears, she thought, utterly fascinated, and he could have perked them up at just the right instant to look for all the world like a dog about to be thrown a bone.

Dorothy nodded. 'At that moment, of course, Mrs Olney glanced up, but I'd already begun to look away.' She said this with some evident relief, and Jenny could understand why. A woman like Dorothy Leigh would have been raised to try and avoid embarrassing little moments as if they were the plague.

The information was definitely interesting and Jenny nodded to herself as she quickly took in its full import, but neither of the policemen seemed to notice. She doubted that they'd picked up on Dorothy Leigh's obvious piece of very clever feminine deduction, either. Namely, that it could only have been from a man. It took another beautiful woman to second-guess someone like Jasmine Olney.

So. There was more to Dorothy Leigh than one might think, the cook mused. But then, wasn't there always more to any woman than a mere man might think?

'Anyway,' Dorothy said, beginning to look a little shame-faced. 'I waited a moment or two and then looked back. I was … well, curious, I suppose. And I saw at once that Jasmine was reading it. The piece of paper, I mean, not the magazine,' Dorothy added hastily.

Rycroft nodded, apparently insensible to the fact that he'd just had his intelligence rather cleverly insulted.

Graves' lips, however, did their usual twitch. So, there was a lot more to the burly sergeant as well, Jenny mused fairly, than was obvious at first glance. Jenny had never been able to understand why the public in general always thought that a big, hefty man had to have a small brain.

She began to wonder whether it might be Graves, and not Rycroft after all, who provided the intelligence for their successful partnership.

'After she'd read it, she sort of turned a few more pages, yawned, and said she was going up for a nap,' Dorothy concluded. 'Naturally, I wondered who the note was from.'

Again the cook nodded to herself. It all sounded very much like Jasmine-Olney-type behaviour to her. She didn't doubt that Dorothy Leigh was telling the truth.

Rycroft pursed his lips. 'Could you see what was written on this note?'

But Dorothy quickly shook her head. 'Oh no, I was sitting several seats away. I can only tell you that it wasn't a very long note.'

Jenny gave a very slight cough. 'Did you notice which magazine it was in?'

Dorothy smiled. 'It was one of those fancy French fashion things. I remember particularly because I've always admired the actress who was on the cover.'

Jenny's eye quickly scanned the room and alighted on the coffee table, on which resided two magazines. Rycroft, catching on, all but sprinted for the table, moving off the spot like an athlete hearing the starting gun.

Jenny, of course, who'd had no intention of making such an undignified dash for the evidence, felt her own lips begin to twitch. Ruthlessly, she firmed them into a hard straight line. Sergeant Graves' example of hidden mirth could be most habit forming.

The junior officer was a handsome man, too, Jenny noted absently and then frowned ferociously. If mixing business and pleasure was a no-no, then how much more of a no-no was mixing murder enquiries with pleasure? She quickly turned away from the sergeant and turned her mind strictly

to Rycroft, who was returning to their position clustered
around the door and riffling the pages of the magazine as he
did so.

Then he gave a soft exclamation and withdrew a single piece
of paper. 'I'd have thought she'd have got rid of this by now,'
he said, avidly scanning the few lines.

As he read the 'B.O'K' signed at the bottom of the note, he
drew his breath in sharply.

'O'Keefe again,' he said, then suddenly remembered that
Dorothy Leigh was still present. He quickly curled the note into
his fist. 'Oh, er, thank you, Mrs Leigh, for bringing this to our
attention.'

Jenny very helpfully poured Dorothy's milky drink for her
and urged her to get to bed.

She was not quite as pale as she had been earlier on, and,
indeed, dressed in a long-sleeved mint-green dress, she now
looked very fetching. But her eyes showed signs of strain, and
the cook didn't urge her to bed merely to help out Rycroft, who
obviously wanted her gone.

As she watched Dorothy move across the main salon, her
husband quickly joined her from the games room. Obviously,
he'd been watching out for her, too. Together the young couple
left the room. As a show of simple togetherness it was touching
in a way you seldom felt about couples nowadays, Jenny
mused with just a little sigh.

Obviously the sergeant thought so too.

'Attractive,' Graves said succinctly, but Rycroft was once
again scanning the note. He handed it to Graves who then, after
a moment's thought, handed it to the cook.

Jenny read the note thoughtfully. It purported to be from
Brian O'Keefe, and it urged Jasmine to go to her room and wait
for him. It asked her to keep a lookout at the door in case her
husband should show up.

It was a very clever note, Jenny thought judiciously.

Very clever indeed.

'Right then,' Rycroft said. 'Let's get O'Keefe in here. I want another word with him,' he added ominously.

But as Graves started off, Jenny halted him in mid-stride with just one quiet, very well-placed word. The word was, 'Why?'

Rycroft and Graves both stared at her. 'Why?' Rycroft squeaked. 'Because I want an explanation for this damned thing.' He rattled the note. 'That's why.'

'But O'Keefe didn't write it,' Jenny said patiently.

Graves returned to the doorway. He looked interested more than upset. Rycroft, on the other hand, was beginning to feel decidedly frayed at the edges.

'Oh? You're a handwriting expert, are you?' he snapped.

Jenny sighed crossly. 'No, I make no such claim. But why, if he was all set to search Gabriel Olney's room, would Brian invite Jasmine Olney to meet him there? He chose lunchtime to do the search precisely because he thought there would be nobody about to disturb him. So he'd hardly invite Jasmine to come and do just that, would he?'

Rycroft opened his mouth and then abruptly closed it again. He stared at the note in his hand, his face openly aggrieved.

'Perhaps they're in it together?' he said tentatively, then instantly corrected himself. 'No, if that were so, there'd be no need for them to pass cute little notes to each other.'

'Then who did write it?' Graves finally asked.

Jenny shrugged. 'I don't know.'

But she was sure that she *should* know. All the clues, she was convinced, were right there in front of her. She just wasn't seeing them clearly. She needed to rearrange them. She needed to sift through the camouflage. She needed to sleep.

'I think we should all turn in,' she said wearily. 'I'm almost asleep on my feet now.'

But Rycroft, terrier-like, had the rat between his teeth once again, and had no intention of giving up shaking it about just yet. 'Well, I for one want a word with Mrs Olney. Graves,' he snapped.

The sergeant dutifully went into the games room and extracted the widow. As soon as she saw the magazine and note in the inspector's hand, she stiffened, then seemed to wilt.

Her smile was somewhat ironic. 'I see you've found the mysterious note, Inspector,' she murmured. But she seemed more amused than afraid. She was wearing a low-cut black evening dress, and her eyes were heavily lined with mascara. She looked both attractive and dangerous. Both men felt themselves put on their mettle.

Rycroft nodded. 'Can you explain it to us, please, Mrs Olney?'

Jasmine elegantly shrugged one white shoulder and raised a hand to fiddle with the single row of pearls at her neck.

Jenny noticed at once that they were real. Then she wondered exactly how much money Gabriel Olney had left, and whether he'd left it all to his wife. Or had David Leigh, in the last week or so perhaps, made up a new will and testament for Gabriel that had left his money entirely elsewhere?

'What is there to explain?' Jasmine shrugged. 'I found the note in my magazine this afternoon, during the darts match. It seems like years ago now, not merely a matter of hours. Anyway, I went upstairs. He never came. And that's the whole story,' she added mockingly.

Her voice, although kept deliberately flat, had an undertone of real anger to it. Jenny, for one, had no trouble in detecting it at once. Nor did it surprise her. Jasmine Olney was clearly not the type of woman who would appreciate being stood up. Her ego was too fragile for such an insult to go unnoticed.

'Why didn't you tell your husband about it, Mrs Olney?' Rycroft asked. 'Or did you?' he added sharply.

The cook saw at once where Rycroft was leading, of course. If Gabriel Olney knew about the supposed assignation, might he have tackled O'Keefe and been killed for his pains?

But Jasmine laughed openly at the question. 'Tell Gabby?

Why on earth would I do that?' She sounded both genuinely puzzled and wary at the same time, like a mouse spying a twitching whisker at the mousehole.

Both men looked distinctly disapproving. 'I see,' Rycroft finally grated through severely clenched teeth. 'So you went upstairs to meet a lover?'

But again Jasmine laughed, relaxing now that she understood the policeman's interest, and apparently not one whit put out by the Inspector's obvious disapproval. 'Hardly that, Inspector,' she drawled. 'I'd only set eyes on Brian O'Keefe yesterday. No, I never intended to let him … do … anything. I was merely curious, that's all.'

Rycroft looked a little mollified at this. 'I see. And you say Mr O'Keefe never showed up?'

'No, he didn't,' Jasmine said shortly.

'Did you hear anything whilst you were in your room, Mrs Olney?' Jenny put in, making Rycroft fume silently at her cheek.

Jasmine glanced at her, surprised by the cook's presence, but she answered her question readily enough. 'No. At least, not when I was *in* my room. But now that you mention it … Just before I got to the door I thought I heard something inside. But …' She shrugged. 'There was nobody there.'

Jenny nodded. Brian O'Keefe had good hearing. Or a guilty man's super-sensitivity to sound. In any event, he'd managed to get out before being caught in the act of searching the room.

'Was the window shut or open when you went in?' she asked, earning herself yet another wrathful look from the inspector. This she met with such calmness that it only infuriated the tiny inspector all the more.

Jasmine frowned. 'Well … now that I think about it, the window was closed. But it had been open previously. Gabriel always liked to sleep with the windows open. He was a solider, you know,' she added, as if this explained any and all of her husband's idiosyncrasies. 'And the day was so hot, I'm sure he wouldn't have closed them for any reason when we got up. Why would he?'

She looked sharply at the two policemen, then at the cook. 'Why do you ask?'

But at this point, Rycroft hastily dismissed her. She went, casting suspicious, thoughtful looks over her shoulder as she did so. And Jenny couldn't help but think that any woman who didn't care what men thought of her was a woman to look out for.

'O'Keefe shut the window behind him, of course,' Rycroft said, when the widow was safely out of earshot. 'He must have heard her coming and bolted for it.'

'Hmm,' the cook made a soft sound of agreement. 'He probably shut the window to help mask the sounds of his climbing down to the lower deck.'

That would have been the starboard deck, she suddenly realized. If she'd followed her usual habit of sitting out on the starboard deck after lunch, instead of going for a walk, she'd have been treated to a very interesting spectacle indeed. Instead, she'd been a good mile away at the time.

Such was the luck of travelling cooks.

Graves nodded. 'So O'Keefe can think quickly on his feet.'

Jenny sighed wearily. There were far too many clever people on board this boat for her liking.

'I'm going to bed,' she said shortly. 'My head's spinning.'

The next morning Lucas suggested a walking party to the village of Carswell Marsh, to buy papers, to phone relatives and explain what had happened and, in David Leigh's case, to phone his employers to make general arrangements for a short leave of absence.

Besides, Lucas wanted to buy some crackers for his parrot.

Rycroft had no objection to this, and at ten o'clock Lucas, Jasmine, the Leighs, O'Keefe and the captain set off on their cross-country walk. No doubt they were all relieved to get away from the boat for a while, not to mention get out of sight of the policemen and all their questioning. Besides, it was a perfect day for such a tramp across the meadows.

Jenny, who was sat out on the starboard deck watching a pair of moorhens and their chicks swimming in and out of the river reeds, had declined the offer. She had no one to telephone, and besides, she had some thinking to do.

It didn't take the policemen long to find her. Graves pulled up a similarly hefty chair to the one the cook had requisitioned, whilst Rycroft perched with perfect ease on a flimsily wooden and canvas folding deckchair.

'Well, Miss Starling,' Rycroft said. 'You're the expert,' he added sarcastically. 'What are your thoughts so far?'

Jenny dragged her eyes from the moorhens and looked at him. She sighed unhappily.

'I think,' she said, 'that someone has either been very clever, or very lucky, or both. Unless….' But the thought that suddenly popped into her head was a little too far-fetched to voice without first thinking it over.

And thinking it over very carefully, at that.

'I don't suppose you've heard from the medical examiner yet?' she asked curiously.

Rycroft shook his head and explained about the railway disaster that had slowed things up.

Jenny sighed. 'A pity. I would have liked to know if Mr Olney had been drugged. I don't believe he was, of course, but … it's nice to be *sure* of these things, isn't it?'

Rycroft blinked. 'Drugged? What made you ever imagine that he'd been drugged? The medico was sure that he drowned.'

Jenny nodded. 'Oh yes, I'm sure that he did too.'

Rycroft slowly leaned back in his chair and took several deep breaths. He hated questioning women. They were so damned … illogical.

'If there were drugs involved, then it was premeditated.' He tried a different tack, and the cook willingly went with him.

'If Gabriel was drugged, yes. But I don't think he was. And I don't think, somehow, that this was pre-planned. It smacks too much of desperation for that.'

Rycroft glanced at Graves to see if he was faring any better. Apparently he was, for he said slowly, thoughtfully, 'You have some kind of problem with the method of killing, Miss Starling?'

Jenny started. There was no other word for it. She opened her eyes very widely and said, with total sincerity, 'But of course I have. Don't you?'

Rycroft clutched the side of the chair until his knuckles turned white.

Jenny stared at them, bewildered. 'I'm sorry,' she said. 'But I thought … I mean, it's so obvious, that I was sure that you must have….'

Aware that she was not exactly earning herself any brownie points, she took a deep breath and started at the beginning.

'On the face of it,' she explained, 'the rope and boot on the port side of the deck suggests that Mr Olney was overpowered, that the killer tied the rope to his foot, hauled him over the side, let him drown, pulled him back and put him in the cupboard. Yes?'

Rycroft let go of the chair, and nodded. 'Yes.'

'But that's so patently absurd as to be laughable,' she said, her voice rising an octave into a near-squeak of incredulity. 'To begin with, how did the killer overpower Mr Olney? He was fit enough, and an old soldier to boot.'

Rycroft was beginning to feel uncomfortable. It occurred to him that whilst he had spent his time *investigating*, Jenny Starling had spent her time *thinking*. And he was beginning to appreciate just how exasperated his colleagues must have felt on their previous murder investigations where she had also been involved.

Now, he shrugged and tried to keep up with her. 'Well, we assumed the killer gave Olney a crack on the head before trussing him up,' he said, somewhat defensively, and looked at Graves, who nodded his agreement.

'But didn't the medical man say he could find no obvious cuts, bruises or outward marks of violence on the body?' she reminded him. 'At least, when I looked at Mr Olney with you, Inspector, I couldn't see anything. Only his fingernails looked a bit broken, and his knuckles looked slightly discoloured. I don't know enough about pathology, of course, to know if bruises can develop after death or not. But apart from that, there seemed to be nothing wrong with Mr Olney at all. Or am I wrong?'

Rycroft ran a finger around his collar. 'No, you're not wrong,' he admitted uneasily. He too had noticed no obvious wounds on the body. And any medico examining a body – even giving it a very quick and preliminary look over at the scene – would have noted any bashes on the head.

'And surely one of the very first thing a doctor checks is a body's head?' Jenny said, eerily echoing his own thoughts.

Rycroft reluctantly admitted that it was so. Looking back, he could see in his mind's eye the police surgeon run his hands carefully over Gabriel Olney's head.

'And he didn't report to you later on any bumps or bangs on Mr Olney's head?' she pressed.

Rycroft frowned, not liking the feeling he was getting that he was being backed into a corner. 'No. He didn't,' he confirmed shortly.

'So I repeat,' the fat cook said. 'How did the killer overpower Mr Olney?'

'He couldn't have. Unless he was drugged,' Sergeant Graves said. 'But you said you didn't believe he was drugged.'

Jenny sighed. 'No. I don't think so, but I don't *know* so. Not for sure. That's why I wanted to know if you'd got the post-mortem report.'

Rycroft grunted. 'Well, say for the moment the killer *did* dope Mr Olney somehow. He tied him up, chucked him over the side, and drowned him.'

But Jenny was already shaking her head. 'Inspector, does that sound reasonable to you?' she asked, and Rycroft was back once more to clutching the side of his chair.

'Consider the difficulties,' she urged, for all the world like a teacher instructing a classroom. 'The killer would have had to have doped Mr Olney sometime in the afternoon. Without being seen. He – or she – would then have had to either hide the unconscious man, or go through the rigmarole with the rope and drowning that you've just described, again *without being seen*. Then the killer would have to hide the body in my cupboard – still without being seen. How? How could all this be done?'

Rycroft swallowed hard. 'We know that at four o'clock the deck was dry,' he began. 'The killer could reasonably guess that the captain would be in the bridge, and O'Keefe in the engine room.'

'Providing it was neither of them that did it,' she put in.

'Right,' Rycroft conceded.

'And he knew that Jasmine would be in her room,' Graves put in brightly.

'Right. The note was a decoy,' Rycroft agreed.

'But by four o'clock Jasmine had been out of her room for a good half an hour or so,' she pointed out, hating to rain on their parade. But facts were facts.

Rycroft groaned. 'But she went back up to her room for a quarter of an hour,' he suddenly remembered. 'To change, or whatever. And at just about four o'clock too.' He was reluctant to let a good theory go to waste, just because the facts didn't fit.

'The Leighs were on the opposite side of the boat,' Graves added, getting carried away with the theorizing now, 'and you were in the galley.'

'So how did the killer get the body into my cupboard?' she asked bluntly.

'When you were taking Dorothy Leigh her tea and toast,' Rycroft said quickly.

Jenny looked from one policeman to another. 'But don't you see how *risky* this all is?' she asked, exasperated. 'What's to stop me from going back to the galley straight after taking Dorothy her toast? The killer couldn't *know* that I would take a stroll around the boat. And besides all that, Lucas Finch was wandering around all afternoon. He could have bumped into the killer at any point in these proceedings.'

'If it isn't Finch we're after.' This time it was Rycroft's turn to put in the little dig.

Jenny ignored this childishness and kept doggedly to the point. 'What's to have stopped the Leighs from leaving the starboard deck? How could the killer know how long Jasmine would be gone? She might only have nipped up to the loo. She could have been gone only a minute or so. But in that time the killer dragged Olney's body to the side, drowned him and carted him back to my cupboard? I don't think so.'

Graves scratched his chin. 'If he or she did, it sounds….' He looked lost for words.

'Desperate?' Jenny supplied one for him helpfully. 'Suicidal? *Risky*?'

'And yet, it worked,' Rycroft pointed out.

'But did it?' she asked sceptically. 'If so, how come the deck was wet, but not the route the killer must have taken to my galley? Why wasn't the galley floor wet? It wasn't, you know. Only the cupboard floor was wet.'

'I know that,' Rycroft snapped, although in fact that detail had totally escaped him. 'The killer must have covered him in something dry.'

'The plastic sheet,' Graves suddenly whooped, remembering the cook's fascination with the engineer's woodpile and its covering and now understanding it. 'It was bound to dry out quickly in the boiler room, and putting it in the engine room meant that it was also out of sight.'

'So the killer must have waited until Brian O'Keefe had stepped out of the engine room,' she said. 'He has to every now and then, of course,' she added thoughtfully. 'I've seen him. He checks in with the captain every so often for a start. Then he checks the paddles at the back. Oils things. But it all takes time. How did the killer know that O'Keefe was going to conveniently leave the engine room and allow him or her time to put the wet plastic over the wood to dry out?'

'But O'Keefe did leave the engine room,' Graves pointed out. 'He was going to ask the captain where they were. But then recognized the straight stretch of river, or so he said. So he was out of the engine room for a few moments at least.' Then he frowned. 'Of course, the killer would still have had to have been nippy. Very nippy now that I think about it.'

'Incidentally,' Jenny put in, 'I hope you realize the significance of that straight stretch of river.'

Rycroft glanced at her. He didn't look pleased. 'Significance?'

The cook sighed. Did she have to point out even the obvious? 'The *Swan* travels at about four miles per hour. On a straight stretch of river, such as the one we travelled down yesterday afternoon, the captain could have tied off the wheel, murdered Olney, and gone back, without anyone knowing. With the boat travelling slowly, the straight stretch could be made to last for at least half an hour, and the boat would be perfectly safe without anyone steering her. Other boats would be sure to see her coming a long way off and steer to either side of her, so there'd be no question of a collision to give the game away. The captain could have left the wheelhouse any time during that period. It's a wonderful sort of alibi to have. Everyone thinks the captain *must* be steering the boat. But that's not necessarily so.'

Rycroft sighed, fighting back the urge to scream. Loudly.

'We've already established that nobody had an alibi for every moment of that afternoon, Miss Starling. I think we can agree that anyone *could* have done it.'

Sergeant Graves shifted uneasily in his chair. 'What exactly are you getting at, Miss Starling? Are you saying that Mr Olney *wasn't* drowned on the port deck?'

Jenny shook her head, more in sorrow than in denial. 'I'm just pointing out how impossibly risky the whole thing must have been, if the evidence is to be believed,' she explained patiently. 'And haven't you asked yourself *why* Gabriel Olney was put in my cupboard? If the killer did heave him over the side, tied by one foot to a rope to ensure that he drowned, why didn't the killer then simply undo the rope and let Gabriel's corpse float down the river? In due course, he'd be noted as missing, we'd quickly set up a hue and cry, and his body would be found somewhere on the Thames. The police would conclude, with no bumps or signs of violence on the body, that he'd simply fallen overboard and drowned. Even if you *did* suspect foul play,' she cut in quickly, as Rycroft opened his mouth to hotly deny that they'd come to such a conclusion so quickly, 'what *proof* would you have? You might suspect that there was something rotten going on, but you'd be more likely to drop it and label it an accident after a diligent investigation, if Olney had been found floating face down by some innocent bystander walking their dog. But by putting the corpse in my cupboard, it was like advertising the fact that it was murder. Why?'

Rycroft was beginning to get a headache.

'Do *you* know why?' he asked hopefully.

But Jenny shook her head. 'It seems to make no sense. But then so many things about this case don't make sense. Haven't you noticed how … *messy* things are?' she demanded, beginning to sound thoroughly exasperated herself now. 'Hasn't it struck you how muddled up everything is? Brian O'Keefe searches the Olneys' room, but somebody sends a note to Mrs Olney that sends her upstairs, and so she almost catches Brian out, forcing him to flee down the balcony. David Leigh forges a suicide note, but the killer goes out of his way to make sure everyone knows it was murder. Everyone seems to be falling over everyone else's feet.'

'Coincidence?' Graves murmured. 'Or something else?'

'If it's something else,' Jenny said gloomily, 'then a whole lot of them are in on it together. But it's too messy for that. Too uncoordinated. If it was a conspiracy, you could expect them to make a better job of it. As it is, it's been like a comedy of errors from start to finish. And yet the murder itself must have been very clever. The rope, the boot, the plastic sheet … the incredible timing. You just can't put it all down to luck on the killer's part.'

Rycroft got briskly to his feet. 'Sergeant, I want you to go to the village and ring up the medical examiner.' It was just his luck his mobile had a dead battery. 'Tell him I want a toxicology test run on Olney immediately. Wait around and keep chivvying them if you have to, but make sure they get on with it, and then bring the results back with you. At least we can clear up the question of whether or not he was drugged.'

Graves nodded and left.

When he was gone, Rycroft looked at the cook thoughtfully. 'I think you'll find, you know,' he said slowly, 'that Olney was drugged. If, as you say, he wasn't knocked on the head, then how did the killer get him to meekly agree to having a rope tied around his leg? Not to mention allow himself to be tossed overboard without so much as raising a shout?' Rycroft shook his ugly head. 'No. If somebody was trying to drown me, I'd scream blue bloody murder.'

Jenny nodded. It was a good point.

'But nobody heard anything,' Rycroft continued. Really, it was amazing how talking things through with the big, handsome woman helped him to see things more clearly. 'And on a boat this size, surely somebody, somewhere, would hear a man cry out? No, Olney must have been drugged.'

But Jenny didn't think so. Jenny, in fact, was pretty sure she knew exactly *how* Olney had died, and it was not in the way the killer wanted them to think.

But that still didn't get her any further forward in finding out *who* the killer was.

She only knew that the killer was clever.

That the killer had been desperate.

That the killer had either been very lucky or very confident.

And that thought, for some reason, made the cook feel deeply unhappy.

THIRTEEN

Jenny put back the last bag of mixed vegetables into the cooler and checked off her list of ingredients. It wasn't anywhere near as long as she'd have liked it to be, but she could still do enough with it to be able to hold her head up high, come the next mealtime. She sighed, put down the pen and pad of paper, and stepped out of the galley.

Luckily, the others must have decided to stay on and lunch at the pub in Carswell Marsh, so she'd only had to prepare lunch for herself and Inspector Rycroft, which would help eke out the meagre rations. Sergeant Graves had not yet returned. It was still only 2.30, however, and she expected him back in time for dinner.

She wondered if he'd think to bring more supplies with him, but doubted it. Men tended to think good food appeared out of thin air. Unless they lived alone, of course, in which case most of them seemed to think it came from a pizza box.

She found Rycroft on the rear deck, staring gloomily at the paddle wheels.

'Inspector,' she said quietly. 'If you want us to spend another night on board, I'm really going to have to get some more food in.'

The inspector sighed but nodded. 'Make out a list. I'll have one of the constables go into the nearest town for it,' he said, still staring at the elegant blades.

Jenny nodded, was about to return to the galley, then hesitated.

Rycroft was looking slump-shouldered and miserable. 'It'll be all right, you know, Inspector,' she said softly, but with rather more confidence than she actually felt.

The policeman turned to give her his usual, all-purpose raised-eyebrow look. The cook sighed and left him to it. No doubt he was under pressure from his superiors to clear up this murder quickly. It was not his fault that this particular case was proving to be a very frustrating, not to mention very oddly executed crime. She only hoped that when Sergeant Graves returned, he brought with him some helpful information.

As it happened, she didn't have long to wait.

She'd just finished writing out a full list of the supplies she'd need, and had already set about making a savoury beef stew for dinner, when she heard the roar of the motorbike returning. She stepped outside to see what was afoot.

Rycroft was still on the rear deck, but now his eyes were avidly following the progress of his sergeant. Graves leapt on board and nodded to his superior. 'Sir.'

Jenny coughed, just to announce her presence, but neither policeman seemed inclined towards privacy.

'You have the test results?' Rycroft asked abruptly.

Graves nodded. 'But only because they sent down some relief from the John Radcliffe and the doc was able to start work on our Mr Olney last night. He confirms there was no knock on the head, and, by the way, he did detail several broken finger-nails and some – but not much – bruising of the knuckles on both of Olney's hands.'

Rycroft rather angrily waved away the confirmation of the cook's sharp eyes. 'Was he drugged?' he demanded impatiently.

Graves shook his head. 'Not that the doc can tell. Of course, not all the tests are in yet, but we can say that Olney certainly wasn't drugged with any of the usual, easily available drugs.'

'And nobody on board has expert medical knowledge, or access to anything more exotic to make a do-it-yourself Mickey Finn,' Rycroft murmured to himself. So that would also seem to confirm Miss Starling's hunch, he admitted to himself grimly.

So how the hell had the killer managed to drown Olney without the beggar putting up a fight? He shot the large woman an angry look.

As if it's my fault, Jenny thought wryly, but had better sense than to let even the ghost of a smile cross her face.

'But that's not all,' Graves said, and from his voluminous breast pocket began to pull out several official-looking police reports. 'Our lads have been busy. And the stuff they've got on David Leigh is quite something.'

By unspoken mutual consent, the three of them walked back into the main salon and spread the papers on the table. The others still weren't back from the village, but Rycroft wasn't worried about that. He'd sent several constables with them to keep an eye out, just in case somebody made a bolt for it.

Now, though, he had other things on his mind.

'First, the handwriting experts confirm that the suicide note was a forgery. It's definitely not Gabriel Olney's handwriting, although the boffin at Brasenose that we use said that it was a very competent, but not, in his experience, a professional job.'

Rycroft nodded. 'So we're dealing with a gifted amateur.'

'We also showed him copies of David Leigh's handwriting, and he gave us the thumbs up. In his opinion, it's likely that Leigh was the forger.'

'In his opinion, it's *likely*, is it?' His lips twisted sardonically. 'They don't like to commit themselves, do they?'

Graves smiled. 'But it gets better, sir. Do you remember Gimsole? The constable who worked on that fraud case over in Banbury?'

The inspector nodded. 'A good man to have on old-fashioned paperwork – especially when it comes to nosing out records that aren't on computer yet. He has a nose for it, I think his superiors said.'

'Right. Well, we had a spot of good luck there. Gimsole was put onto tracking down David Leigh's past doings. Any other PC might have missed it. But Gimsole's a thorough little nerd,' he said affectionately. 'Now, it appears that some old retired general or other had retained Leigh to look into some past military records for him. He was writing his memoirs, or something, and he had friends at the War Office and at the local branches of ex-soldiers' clubs—'

'Get on with it, Graves,' Rycroft snapped. He was obviously not in the mood to appreciate the finer details.

Graves nodded, not a whit put out by his superior officer's crabbiness. 'Right, sir. It appears that when he was doing this rather sensitive digging for the general, Leigh stumbled onto something that hit rather closer to home. Gimsole was able to follow the paper trail Leigh left behind, although he'd tried to cover his tracks. Gimsole was really very clever….'

'Graves,' Rycroft gritted. Nor was he in the mood to appreciate Glimsole's famous 'nose' either, it seemed.

'Sir,' Graves said apologetically. 'It seems that the memoirs-writing general, our Colonel Gabriel Olney, and a Lieutenant Arnold Leigh – David Leigh's father – were all involved in the same regiment. As you know, a lot of local lads were part of the—'

'Graves,' Rycroft positively growled now.

Which in itself was some feat, Jenny thought in startled appreciation, given the fact that the inspector's natural voice was practically falsetto.

'Sorry, sir,' Graves said yet again, obviously wondering what had happened to put his superior in such a bad mood. 'The upshot is,' he carried on, pretending not to notice Rycroft roll his eyes in relief, 'that Gabriel Olney was in the Falklands conflict, and in charge of a group of men which included Arnold Leigh. It seems that Gabriel sent Leigh off on a suicide mission. He later told his superior officers that he needed to get a written message through the lines as he believed the usual channels had been compromised, but no message was found on Leigh's body when he was picked up by the medical team. He died in the ambulance before he could be got to the military field hospital by the way. Anyway, nothing was done about it immediately. Olney was not the only colonel by a long shot to make a mistake and get one of his people killed.'

Rycroft had begun to look interested now, as had Jenny.

'You say that David Leigh uncovered all this?'

'Glimsole says that he did. Oh, he started off chasing down proof of the general's daring deeds, but when he came across the reports on Arnold Leigh, his own father, he abandoned his client's interests to satisfy his own curiosity. Apparently, the official version of his father's death had differed somewhat from what the family had been told,' he added dryly.

'Understandable,' Rycroft said shortly. 'But I have a feeling there's more to this than meets the eye.'

Graves nodded. 'There is,' he confirmed, his voice going a tone harder now.

Jenny shifted uncomfortably on her seat, already sensing that something very nasty was about to rear its ugly head.

'A sergeant … one …' Graves quickly checked the report. 'Watt Gingridge, who was a friend of Arnold Leigh's, wrote to a friend back home saying that Gabriel Olney had deliberately sent Leigh off on the mission, knowing that he'd get killed, and that he lied when he said he'd given Leigh important papers to carry. He further wrote that Arnold Leigh had told him that he'd seen Olney desert the platoon earlier that day, when the firing was most intense.'

Rycroft scowled. 'There were some nasty skirmishes in the Falklands,' he recalled, his voice grim.

Graves ignored the interruption. 'He also told Gingridge that he believed that Olney *knew* that Leigh had seen him run away, and was afraid that Leigh would report his cowardice to the general. This Watt Gingridge alleged that Arnold Leigh had come to him after Olney had given him the orders to try and get through enemy lines, and told Gingridge that Olney was deliberately sending him to his death to keep him quiet. He wanted Gingridge to give a sort of "goodbye" letter to his wife. Apparently, though, he never told her of his suspicions in the letter. Perhaps he was scared that if he did, and she went after Olney in the courts, they'd give her a hard time. You know how the army likes to keep their disgraces strictly on the Q.T. Anyway, Gingridge took the letter and duly sent it to Leigh's widow when Arnold had been confirmed missing and then killed in action.'

Rycroft swallowed hard. 'What a bastard,' he said quietly. But there was such a wealth of feeling behind the simple sentence that it made a cold shiver sneak across the cook's spine.

Graves nodded. 'But it didn't end there. The friend that Gingridge wrote to had another friend in the War Office and he passed the letter on. Unfortunately, by that time, Gingridge himself was reported killed, and although the MPs had Olney in and questioned him, they could prove nothing. Besides, the powers-that-be had troop morale to think of, not to mention the kind of bad reaction that would follow in the press if it ever came out. And it seemed that once Olney had been given the requisite short sharp shock, he apparently knuckled under and acquitted himself reasonably well until the fighting was over.'

'Unless he fled under fire again, and this time there was no poor sod to see him do it,' Rycroft grunted. 'Once a coward, always a coward, I say.'

Graves nodded. 'Anyway, Leigh uncovered the original Gingridge letter, and the notes of the interview between the tribunal and Olney. Like I said, the old general who'd hired him to help with the memoirs had clout, and since it was his lads and his regiment in the first place, Leigh got access to stuff they normally keep under very close lock and key. Of course the general whose memoirs Leigh was helping to research knew nothing about what Leigh was up to, or he'd have put a stop to it. And I daresay Leigh wouldn't have been in any hurry to bring it to the general's attention either. I reckon he didn't want it to get official or become public any more than the army did. He obviously decided he was going to go about things very differently,' Graves concluded flatly.

It was impossible to tell from either his face or his tone of voice whether he approved of David Leigh's desire for personal revenge or not.

'So David Leigh knew that Olney was a coward who'd deliberately killed his father?' Rycroft sighed. 'No wonder he wanted to take matters into his own hands.'

'Just think of it,' Jenny said softly, her voice thick with compassion. 'David Leigh would have been spent years thinking that his father was a war hero. That he'd willingly sacrificed his life for his country and comrades. That his death had been tragic but heroic, and most of all, accidental. Other men died in the Falklands, after all, and his father had just happened to be one of the unlucky ones. But then to suddenly find out that it had not been fate, nor an accident or bad luck after all, but a deliberate act by his commanding officer....' She let her voice trail off.

She felt, in fact, rather sick. And she was obviously not the only one to feel that way.

'Olney deserved what he got,' Graves suddenly said. 'My granddad was a fighting man too, in the last war. He told me what it was like out there in the thick of it. You had to rely on your officers. You had to keep faith with your mates and trust that the bigwigs knew what they were doing.'

Rycroft shook his head. 'Olney abused his power,' he grunted. 'No two ways about it.'

'Couldn't Arnold Leigh have refused to go?' Jenny suddenly asked. 'If Olney didn't give him any papers, but just ordered him across the lines....' She trailed off as both men looked across at her. It was not a scornful look they gave her, but rather a sad one.

'Olney could have had him court-martialled for disobeying orders.' Rycroft took it upon himself to educate her.

'Or had up on charges of cowardice,' Graves added. 'And that would have haunted him for the rest of his life. No, poor Arnold Leigh was finished whatever he did. In the end he did the only thing he could. The thing that I would have done if I'd been in his place.' Graves shook his head, with infinite pity for the dead soldier. 'He told a good mate what was happening, and wrote a letter home.'

Jenny shivered. 'No wonder David Leigh hated him so much.'

'And killed him,' Rycroft said, glancing at Graves, who looked as unhappy as his superior. 'We have proof that he wrote the suicide note – or as much proof as we need. A jury will believe our Brasenose don all right – he makes an impressive witness in the stand. And David Leigh was on board the boat when it happened. He had both motive and opportunity.'

Graves withdrew a long document from his pocket and handed it over. 'I took the liberty, sir, of getting a warrant for Leigh's arrest.'

But he didn't sound happy about it and Rycroft took the document looking equally miserable. 'Right,' he said reluctantly.

Jenny coughed. 'I think you're forgetting something,' she said quietly.

Rycroft, who'd had just about enough for now, turned on her angrily. 'Look, Miss Starling, I know you're used to being the centre of attention whenever somebody's been murdered, but this time you'll just have to accept the fact that we, the police, have solved this case, and not you. Now, I've got to make arrangements to arrest a man who, in my own personal opinion, was fully justified in doing what he did. So give me a break, will you?' he snarled, and took a deep, shaky breath.

The Junoesque cook was silent for a moment. She was very much aware that Rycroft was genuinely upset, as was Graves. But they were thinking with their hearts and not with their heads, and might be about to make a very costly mistake.

'Inspector,' she said patiently. 'I think it's obvious that David Leigh came on board this boat determined to kill Gabriel Olney. I think it's also obvious why. We also know he forged a suicide note and put it in Olney's room. I think he did it yesterday morning. I myself saw him coming out of the Olneys' room. I'd had a bath, and noticed him leaving.'

Rycroft nodded. 'That'll be useful evidence, Miss Starling,' he said flatly. 'The case against Leigh is building up nicely. He could have killed Olney any time between 4 and 4.15. We only have his wife's word that he stayed with her, and that's less than worthless. They're devoted to each other, that's perfectly obvious to anyone who sees them together – either one of them would lie their heads off to protect the other.'

Jenny sighed. 'I agree. But answer me this. If David Leigh planned to kill Gabriel Olney and fake it to look like suicide, *why did he put Olney's body in my cupboard*? What kind of suicide is that?'

Rycroft, who'd risen to give orders to a constable to take him to Carswell Marsh to arrest David Leigh, suddenly sat down again. He stared at the cook, his face a mixture of relief, bewilderment and, lastly, sheer frustration.

'Only an idiot would do something that so obviously pointed to murder,' Jenny carried on ruthlessly. 'If David Leigh had killed Olney, he would have simply let his body fall overboard and be taken away by the river. What evidence would there be then to say that Olney hadn't committed suicide? That, surely, must have been his plan, yes?'

'But Leigh had the perfect motive,' he finally said mournfully.

'So did Mrs Olney, sir,' Graves put in. Like his superior, he too felt a certain relief that the cook was standing up for David

Leigh so strongly. He himself would have been tempted to kill Olney, if he'd discovered that the ex-colonel had deliberately sent his own father to his death. And like Rycroft, he also hadn't felt any of the usual pleasure and satisfaction that normally came when you were about to arrest a murderer.

Now Rycroft looked at Graves. 'You have something else for me?'

Graves nodded. 'The Olneys were well off, but not rich. Olney knew that Lucas wouldn't part with the boat unless Olney offered him a good price for it. Lucas wouldn't value his reputation to *that* extent! But Olney wanted the *Swan*, and he was prepared to wipe out his bank balance to do it.'

Graves handed over the banking material that clearly showed the amount of money Olney had been worth, and Rycroft pursed his lips in a silent whistle. 'Olney *would* have been wiped out,' he said, surprised.

The forensics boys had pieced together the pieces of torn cheque they'd found in Olney's wastepaper basket and Graves had affixed it to the banking documents. 'I reckon Olney would have had to sell the house, sir, just to keep this boat running,' Graves pointed out. 'And Mrs Olney has expensive habits,' Graves added, handing over yet more paperwork, this time in the form of bills, receipts and expenditures.

This time, Rycroft whistled out loud. 'She spent more money on clothes in one week than I earn in a month,' he said, his voice a scandalized squeak. 'Theatre tickets, travel expenses to Paris … good grief. No wonder she tore up that cheque. I'm assuming she was the one who found it and tore it up?'

'I think that's a fair assumption, sir,' Graves said, his lips once more twitching.

'So if her husband spent all his money buying this boat, and sold the house to pay for the *Swan*'s upkeep, she could expect to see her pretty and expensive little habits sent down the tubes, and no messing about.'

Graves nodded. 'And she was keeping a man, sir – a very

handsome bloke who is supposed to be some sort of an artist. Not that Constable Greenly was able to find any gallery or individual who'd actually bought one of his pieces.'

Rycroft read through the report on Jasmine Olney's London flat and extra-marital activities with a look of fastidious distaste on his face. As usual, he got straight to the point. 'You had someone check out Olney's solicitors?'

Graves nodded. 'Very interesting, sir. For a start, Olney used David Leigh's firm, as you know. Pringle, Ford and Soames. It was Mr Ford who confirmed the contents of Olney's will for us. It all goes to the widow, although Olney had made an appointment for next week to make an alteration to his will and also to discuss a totally different subject.'

'Oh?' Rycroft asked, his nose almost twitching as he scented a new hare.

'Hmm,' Graves said. 'Mr Ford, when pressed, admitted that Olney had indicated that he wanted to make out a new will, cutting out Mrs Olney altogether. He also said that he'd asked Ford if he would take on his divorce case for him.' Graves smiled grimly. 'He was about to give her the old heave-ho. And I think, given the type of woman she is, she must have at least suspected as much.'

Rycroft sighed. 'So. The widow had a motive every bit as strong as that of David Leigh. As you say it's hard to imagine that she would have missed the clues that indicated that her husband was about to divorce her and cut her out of his will.'

Nobody objected to Rycroft's logic.

'And she says she was in her room at 4 o'clock to 4.15, changing and putting on make-up, but nobody saw her. She could have killed him—' Here Rycroft suddenly broke off. 'Damn! No, she couldn't. I know Olney wasn't a big man – he was built like a whippet. But even so, I can't see a woman being strong enough to overpower him, drown him, and then cart his body about and shove it in Miss Starling's cupboard. We've *got* to be looking for a man.'

Graves sighed. 'Lester could have done it. As Miss Starling pointed out, there was that long straight stretch of river. He could have tied the wheel off, killed Olney and shoved him in the cupboard. The same can be said of O'Keefe and Lucas Finch. And speaking of motives …'

Rycroft nodded. 'In getting rid of Olney, Lucas gets to keep his blessed boat and get rid of a blackmailer.'

Jenny heaved a massive sigh. 'So many people wanting Gabriel Olney dead,' she said thoughtfully. 'So many of them….' And then, suddenly, like a bolt from the blue, it all made perfect sense.

Everything she'd seen, and not realized she'd seen. Everything she'd heard and not truly understood. What she'd already surmised about the murder method. It all combined to suddenly collide in one brilliant kaleidoscope to make total and utter sense.

In one instant, she saw it all. From start to finish.

She got up abruptly. 'I think I'll make a cup of tea. Who wants one?'

'What? Oh, yes, please,' Rycroft said. He was going over the papers again, trying to sort it all out into some kind of order. But Sergeant Graves had been watching the cook. He'd seen her suddenly stiffen. He'd noticed her eyes go round in shock. He'd seen her go suddenly pale.

'I'll give you a hand, Miss Starling,' Graves said firmly, pretending not to notice the go-away look she gave him.

She needed to think, damn it. She *had* to think!

Just then, the sound of cheerful voices floated across the fields, and the party of boaters suddenly appeared through the gap in the hedge.

'Better make that teas all round,' Rycroft said drolly. 'The wanderers have returned.'

Jenny could have screamed. She'd never known a worse case of bad timing.

She walked crisply to the galley and set about making the tea. Behind her she heard the door close quietly. When she turned, Sergeant Graves was leaning against the door, and was in the process of folding his arms across his chest. His handsome, blunt face looked at her in open admiration. 'You know, don't you?' he said simply.

Jenny firmed her lips and reached for the teabags.

Graves watched her in silence for a minute, and then said quietly, 'Are you going to let me in on it?'

The cook smiled grimly. 'That's rather a telling slip, Sergeant Graves. Am I going to let *you* in on it. Not *us*?'

Graves' lips twitched. 'Inspector Rycroft is a fine officer.'

'But you're a better one,' she shot back.

'You're stalling, Miss Starling,' Graves said quietly, shaking his head and forcing the cook to stop her frantic tea making and look at him more closely.

'You really *are* good,' she said at last, sounding just a little – not much, just a little – surprised.

Sergeant Graves smiled. 'Thank you,' he said simply. 'But you're better – is that what you're waiting to hear? Now – out with it. Who did it?'

Jenny turned back abruptly to the kettle and fiddled with the gas. She didn't like to be hurried. She wasn't being given time to mull it all over. And she needed time.

'Miss Starling,' Graves pressed her firmly. 'I want that name.'

Jenny slowly put down the kettle, turned, and took a deep breath.

'You're not going to like it,' she warned him.

Graves' face tightened. 'Nevertheless,' he said simply, 'murder is still murder.'

Jenny stared at him for a long, long moment. Then she sighed. 'Yes,' she agreed sadly. 'I suppose, when all's said and done, murder *is* murder.'

The kettle began to boil and she turned and poured out the tea. She put the cups, milk and sugar onto a huge tray, added the full teapot and lifted the whole into the air. When she turned, Graves was still standing firmly in front of the door.

Jenny thought for a moment, then gave a brief nod. 'All right,' she said flatly. 'Do you still have that warrant for David Leigh's arrest?'

Graves paled, but nodded calmly. 'Yes.'

'Then I suggest you use it,' she said fatalistically.

Graves paused, then inclined his big head and opened the door for her. Jenny went through, into the main salon, and put the tray down on the table. Now the whole cruise party was gathered together once more. After their long, hot walk, everyone gathered around it eagerly.

As Graves bent over Rycroft and whispered something in his ear, David Leigh poured a cup for his wife and took it to her where she sat on the sofa. There he rested it on the wide wooden armrest for her to allow it to cool, before returning for his own cup.

Rycroft cast the cook a quick, searching look, then nodded at Graves. Graves extracted the warrant, which he'd returned to his coat pocket, and straightened up.

Brian O'Keefe, who'd grabbed a mug of tea and was about to scarper back to the engine room, caught the look on the sergeant's face and froze. Tobias Lester and Lucas Finch stiffened as Graves suddenly coughed very loudly.

Everyone turned to look at him.

Graves moved a little to his right, just to be within grabbing distance of David Leigh should he decide to try and make a run for it.

'Mr David Leigh,' he said, his voice as grave as his name. 'I have a warrant for your arrest on the charge of murder. You do not have to say anything....'

David Leigh stared at him, slack-jawed. As a solicitor, of course, he was probably more aware of his legal rights than the policeman arresting him, but he looked so surprised and stricken that Jenny wondered nervously if he was even taking it in at all.

She felt a fierce thump of contrition hit her. Then, just as the cook had known she must, Dorothy Leigh suddenly jumped to her feet, knocking over her cup of tea to the ground.

Nobody noticed the minor mishap. Everyone was too trans-fixed by the drama being played out in front of them to pay any attention to such a small thing.

'No!' Dorothy cried out desperately. 'You can't!'

Lucas made an instinctive move to go to her, but Dorothy was already rushing towards her husband and Sergeant Graves.

The others continued to stand, frozen in shock. Ever since the body had been discovered, each and every one of them had known that a killer was amongst them. But although they might have suspected each other in turn, none of them had ever really thought that the police would make an arrest.

Now, they could only watch in helpless fascination as one of their number – the quiet, handsome young solicitor – was being culled from the herd.

'… anything you do say will be taken down and can be used in evidence against you,' Graves continued, ignoring Dorothy's shouted denials. 'If you choose not to say anything, that you later rely on in court …'

Dorothy had now reached her husband's side, and she clung to him, grabbing his arm, thrusting herself forward to stand between the man she loved and the forces of the law.

'Mrs Leigh, please move out of the way,' Inspector Rycroft said, anxious to avoid any rough housing. Mrs Leigh, in her condition, could seriously hurt herself if she accidentally got in the big sergeant's way.

He reached for her arm, but she shook him off angrily. Her blue eyes blazed like lightning bolts. 'No!' she shouted again. 'You can't arrest him. You can't.'

'Mrs Leigh, please,' Rycroft said. 'We have proof that your husband forged the suicide note we found in Mr Olney's room. We have proof that Olney was responsible for his father's death during the Falklands war, and that Mr Leigh knew about it. We—'

'No, you don't understand!' Dorothy all but screamed now, as she listened in mounting panic to the evidence that was being piled up against him.

As it began to sink in, *really* sink in, that they meant to try her husband for murder, she bit back the useless urge to scream out loud. Instead, she forced herself to try and explain. 'You can't arrest him. He didn't do it!'

Unnoticed by everyone, Jenny Starling slowly sank into a chair. She was beginning to feel sick again.

And she was beginning to feel guilty.

But, as Graves had said, murder was murder.

'Mrs Leigh, why don't you go and lie down?' Rycroft said, his words at last bringing David Leigh out of his fugue of shock.

'Yes, darling, you mustn't upset yourself,' he said anxiously, looking around for help and settling on Lucas. 'Lucas, you must take care of her. Get her a doctor or something,' he said vaguely. Even in his own perilous position, his thoughts were all for his wife.

But Dorothy almost snarled at Lucas as he went to take her arm. 'Let go of me. Oh, don't you see?' She looked at Tobias, then at Brian, then at Jasmine. 'They've got it all wrong! David didn't kill Gabriel. I did!'

She rounded on Rycroft. 'You've made a mistake. I killed Gabriel. I did. I did!'

Rycroft nodded soothingly. 'All right, Mrs Leigh,' he said, still trying to manoeuvre her from between her husband and his sergeant. 'Why don't you calm down and then you can tell us all about it, hmm?'

Dorothy, aware that she was being patronized, and worse, that she wasn't being even remotely believed, stared at him in helpless horror.

It was left to Jenny to come to her aid. Into the tense silence that followed, the cook's words dropped like stones. 'I would listen to her, if I were you, Inspector,' she said quietly. 'Mrs Leigh knows what she's talking about.'

And then Sergeant Graves' head whipped around, his handsome face paling as he fixed the cook with an accusing and then slowly comprehending look.

Jenny nodded. 'Yes,' she said simply. 'Dorothy Leigh.'

And then, haltingly at first, but with growing desperation, Dorothy Leigh proceeded to tell them all just how she had murdered Gabriel Olney.

FOURTEEN

'WELL, SO LONG, love,' Lucas said to Jasmine, wondering if he should give her a hug. On the one hand, she was a very tasty piece, and he hugged tasty pieces almost as a matter of course. However, on the other hand, she *was* a widow, whose husband had just been murdered whilst on his boat.

Jasmine solved the problem for him by nodding rather briskly at him and then firmly picking up her case. She tolerated Brian O'Keefe's helping hand on her elbow as he guided her across the wooden planking onto the riverbank, then just as briskly nodded at him and marched off.

She was smiling, however, as she did so. As well she might. She was free, rich, and had a handsome lover waiting for her.

Jenny watched her go, then sighed.

It was late afternoon and all the fuss and excitement was over.

Instead of having the inconvenience of accompanying their prisoner across the fields to Carswell Marsh, Rycroft had ordered Lucas and Tobias Lester to sail the *Swan* on down to Swinford, as had been originally planned, where he'd arranged to have a police car waiting for them.

It had been a short but odd journey. In deference to her condition, Rycroft had allowed Dorothy Leigh to go to her room and lie down. Naturally he'd had Graves stand guard outside the door, but her husband had been allowed to sit with her, just to make sure she didn't do anything silly.

No doubt they'd also made good use of the couple of hours' peace and quiet left to them to discuss her defence and map out a strategy for her trial.

Jenny hoped so.

As soon as they'd docked, Graves and Rycroft had left with their prisoner, David Leigh following on close behind, and Jenny had taken advantage of the peace and quiet to give the galley a thorough clean and to pack her case.

Lucas had sent Francis back to Buscot to ready the house for his return, so the silent valet was no longer on board. Jenny was glad. She still found him creepy.

'Well, then, ready for the off, Miss Starling?' Lucas asked, coming to rest by the port deck rail, once more back to his relaxed and normal self.

The parrot hopped off his shoulder and waddled along the railing towards the big cook, who reached into her handbag to withdraw six thin wafer biscuits. She'd cooked them especially for the bird whilst the *Swan* was sailing to Swinford.

The parrot took the offering with a solemn blink of his eye, and proceeded, surprisingly neatly, to scoff the lot.

'I'll have to get a lift back to Buscot to pick up my van,' Jenny agreed. 'But I can't say as I'll be sorry to get off the boat,' she added archly. 'After you've paid me my fee, of course.'

Lucas grinned at her, then produced his wallet and counted out her wages. Jenny thanked him and put the money safely away in her handbag. Just as she snapped the catch closed, she heard a car pull up and watched it park neatly on the grass verge.

She was not particularly surprised to see Rycroft and Graves emerge.

'It's all right, sir, she's still here,' she heard Graves say. A moment later he negotiated the planks and stepped through the boarding gate. The look he gave Lucas was enough to send him, and his parrot, scurrying off into the main salon, and well out of the way.

Inspector Rycroft joined his sergeant and the cook on the port deck, and grabbed the only deckchair. He looked rather frayed at the edges.

'Everything ... done?' she asked delicately.

Rycroft grunted. 'When we got to the station, David Leigh forbade his wife to make a statement and immediately got on to some big-shot silk he knows in London. A QC who's never lost a case, or some such thing. When we left, Mrs Leigh had been charged, and was awaiting the doctor. I thought it best to call one in.'

Jenny nodded. 'A good idea,' she concurred.

Sergeant Graves, who'd left to purloin the solid chairs that were still sitting out on the starboard deck, returned at that moment and very firmly set them up.

The cook took the hint and sat down, resting her packed suitcase at her feet.

'Now then, Miss Starling,' Rycroft began, settling himself back in a chair, for all the world like a boy scout settling around a camp fire, all set to hear the best ghost story ever told. 'I want to know exactly how you deduced that Dorothy Leigh was the killer. Or was it just a good guess?'

'A good guess?' she squeaked, so indignantly it set all her magnificent flesh aquiver.

It was, Sergeant Graves had to admit silently to himself, a most impressive sight.

'Sorry,' Rycroft said hastily, realizing he'd rather badly over-stepped the mark. 'But I do want to know how you knew she was the culprit.' He himself had never seriously even suspected her.

Jenny sighed, but was mollified. 'Well, for a long while I didn't know it was her,' she began, scrupulously honest, even to the last. 'Even when I discovered *how* the murder had been committed, it didn't tell me the *identity* of the murderer.'

'Yes,' Graves broke in, unable to contain himself. 'But just how the Dickens did you get onto *that* in the first place?'

Jenny shrugged. 'Well, right from the first, I found that rope and boot very suspicious. As a way to drown a man, it seemed so far-fetched and needless. Why not just cosh Olney over the head and heave his body into the river? That made much more sense. It could be argued that Mr Olney had somehow fallen overboard, banged his head on the side of the boat on the way in and drowned. But the rope and boot was so theatrical. Tying a man up by his ankle, dangling him over the side of a boat and drowning him. It was so outlandish. And when I saw the body for myself the second time, and I was able to take a more detailed look at it, and could detect no bumps on the head … Well, I began to doubt the scenario the killer had set up even more. So, when the medical examiner confirmed that Gabriel hadn't been drugged either, I was absolutely convinced that the rope and boot had been deliberately planted.'

'The classic red herring so beloved of classic detective fiction, in fact,' Rycroft murmured appreciatively. Now that the murder had been solved, he could afford to relax and be magnanimous.

Jenny nodded. 'Yes. Exactly. But the police surgeon told you that Mr Olney *had*, in fact, drowned.' She paused. 'And his corpse was undoubtedly wet, and had left a pool of water in the cupboard. So, the facts pointed to drowning as the murder method. But not in the way the murderer wanted us to think. It was obvious, then, that I had to think of another way in which the murder had been committed. How else could Gabriel Olney have been murdered by drowning?'

'And you came to the conclusion that he must have been drowned in the freshwater butt,' Graves murmured, his excitement every bit as intense as that of his superior now.

Jenny smiled. 'I didn't just grab that conclusion out of thin air, you know,' she said, trying to curb their eagerness. 'I did have a few clues pointing me in that direction.'

Rycroft leaned forward in his chair. 'It had something to do with the way you sniffed the body, didn't it?' he demanded, his rather indelicate way of putting it making the cook colour slightly.

'Er, yes,' she agreed. 'I was puzzled by the fact that I couldn't smell the river on him, you see. Even a river as clean as the Thames smells … well, like a river.'

Rycroft leaned back in his chair, his expression sublime. 'Ah. That's what you meant when you asked me if I could smell anything. And when I said I couldn't—'

'Exactly,' she said. 'Only freshwater would leave no odour at all. And then there was the fact that Mr Olney's body had dried out in such a *clean* way. I looked and looked at him, but I couldn't see a bit of river weed, or slime, or even a smidgen of river mud on him.'

'So that's why you stared at him with such a puzzled look on your face,' Rycroft mused.

Jenny nodded. 'Exactly. So, because there was no river smell on him, or weed or mud, I came to the conclusion that he must have drowned in clean, fresh water, and not in the river at all.'

Graves nodded and, like so many police officers before him, said thoughtfully, 'It all makes perfect sense, now that it's been explained to you.'

'Yes, but I still don't see how you came to suspect Mrs Leigh,' Rycroft said impatiently. 'Why not her husband? Or Lucas? Or any of the others. They all had equally strong motives.'

Jenny nodded. 'Yes, they did. And that's what started me off looking in the right direction,' she added, once more confusing the other two. 'You remember when we discussed how risky it all was, how the murder itself smacked of such desperation?'

Both men nodded.

'Well, I kept asking myself, what made the killer so sure that he, or she, could possibly get away with it? On the face of it, the murderer seemed so reckless and very willing to take as many risks as he or she needed to. Anybody could have caught them out. I asked myself, if I were the murderer, would I be so willing to leave everything to chance, even if I were as desperate as desperate could be? And I came to the inescapable conclusion that no, I wouldn't.'

Rycroft frowned but said nothing. He was following her thinking but still, for the life of him, couldn't see how the cook had made the jump (and the correct jump, as it turned out) to Dorothy Leigh.

'So, I put myself in the killer's shoes,' Jenny continued. 'If I took it for granted that the killing wasn't *quite* as reckless as it looked, then the killer must have done something to lessen his or her chances of getting caught. So I looked out for anything that would point in that direction. And, of course, there was one obvious, in fact, *glaring* example.'

Rycroft blinked.

'The note to Jasmine Olney,' Graves said matter-of-factly.

'Exactly,' Jenny said. 'Somebody had ensured that Jasmine Olney would go to her room and stay there, for some considerable time, because she was expecting Brian O'Keefe to pay her a visit. Now the writer of that note could have been anybody, of course. Everyone (including Dorothy Leigh) had seen how Jasmine ogled the engineer. It could safely be assumed that Jasmine would take the bait. But we knew that O'Keefe didn't send the note, because he was searching her room at the time and nearly got caught. No, it was a fair bet that it was the killer that sent it.'

'So you eliminated Jasmine as a suspect?' Graves chipped in.

Jenny nodded. 'But there was also one other point about that note that struck me quite forcibly at the time.'

She glanced at Graves, who reluctantly shook his head.

'The writer was at pains to make sure that Jasmine stayed *near the door*,' she emphasized.

'That's right,' Rycroft agreed. 'In case the husband came up,' he added, remembering the note in perfect detail.

'Yes. But why would the killer want Jasmine to stay near the door?' the cook asked. 'At the time, I had no idea, but I always kept it in mind.'

'All right,' Graves said, his big hands interlocking in his lap as he followed her reasoning through. 'The killer managed to get Jasmine out of the way. But nobody else, as far as I can see, was lured into any kind of trap.'

Jenny smiled. 'Except David Leigh,' she chided mildly. 'Dorothy urged him to go to his room to work on the will he'd brought with him. As a solicitor's wife, she knew it would keep him busy for nearly an hour or so. And the last person Dorothy wanted hanging around was her husband. She adored the man. For a start, she wouldn't want to involve him, and for another thing, she was terrified that if he realized what she'd done, he might be so disgusted with her that he'd leave her.'

'But the man adores her,' Rycroft snorted.

'Yes, but she was willing to take no chance of losing him. That's the reason she killed in the first place. And in that, I think I was a little at fault there,' Jenny said, with genuine regret and self-horror. 'I was the one who pointed out to her that there was more than just an annoying flirtation behind Gabriel's pursuit of her. I more or less came straight out and said that the man was planning on dragging her name through the divorce courts – or at least, bandying it about in a very pubic manner.'

Sergeant Graves shook his head. 'You can't blame yourself for that, Miss Starling,' he said. 'You weren't to know how unstable she was. Besides, if Olney had gone ahead with his plans – and knowing the kind of man he was, I'm sure that he would have done – she'd soon have realized for herself what was afoot, and killed him anyway. She'd just have done it a little later than she did, that's all.'

Rycroft shifted impatiently on his seat. 'All right, so you realized the killer had got Jasmine out of the way. And David Leigh was sent off to his room to work on the will, so that was him out of the way. Did....' Rycroft suddenly sat bolt upright. 'Wait a minute. Jasmine was in her room from about 2.15 to 3.10. The same as David Leigh. But the rope and boot and the wet planking on the port deck wasn't discovered until 4.15!' Rycroft was almost incandescent with disbelief. 'The timing's all wrong.'

Jenny and Sergeant Graves both smiled at the ugly little man with almost identical, patient smiles.

'But, sir,' Graves said, not wanting it to be the cook to explain the obvious, 'if the rope and boot were fakes, so was the wet deck. Mrs Leigh faked the *timing* of the murder, just as she faked the method of the murder.'

'Oh.' Rycroft leaned back. 'So when Miss Starling went back to the galley after asking her if she wanted some dry toast and a cup of tea, she slipped away from her husband and set up the rope and boot and wet the planking *then*?'

Jenny nodded. 'Yes. Luckily for her, though, Jasmine Olney had chosen that moment to slip upstairs to change. Other than that, it was as simple as ABC. There were plenty of places on board she could have hidden Olney's boot and a length of rope. No doubt she told her husband she was just going upstairs to get an aspirin, or to nip to the loo or something. It wouldn't have taken her a minute to set up the rope and boot and lower a bucket down on the rope to slosh water all over the deck.'

'Or her husband might have known what she was up to,' Rycroft said darkly, then just as quickly shook his head. 'No. No, of course he didn't. She didn't want him to know, as you said, and he couldn't have faked his shock on hearing her confession.'

Jenny nodded.

'You were talking about how the killer lessened the odds on being discovered.' It was left to Sergeant Graves to get them firmly back on track. 'You've proved she kept Jasmine Olney and her own husband out of the way. But what about the others?'

Jenny sighed. 'I couldn't find any proof that any of the others had been deliberately waylaid.'

Rycroft pursed his lips. 'So that still left Lucas, Brian O'Keefe and Captain Tobias who could have come across her killing

Olney?' He whistled softly. 'She was still taking an awful lot of risks. By his own admission, Lucas had been wandering around the boat at random. He could have come across her at any time.'

'Ah,' Jenny said, 'but that was one of the other things that made me realize that Dorothy Leigh was the only one who could have killed Mr Olney.'

This time it was Graves who frowned in puzzlement. 'I don't follow you, Miss Starling. How do you come to that conclusion?'

Jenny smiled. 'Tell me, Sergeant, just what do you think Lucas would have done if he *had* seen Dorothy Leigh kill Gabriel Olney? Bear in mind that, with Olney dead, he gets to keep his boat, and be rid of a blackmailer. And keep in mind too that Lucas was very fond of Dorothy. Do you think he'd turn her in, or pretend he'd seen nothing and keep his mouth firmly shut?'

Graves opened his mouth, then shut it again.

Jenny nodded. 'Now, what do you think would have happened if *Brian O'Keefe* had seen her? Could you seriously see a good Irish God-fearing Catholic handing over a pregnant woman to the cops? Bear in mind too that Brian O'Keefe, like most men of his sort, do their best to avoid the police as a matter of principle. Much the same could be said if Tobias Lester saw her. Both Lester and O'Keefe stood to lose their jobs and their homes. But with Olney dead....'

Rycroft nodded. 'I begin to see what you're getting at. She relied on the fact that everybody had reason to want Olney dead.'

'And that nobody – or at least, none of the *men* – would want to see a pregnant woman go to prison for it,' Graves said. 'Not if avoiding it meant that they only had to keep their mouths shut.'

Jenny nodded. 'Right. As outrageous as it might sound in this day and age, she was actually relying on male gallantry to keep her safe, if she was seen,' she admitted. 'But that's not really out of character for her. For all her life, Dorothy Leigh has been treated like delicate china. Her petite build and fair delicate colouring has guaranteed that men have always placed her on a pedestal. She'd take it for granted that, if the worst did come to the worst, and she was seen killing Olney, that the men would band together to protect her. Especially when she could tell them what Olney had threatened to do to her and David. Only Jasmine Olney might want to see her husband's killer get caught,' the cook pointed out, 'and then, not so much out of a desire for justice, but more likely because it would put her in the clear.'

Jenny thought about the widow for a moment and smiled wryly. 'That's why Jasmine *had* to be got out of the way. And, incidentally, why the note stressed that Jasmine should stay by the door. Dorothy wanted her as far away from the window as possible. The fresh water butt, remember, was on the starboard deck. It was the one thing that could have caught her out if Jasmine had happened to hear anything outside. But even in that, Dorothy Leigh was lucky. Brian O'Keefe *shut the window* as he escaped down onto the lower deck. So, as it was, Mrs Olney didn't hear a thing as her husband was being drowned just yards away, more or less right under her window.'

Graves sighed. 'That's another thing that gets me. In fact, it's the only thing that makes me glad that we actually caught her. It was such a cold-hearted way to kill a man.'

Jenny sighed. 'She was desperate. And, no matter what you feel about it, you have to admit that it *was* very clever.'

Rycroft nodded. 'How do you think it was accomplished, Miss Starling?'

The cook shrugged. 'Very easily, I should imagine. She got the trolley and the plastic sheet from the engine room when O'Keefe was elsewhere and took them to the water butt. Then she hunted out Gabriel and told him some pretty story – probably that an earring had dropped off and fallen in the water butt and that her arms weren't long enough to reach the bottom, and could he help? You must remember that Olney had been pursuing her for some time. He'd jump at the chance to perform such a simple, gallant little task. It would earn him brownie points with the lady, if nothing else. And you must remember the kind of man Olney was – he no doubt thought it was only a matter of time before Dorothy Leigh fell for his charm. He probably thought that her request to come to her aid was just *her* way of flirting with *him*.'

Graves snorted. 'So she takes him to the water butt, and he leans in and starts fishing around for the bauble, but can't find it.'

'So he has to stand right up on tiptoe and lean even further in. Yes,' Rycroft said softly. 'I can see how that would work.'

'Then,' Jenny finished, 'it was a simple matter to grab his legs and upend him head-first into the butt.'

'I wouldn't have thought she'd have had the strength though,' Rycroft said dubiously, even though the lady herself had admitted, in her rush to clear her husband, that that was indeed exactly what she *had* done.

'Oh, but there you fall into the usual trap of all men,' Jenny said complacently. 'You assume that if a woman is thin and dainty, then she must also be mentally and physically weak. Whereas, in fact, Dorothy Leigh was neither. I saw for myself how good a swimmer she was, that first day on board the *Swan*. And she said herself that she often took their dog for long walks. She may have been three months pregnant, but she was also an extremely fit young woman. Besides, as you pointed out yourself, Gabriel Olney was a thin man. It wouldn't have taken much just to hold his legs whilst he thrashed about in the water butt. The butt itself is four feet deep and narrow. A man, submerged head-first, with somebody pinning down his legs so that he can't get a good purchase, would very quickly drown. He would have only his hands with which to try and lift himself up anyway, and on a smooth-sided, round, wooden barrel … well. As the medical examiner said, he broke some fingernails and bruised his knuckles. But that was all. It would have been over very quickly.'

Both men were grimly silent. Then Rycroft stirred. 'But how did you figure out what she did next? Even as fit as she was, she wouldn't have had the strength to drag his dead body out of the butt and cart him to your cupboard. Not quickly, anyway.'

Jenny smiled. 'Ah, there I had the advantage over you,' she admitted. 'When Mrs Leigh first came on board, Brian O'Keefe was carrying a block and tackle over his shoulder, and Mrs Leigh admitted that she knew what it was. She explained that her father had worked on a building site all his life and that she, like so many fond daughters, as a child had loved to visit him and watch him work. It was obvious that she would know how a block and tackle was used. Then, when we were out on the starboard deck, we both observed Brian O'Keefe use the equipment box. Which, incidentally, is conveniently situated right next to the freshwater butt. And, as a final cherry on the cake, your own forensics man, when giving you a run-down on the condition of the ship, told you that the life belt ring above the equipment box and right next to the water butt, was hanging on a particularly strong bracket.'

Graves smiled. 'So you knew that Dorothy Leigh would be able to use the strong bracket to set up the block and tackle to haul Olney out of the water butt and….' He trailed off, not yet quite sure of his ground after that.

Jenny happily came to his rescue. 'She would have put the plastic sheet onto the trolley and lowered the body onto it. Remember, she'd be at pains to keep the deck, and the trail to my galley, totally dry. Then it was just a question of wheeling the body to the cupboard, upending the trolley – those railway-porter type trolleys are so good for that sort of thing – and shutting the cupboard door quickly, before he could fall back out. Not forgetting to take the plastic sheeting back to the engine room to dry off, of course.'

'But why hide the body in the cupboard at all? Why not use the block and tackle to put the body over the side?' Rycroft asked suddenly.

But Jenny was already shaking her head. 'No time. She'd have had to winch the body sideways, swing him out, and drop him overboard. It would take much longer, and besides, with both Jasmine Olney and David Leigh in their rooms above her, one or the other of them would be bound to hear the splash as his body hit the water and look out. On board a boat, a big splash would be a dead giveaway that someone had gone overboard. And how would she be able to explain then what she was doing out there, with the block and tackle all set up? No, silence and speed were her main requirements.'

'So she hid the body in the only place she was sure where it wouldn't be found too soon.' Graves nodded. 'Your cupboard.'

'Right. There aren't many places on a compact boat where you can hide a corpse, after all. And she knew I was out on my walk at the time,' Jenny reminded them. 'Of course, during all this time, Dorothy was supposed to be upstairs in the bathroom, suffering the pangs of morning sickness.'

'Faked, I suppose?' Graves said.

Jenny shrugged. 'Perhaps. But perhaps not. I think the thought of what she was about to do probably did make her feel genuinely ill. And the shock and strain she showed afterwards was certainly real enough. She was not a natural-born killer, after all. Just desperately in love with her husband and terrified of losing him.'

'So that was how you figured it all out?' Rycroft said, full of admiration and awe in spite of himself.

Jenny smiled wryly. 'That, and one or two other things. Something Jasmine Olney said, when giving you her statement, stuck in my mind, for example.'

'Oh?' Rycroft said, frantically casting his mind back. 'What?'

'She said that when she left her room and bumped into the Leighs on the landing, Dorothy obviously wanted to go back to her room, but her husband insisted that she went back downstairs for a cup of tea.'

'So?' Rycroft said. 'I don't see any significance in that.'

The cook sighed. 'No, neither did I, but I should have done Especially as I'd noticed the dress Dorothy was wearing, and had seen with my own two eyes what should have been so obvious.'

'Dress?' Rycroft echoed, glancing at his sergeant, who, for once, looked as puzzled as himself.

Jenny obliged. 'On the morning of the murder, Dorothy was wearing this pretty, powder-blue dress. I remember thinking how much like a meadow blue butterfly it was in colour. But later that afternoon, *after* the murder had been committed, when I came to give her her tea and toast, I remember thinking how much *darker* it looked. I put it down to the fact that she was sitting in the shade, but really, I should have remembered that pastel colours, when *wet*, look much darker.'

'And in all the business around the water butt, getting Olney out and onto the plastic, she'd be bound to get a little wet,' Graves breathed.

'Exactly. So when she went back upstairs, with Olney dead and safely in my cupboard, all she must have wanted to do was go and *change her dress*. Just in case anybody noticed, and later remembered that she had got damp for some reason at some point that afternoon.'

Graves snapped his fingers. 'And she did go upstairs later on,' he said. 'Do you remember, sir, when we first got here and started taking statements, you had to send me upstairs to go and get the Leighs?'

Rycroft nodded. 'And, if my memory serves me right, Mrs Leigh wasn't wearing a blue dress then, but a skirt and a fluffy pink sweater.'

Jenny nodded. 'I thought at the time she'd changed into something warmer, because the shock of finding that Mr Olney had been killed had made her feel cold. I even remember thinking how sensible it was of her, especially in her condition, to change into something warmer. Later, of course....' She shrugged.

Thinking of the woman's cleverness, Graves slowly shook his head. 'She'll get prison, of course,' he said, but didn't sound at all happy about it.

'But not for life,' Jenny said matter-of-factly. 'That husband of hers is no fool. And that fancy QC he's retained won't be either. Together, they'll arrange for her trial to start just when she's heavily pregnant. And they'll have no shortage of witnesses to testify what a bad lot Gabriel was. And what jury, when faced with a pretty, fair, petite, heavily pregnant woman will go hard on her, when she murdered a man who threatened to destroy her life? Who threatened to have her husband dismissed from his job and – far worse – who threatened to tell her husband, quite untruthfully, that the child she carried wasn't his?' Jenny shook her head. 'No. Gabriel's attempted blackmail of Lucas will come out, and David Leigh will be at pains to point out that Gabriel Olney was a coward, a deserter, and a murderer himself. He as good as murdered Arnold Leigh, after all, and the jury will see it the same way. Maybe the QC will even put forward temporary insanity as a defence. Any man can argue that a pregnant woman is prey to depression. No, they'll pull out all the stops and get it down to manslaughter I should think.'

Graves found himself hoping that the cook was right. He had no desire to see Dorothy Leigh spend the rest of her life in jail for doing away with Olney.

'I think you're right,' Rycroft agreed. 'If ever there were mitigating circumstances, this case is full of them. Well....' He rose to his feet and stretched. 'We have to get back to the station. Can we give you a lift, Miss Starling?'

But the cook shook her head, and explained how she needed to get back to her van. Best to call a taxi. She waved the two policemen goodbye, giving the burly, handsome sergeant a slightly wistful, final look. Then, when the car was out of sight, she lifted her case and walked slowly down the deck.

The sun was just beginning to redden as she stepped onto the lush green river bank and started towards the village and a telephone.

Suddenly there was a loud squawk, and a scarlet and blue flash shot past her to land on the limb of a nearby tree.

Jenny looked at it fondly. 'So long, featherbrain,' she called cheerfully.

'Goodbye, sweetheart,' the parrot said, and gave her a long, low, flattering wolf whistle.